ANTHROTERRA

THE STAG SENATOR

Anthroterra

THE STAG SENATOR

Ratthew K. K.

Published in the United States by Binary Starium LLC.

The Cataloging-in-Publication Data is on file at the Library of Congress. LC record available at https://lccn.loc.gov/2023922847

LCCN 2023922847
ISBN 979-8-9896139-0-8 (Amazon paperback)
ISBN 979-8-9896139-2-2 (trade paperback)
ISBN 979-8-9896139-1-5 (ebook)

*For those who seek the courage to
embrace and reconcile with their true selves.*

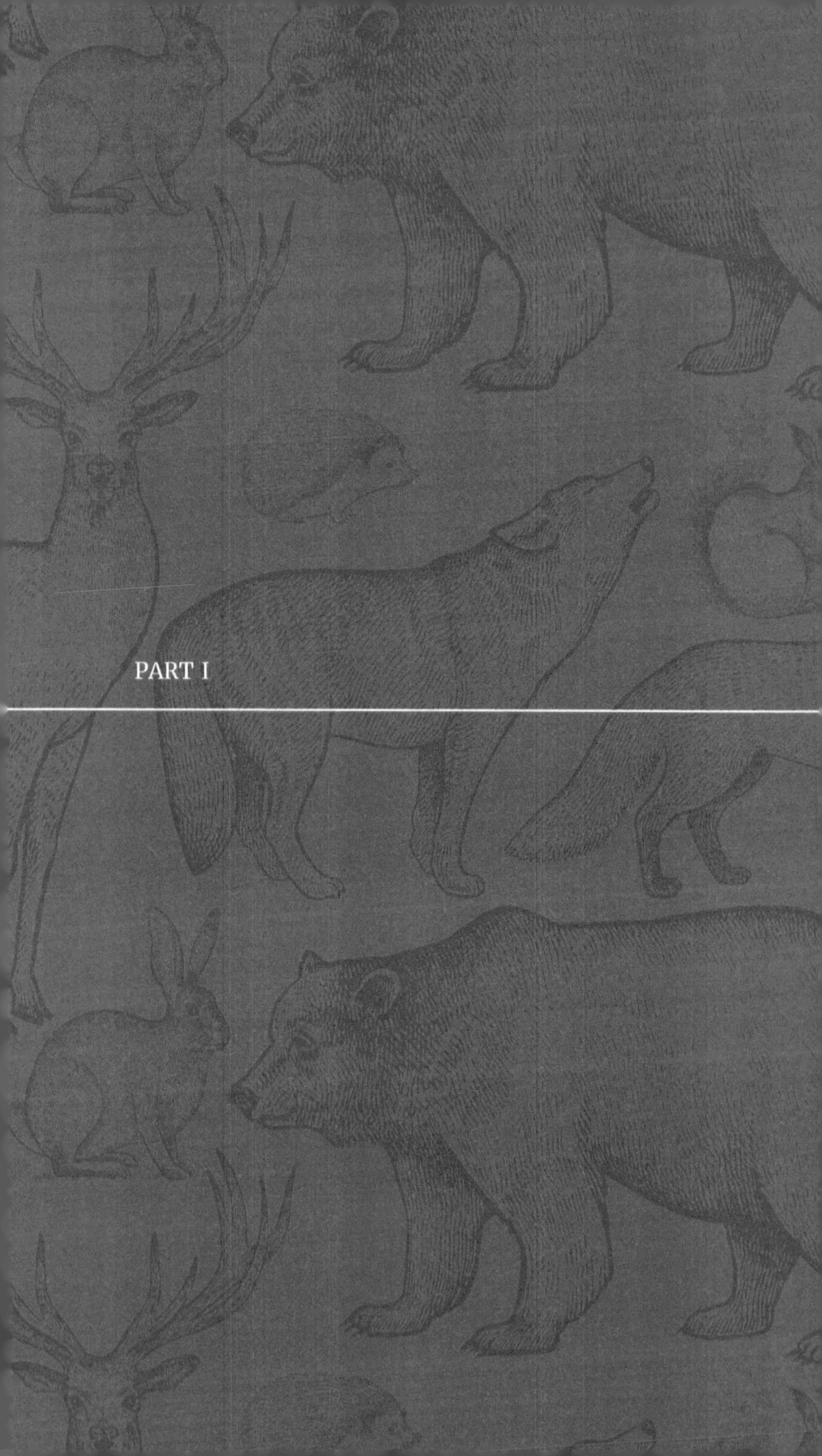

PART I

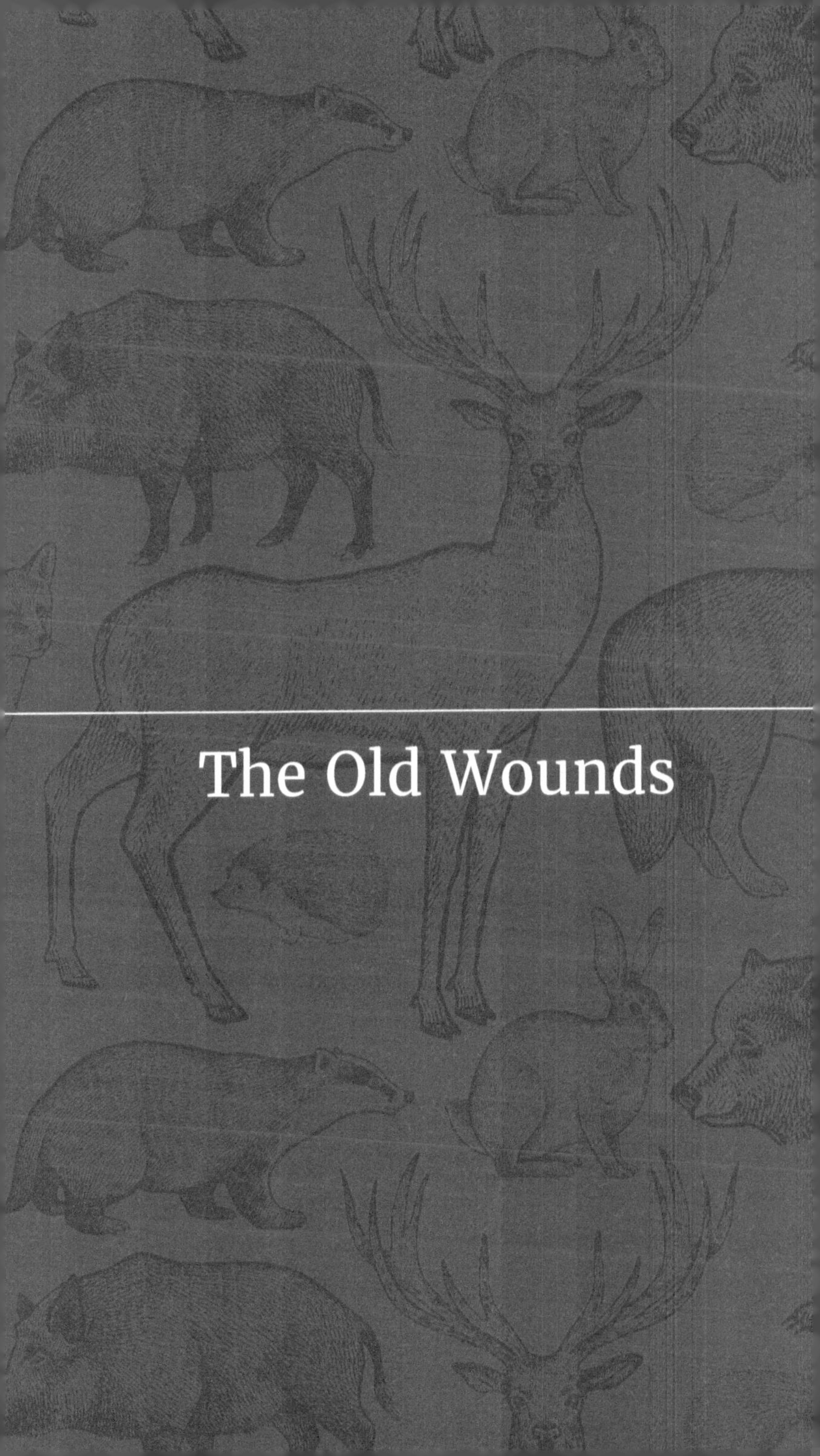

The Old Wounds

The Reunion

Having a complete set of antlers, particularly those with a thick beam and well-balanced crown tines, was a mark of privilege and an emblem of the authority one held. Hart knew this well, and he tried to remain appreciative of his status, even when faced with minor inconveniences, particularly during his weekend visits to the towns in Wilfen district.

However, when he found himself awkwardly wedged just beyond the doorway of a newly opened bookstore, his velveted antlers threatening to topple an entire shelf of books, it was hard to keep his gratitude for being stuck with cumbersome antlers.

"My apologies," said Hart, endeavoring to keep his head steady, with an awkward smile on his face. He was acutely aware his antlers wouldn't fit well through the narrow entryway, yet he couldn't decline the owner's warm invitation to step inside. He could feel the blood rushing to his face, turning his human ears red. He hoped his beard would conceal the rising flush of embarrassment.

Meanwhile, his aide was diligently gathering the scattered books, offering soothing words to the apologetic owner family with reassurances that incidents like these occasionally happened and that they would pay for any damages.

This is not good, Hart thought. Being trapped in a tight space, with no room to maneuver or strategize an exit, was far from ideal. The entrance was mere steps away, yet it felt unreachable.

His heightened senses, a legacy of being raised by a wolf terrian, were on high alert. These instincts, coupled with his innate herbivore caution, had been honed over the years and remained deeply ingrained, even long after the wolf's protective presence had faded.

Suddenly, an uncanny prickling sensation erupted at the nape of Hart's neck. His furry ears, nestled near his antlers, instinctively turned into a rustling movement behind him, alert to the impending danger.

Without a moment's hesitation, he twisted and moved out of the entryway, unwillingly sacrificing a few books as his hurried antlers knocked them from a decorative shelf near the doorway.

Before Hart could fully grasp the situation, the attacker was in motion. A bear terrian lunged at him with all the predatory fierceness. Caught off guard, Hart was swiftly pinned to the ground, the bear's looming presence and unnatural strength rendering him helpless under the sudden onslaught.

The bear's eyes were unnaturally dilated, their bloody-red hue piercingly vivid. Saliva dripped from his mouth as he snarled like a rabid beast. It didn't take much to realize he was overdosing on *Wild*, an illegal substance that had been wreaking havoc among the carnivores of Anthroterra, including those in Hart's own district, over the past several months.

Okay, this is pretty bad, Hart thought to himself, his face and neck stuck in an awkward angle due to the antler. He realized his revolver was out of reach due to the attacker's position. His mind momentarily drifted back to numerous instances where his aide had expressed concern about the potential need for a security guard ever since he was elected as a Senator not too long ago.

As he shielded his face and neck, Hart's thoughts raced to the location of the security officers who had been stationed for his visit. He could only hope they would reach him in time as he tensed, preparing for the bear's next move.

But it was a swift, silent figure that emerged from the crowd that intervened. In the blink of an eye, this figure had pounced on the bear, wrestling him to the ground after a brief but intense struggle. From just a foot away, Hart observed the scene unfolding before him, momentarily transfixed by the figure's fluid, graceful actions.

The hood of the cloak slipped off amidst the scuffle, revealing a face that made Hart's heart skip a beat.

"Lupus?" Hart murmured quietly, his whisper ladened with disbelief. *Am I dreaming right now?* he wondered, his ears perking forward, honing in on the wolf. A wave of unbidden longing washed over him at the sight of this long-missed figure from his past. He couldn't tear his gaze away from the now older wolf terrian. The passage of time was etched in the crow's feet at the corners of Lupus's eyes and the streaks of gray in his hair and fur. It had been over a decade since Hart had last seen him.

With the help of a couple of large terrians nearby, the attacker was subdued and pinned securely to the ground just as the officers arrived on the scene. Lupus stepped back, his attention briefly on a minor scrape on his immaculately shaven chin that had started to bleed.

His gaze, however, was riveted on Hart. It had been precisely 14 years and 9 months since their last close encounter, face to face. While he had watched Hart from a distance, up close, he appeared even more distinguished, having matured into the respected member of the senate he now was. His majestic antlers stood as an emblem to his stature.

Lupus noticed that patches of velvet on Hart's antlers were abraded, possibly from his rushed exit from the narrow storefront, coupled with the abrupt bear assault. "Are you alright?" There was unmistakable concern in Lupus's voice. He reached out to assist Hart, who remained somewhat dazed on the cobbled pavement.

Their gazes met—Lupus's emerald eyes, the eyes of a predator, under prominent eyebrows framed by scars, silent witnesses to past battles. Yet, those eyes held a warmth and worry that was deeply caring.

That look, ironically, yanked Hart back to reality, re-igniting the pain and resentment he harbored against Lupus, who he once considered family. His brows knit together in a frown, and his expression hardened. *What the hell is this wolf doing here?*

"I'm fine," Hart retorted, his ears pinning back in a display of cold defiance as he rose to his feet, declining Lupus's offered hand. In addition to his towering red deer stature, the antlers adorning his head further amplified his intimidating appearance as he glared down at Lupus.

A multitude of questions surged in his throat, but he found himself unwilling to voice any. The agony he wished to forget lingered, its fiery resentment searing his heart. Hart could feel his tail flaring, responding to the raw, untempered resentment gnawing at his core.

Without another look, Hart turned around to face the aide, who was looking between Hart and Lupus, seeming shocked by what had happened, with her furry rabbit ears standing at attention in evident shock.

"We're done here, Ms. Longfoot." Hart declared, reclaiming his professional demeanor. He lightly tapped her shoulder to catch her attention, before making his way towards the main road where his carriage awaited, not waiting for her to respond. As he walked, he clenched his jaw, acutely aware of his racing heartbeat resonating in his trembling fingers, with strong emotions washing over him.

Lupus watched as Hart disappeared into the group of onlookers, his tail flared in unmistakable anger. A knot of deep emotion tightened his throat, causing his lupine ears to droop in resignation. A small part of him had hoped Hart would be happy to see him, but the reality of the situation only weighed his heart down further. No battle wound hurt more than seeing Hart's earthy brown eyes, once filled with affection and joy, now frosted over with the pain and agony that Lupus had caused him.

The illusion of closeness that he had clung to over the years, observing Hart from the shadows, witnessing his rise from an Academy student to a senator, had turned into a blade that now pierced his heart, severing the last thread of hope for reconciliation.

I should never have revealed myself to Hart, anyway. Lupus thought, his tail drooping with a heavy weight of regret. With a heavy sigh, he began to navigate through the thinning crowd, pulling his hood over his head to conceal the sorrow etched on his face.

"Sir," a soft grasp on his wrist caught his attention, almost a desperate plea. Startled yet unperturbed without sensing any threat or danger, Lupus turned around to see the rabbit terrian. Dressed in a crisply tailored suit, he recognized her. She had been by Hart's side since his days at the Academy, now serving as his aide.

"Thank you, sir, for saving the Senator's life." The rabbit began, a hint of confusion clouding her eyes as she released Lupus's wrist, conveying her gratitude for his timely intervention. "I'm Robin Longfoot, Senator Redfern's aide."

Her gaze briefly chased after the direction Hart had gone, her brown eyes clouded with concern. "Please accept my apologies for his behavior—it was out of character. The attack must have deeply shaken him.

Under any other circumstances, he would have expressed his gratitude personally."

"There's no need for apologies, Ms. Longfoot. I did what was necessary," Lupus replied with a reassuring warmth, offering a gentle pat on her shoulder. Meeting his gaze, her ears eased back, and a sincere smile touched her lips.

Robin's attention then fell to an old, knife-shaped tattoo on Lupus's wrist. The design, with its faded edges crossing over three bold lines, marked him as a war veteran. "Thank you for your service," she said, her voice carrying a newfound respect for the depth of his past sacrifices.

Lupus acknowledged the thanks with a nod, ready to depart, when she added, "If you're interested, we are seeking a security guard for Senator Redfern. Sooner rather than later, especially given what just happened." She offered him her business card.

The thick cardstock bore the gleaming gold emblem of Anthroterra Central. Taken aback, Lupus accepted the card. His thumb traced its texture, and his gaze was drawn to the bold title above the contact details:

The Office of Senator Hart Claude Redfern
Wilfen District

A flutter of warmth filled his chest as he felt a small connection to his former family, even though it was just a piece of paper. He looked up, intending to decline politely, to suggest that the senator might not welcome his involvement.

However, he only caught a glimpse of her retreating figure, her ears bobbing above the crowd as she darted towards an open carriage waiting for her.

For a moment, Lupus thought he caught Hart's eye seated within, but he couldn't be certain as the horses began to trot at the gentle urging of the terrian at the reins.

I'm proud of you, Hart. Lupus mused silently, his fingers still playing over the card's embossed emblem. His gaze lingered in the direction the carriage disappeared for a while.

"What were you two discussing?" Hart's voice broke the prolonged silence that had settled within the carriage. He strove to maintain his professional demeanor, yet the hardened expression etched onto his face betrayed his inner turmoil.

Rob responded with a steady voice, "The security guard position. I asked if he was interested." It seemed Hart was teetering on the edge of a response, but he checked himself, turning his gaze to the world outside the carriage, his arm resting atop the door. His fingers betrayed his composure, rubbing and twitching against his thumb, clenching and unclenching in a rhythm of contained agitation.

Rob watched Hart with a careful, yet discreet, scrutiny. She had known him for over a decade, their history stretching back to their academy days, yet she rarely witnessed such a crack in his usually impeccable facade.

"Who is he?" she probed gently, her eyes keenly observing Hart's body language for any telltale sign. "Nobody," came Hart's terse response, his voice flat, his eyes never leaving the passing scenery.

Rob recognized the all-too-familiar barriers going up, the ones Hart always erected when the conversation veered too close to the personal. She gave a simple nod and settled back into her seat, her thoughts already turning to the myriad tasks that awaited her at the office.

She knew Hart well enough to understand that he wouldn't discuss any private details unless he felt compelled to do so, and she respected that boundary, knowing any further questioning would be futile.

As the carriage rolled on, Hart's gaze drifted aimlessly over the fleeting landscape, but his mind was ensnared by the past, replaying the fateful confrontation with Lupus that remained as vivid as if it had happened only moments ago.

"You're lying. I saw you at the Capitol just last week," Hart growled in simmering anger and disbelief, "There was never any urgent mission, was there?" The words weren't a question but a bitter realization. His furry ears pinned back, a clear display of his rising ire, an emotion he hadn't felt so intensely in years.

Lupus's eyes, usually a warm and gentle haven, now widened in shock. Color drained from his face as the weight of Hart's accusation settled upon him. The soft smile that Hart had come to associate with his guardian was nowhere to be seen, replaced by a look of genuine surprise and dread.

The memory from just days ago replayed in his mind with agonizing clarity—spotting Lupus among a bustling crowd, strolling down the main road in the Capitol alongside a beautiful white wolf, at a time when he was supposedly deployed abroad.

Hart wouldn't have opposed giving Lupus some personal space if that's what he needed. All Lupus had to do was be honest, like he had always taught Hart himself. There was no need for him to fabricate an 'urgent mission' in the middle of a stormy night and leave a hastily scribbled note as their farewell. Their usual goodbyes, a tight embrace and the exchange of assurances for safety, seemed to have become a luxury.

Lupus's infrequent returns home, brief and fleeting, made it feel as if visiting Hart was just another errand he had to run because of his legal obligations as a guardian. It felt as if Lupus didn't trust Hart enough to share the truth, or worse, as if he was deliberately distancing himself. Hart felt a sickening twist in his stomach at the thought.

"Hart, listen..." Lupus carefully rose from his seat at the dining table with his furry ears completely flat on his head and tail almost tucked between his legs.

What is he scared of? Hart wondered, his heart pounding as he observed Lupus's nervous demeanor. He could tell Lupus was holding back, reluctant to reveal the truth.

"I'm listening." Hart held Lupus's gaze with a serious look, while internally battling to calm himself down.

He had known Lupus his entire life. Lupus had been a constant in his life, a figure of strength, trustworthiness, and kindness. Since the day Hart had found Lupus in the Capitol, he had grappled with conflicting emotions, clinging to his belief in Lupus's integrity, convincing himself there had to be a justifiable reason for the wolf's secrecy.

Yet, in the oppressive silence of his lonely home, shadows of doubt crept in, stirring fears he had long dismissed as echoes of past misunderstandings and years of rebellious thoughts. The fear that Lupus never truly wanted to be part of his family, that Hart was nothing more than an obligation left behind by the wolf's deceased friends. The fear that Lupus yearned for the company of his own kind, a life away from the red deer he was bound to protect. The fear that this—the absolute loneliness, without anyone in his life—would define the rest of his existence.

Night after night, he lay quivering with shallow breaths, the weight of solitude pressing down on him, his soul eroding under the relentless tide of insecurities. He learned to count the ticks of the floor clock that punctuated the stillness, each tick a reminder to breathe, to stay grounded, to let go of his fears. His only comfort was the belief that Lupus, when confronted, would reassure him of the truth of their bond, that they were indeed family.

But now, the nervous wolf before him, hesitating to speak the truth, injected dread into Hart's veins like venom. *He's a wolf, and you are not.* The insidious whisper gnawed at the edges of his mind. Hart fought back the tears, pushing down the rising tide of emotions.

Lupus's reply seemed to stretch into an eternity, a span that was, in reality, less than a minute. To Hart, it felt like a lifetime. Lupus was caught in a repetitive cycle of opening and closing his mouth, his uncertain gaze flickering between Hart and the floor, his ears nervously twitching.

"You will be an adult soon, Hart," Lupus finally said, his voice laced with hesitancy, avoiding Hart's earnest gaze.

The gravity of his words hit Hart with an unexpected force, confirming his worst fears. As reality sank in, Hart's eyes widened in disbelief, scouring Lupus's face for explanations.

With a jaw set firm, Lupus met Hart's stare, his eyes reflecting a resolve that left no room for argument. "You don't need me around anymore."

Something inside Hart shattered at those words.

"LIAR!" he exploded, his tail flaring in a raw anger. He surged to his feet, his hand slamming down on the dining table with force. The dining chair screeched against the floor as he pushed it back, before it tipped over with a loud crash. The vase, filled with wildflowers Lupus had brought home just an hour before, toppled and sent blooms scattering across the table.

As Hart's stormy eyes locked with Lupus's, time seemed to freeze. Tears began their descent down his cheeks, but his pride was drowned out by the tide of fury.

"This is not about me, is it? This is about you. *You* don't want me around now that I'm old enough," Hart snapped, his voice choked by the overpowering emotions that were threatening to consume him. Each syllable felt like a weight on his chest, and his eyes sought validation in Lupus's. It was a plea for Lupus to deny his accusations.

Lowering his gaze in the wake of the words, Lupus clenched his jaw and remained silent for a heartbeat that felt like an eternity. The air in the room felt heavier, each breath feeling like labor.

When the wolf finally lifted his gaze, his eyes were brimming with tears, and he struggled to calm his shuddering breaths. "This is for your safety, kid," he hesitated, his voice quivering. "I'm a wolf, and you—"

"I KNOW WHAT I AM!" Hart's voice sliced through the air, sharp and laden with pain, causing the wolf to flinch. He felt like an outsider, and the sting of that realization cut deep. *Hart Redfern was not a wolf, but a mere red deer.* Lupus, the only family Hart had ever truly known and trusted, never saw him as one of his own.

In that moment, everything Hart had held dear, everything he had believed in, seemed to crumble around him. The lump of emotion lodged in his throat was like a thorn, scratching his insides as it erupted into a raw sob. "You have been my only family for as long as I can remember. Do you seriously expect me to believe you are suddenly worried about my safety, because you are a wolf? When I'm merely weeks away from becoming an adult?"

An avalanche of memories involving Lupus swept over Hart, accompanied by the torrent of emotions that

reflected the peaks and valleys they'd weathered together. Beyond the faded memories of his parents, it
had always been Lupus who anchored him through the
tumultuous waves of life.

In Lupus, Hart found a guardian he admired who guided
him like a parent, a confidant he trusted who stood with
him as a brother, and a companion he cherished who
shared life's ups and downs like a true friend. Lupus
had been his pillar, his sanctuary, his warmth that Hart
had sought and desperately needed in his life.

After nearly losing Lupus a few years prior, Hart resolved
to mature, to relieve the weight he felt he'd placed on
Lupus's shoulders. He yearned to evolve from a responsibility into a source of strength for Lupus, someone
the wolf could trust and lean on, just as he had relied
on Lupus all his life.

*Was all of that just an illusion? Is my existence so burden-
some, so unbearable, that Lupus can't stand it?*

Hart could feel an emotional storm within him about
to swallow him whole, turning everything he held dear
into an unsalvageable wreckage. His body trembled
with the force of his despair, his ears drooping as his
anger gave way to the terror of abandonment, the very
darkness he had been fleeing each night.

"Did..." His voice emerged as a quivering whisper,
fractured by the weight of his emotions. "Did I do
something to upset you? To make you want to leave?"

His mind raced, frantically sifting through memories, searching for any overlooked sign that he might have unintentionally hurt his only family. Memories of his rebellious youth, of harsh words hurled at Lupus, of cold shoulders turned, and the unmistakable pain and sorrow in Lupus's features that he had caused, all surged back. They had reconciled long ago, but the guilt and regret still clung to him, suffocating.

"No, Hart, you've never…" Lupus began hastily, his words faltering, stifled by the surge of his own emotions. He seemed to ache with the need to offer Hart solace, as he had so many times before. Yet now, the wolf could only avert his gaze, the heart-wrenching pain in Hart's brown eyes too much to bear.

"Can you at least tell me why you're pushing me away?" Hart implored, his eyes seeking Lupus's. Those green eyes, which had always met his own so effortlessly, now evaded him. "Please?" His plea was barely audible, a delicate thread reaching out for reconciliation. Tears flowed unrestrained down Hart's cheeks, dotting his trembling fists and staining the tabletop.

As Lupus blinked quietly, heavy tears broke free, tracing glistening paths down his cheeks and falling to the floor. "I'm… sorry, Hart. I truly am," he managed, his voice laden with sorrow.

Hart felt blood draining from his body.

Lupus, the one being who knew him better than any other, deemed him *unworthy* of companionship, eager to be rid of him once the legalities of guardianship dissolved.

"*Get out.*" Hart demanded, his voice a cold snarl. The fragile hope that had lingered in the recesses of his heart was now replaced by a tempest of pain, betrayal, and growing resentment directed at Lupus.

The wolf's breath hitched as his eyes trembled, the weight of Hart's cold dismissal pressing down on him. Hart's jaw clenched, each grind of his teeth amplifying the storm of anger within.

"I've never doubted you were my family. It seems I was the only one." Hart's voice, thick with pain, wavered, and a bitter smirk tugged at the corner of his mouth. Tears continued their path down his cheeks. "You don't need to waste more of your precious time lying to my face, pretending to care for a poor little fawn who's now grown into an adult stag that no longer requires a guardian."

Hart's trembling fists clenched, his words cutting deep, lacerating his own heart as they spilled forth. "Leave me the fuck alone and get out of this house. *Now.*" he growled, as his brown eyes, aflame with pain, bore into the teary greens of Lupus. "I don't need your fucking pity."

And the wolf did just that, without a word of denial. Lupus clenched his jaw, offering a quiet, pained nod in acknowledgment. He retreated toward the front door, his fingers wrapping around his jacket that hung limply by the entrance.

Lupus cast one final glance towards Hart, his gaze laden with unspoken words and regrets, and then stepped out of the house, leaving Hart in the echoing solitude of their once-shared home.

The deafening crash of a vase shattering against the wall, splintering into countless fragments, was the final memory Hart could recall from that day.

The days that followed were hazy, a blurry sequence of sleepless nights punctuated by tear-streaked cheeks and haunting echoes of the past.

Not long after, his juvenile set of antlers were shed, signaling the close of his tumultuous adolescence. Along with them, he cast aside the tainted memories of his past, leaving behind nothing to cling to.

Walking on the Ice

Hart lifted a thin stack of documents emblazoned with the bold title: 'Formal Proposal for the Authorization of Security Guard: Budgetary and Terrian Considerations Approval.' It was just one of many files Rob had handed him earlier, each clamoring for the senator's attention. His eyes narrowed, as his brown gaze lifted to his aide. "What is this?" he asked, his voice edged with a blend of suspicion and barely concealed ire.

Unfazed by the senator's displeased expression, Rob placed her bundle onto the pristine desk. "Do you recall the incident that happened last weekend, Senator?" she countered, her hand subtly gesturing towards the document he held, highlighting the obvious. Attached to the back was a clipped article from the Wilfen Daily, recounting the tale of a war veteran wolf terrian who had saved the young senator's life from a feral carnivore attack.

Hart exhaled a weary sigh and let the stack of papers drop with a muted thud onto the desk. "You *know* that's not what I'm asking, Rob," he snapped back, a note of frustration creeping into his tone.

Rob was well aware of the senator's actual concern, yet she chose to sidestep the more sensitive issue at hand. Hart's reluctance to publicly acknowledge the wolf's heroism was unmistakable, a personal barrier he seemed unwilling to cross. But Rob understood there was a deeper, unspoken tension between the senator and the wolf.

Yet, the experience and skills of Lupus Greyfang, which were briefly described in his letter expressing his interest in filling the position, were undeniably stellar. As Hart's public upcoming engagements multiplied, Rob, in her dual role as aide and friend, was convinced of the pressing need for a proficient security detail. In her eyes, Lupus was the prime candidate, Hart's personal apprehensions notwithstanding.

Rob squared her shoulders, her arms folding across her chest in a display of resolute defiance. Her typical pragmatic aura surfaced, reinforcing her stance.

"This is about protocol, Hart. You're as aware of that as I am." Her voice was firm, determined to keep the senator's personal sentiments from clouding professional imperatives.

Hart's gaze was unwavering, tinged with a hint of exasperation. "We can't afford to squander our resources on something like this. I've managed before, and I can manage now." Hart insisted, crossing his arms and reclined into his seat to rest his antlers, with his gaze shifted upward to meet his aide who stood across the desk. His face was a mask of practiced neutrality, but the tension in his posture betrayed his deeper feelings.

Rob held his gaze, her voice steady. "If he hadn't intervened that day, our district would have been burdened with a cost at least tenfold the budget suggested on that document to facilitate special elections, appoint a new Senator. Not to mention the absence of representation in the Senate until then."

She paused, allowing the gravity of her words to settle, her eyes never straying from Hart's. She watched the gears turn in his mind, the logic of her argument steadily eroding his resistance. "Besides, I'm fairly certain he is the best we could get for the salary he's quoted," she added, observing the senator's facade crack, a flicker of disbelief crossing his features as his brow arched.

Hart leaned forward, rifling through the papers to locate the budget breakdown. His furry ears twitched in surprise at the proposed salary. "He's asking for this? For a full-time role?" He murmured, almost to himself, the figure starkly modest, nearly half the standard wage.

When he finally met Rob's eyes again, his usual stoic senatorial mask was replaced by genuine confusion. Rob's shoulders lifted in a subtle shrug, her face alight with a blend of victory and playful satisfaction.

Hart's gaze danced over the pages, his mind meticulously cataloging every detail. He knew Rob was right. It wasn't about him—it was about the lives of countless constituents relying on his leadership.

And, as much as it pained him to acknowledge, the wolf was undeniably the best candidate for the job. Not as Hart Redfern, the orphaned red deer once found solace in the wolf's company, but as Senator Redfern, who needed proper protection against the looming threats over his position.

"Very well," he conceded, his voice carrying a low note of resignation. "I'll sign it." *This is nothing more than a professional arrangement*, Hart reminded himself, mentally bracing for what was to come.

"Just remember, once he's on board, you can't just let him go without a solid reason," Rob advised, her sharp eyes observing the senator as he scrutinized the paperwork.

Hart nodded in understanding, his eyes scanning the documents one final time with great attention. With deliberate strokes, he made a few annotations and signed where necessary, each pen mark feeling like a concession. Handing the stack back to Rob, he exhaled a long, weary sigh, the weight of the decision pressing down on him.

"Thank you, Senator." Rob expressed her gratitude with a tone rich in sincerity. She paused to observe Hart, who seemed to retreat into his thoughts, his hand absentmindedly covering his mouth as he stroked his bearded chin. His ears tilted down, as if to hide his thoughts from the world.

As she exited the room, Rob hoped that the senator's life would not have any more close calls in the future.

A knock on the door drew Hart's attention away from the towering stack of documents that had consumed his focus. A quick glance at the desk clock confirmed the arrival he had anticipated yet relegated to the back of his mind, submerging himself in work to avoid the thought.

With a subdued sigh, Hart swiftly tidied his desk, pushing the papers into a neat pile. "Please come in," he called out, maintaining an upright posture as he addressed the knock. A flutter of unease sparked within him, and his jaw tensed as he watched the office door swing open gradually.

"Senator Redfern," Lupus greeted with a warmth that belied the formality of the moment, his voice carrying the gentle curve of a polite smile. He was fully dressed in a stark black suit and tie, contrasting his casual outfit from their previous encounter. The door closed softly behind him as he approached the senator's desk with measured steps.

Hart held the silence for a moment longer, his gaze fixed on Lupus's, striving to keep the interaction strictly professional, to barricade his memories and emotions from creeping into their exchange. "Welcome, Mr. Greyfang," Hart finally said, his voice cold, almost detached. "I trust Ms. Longfoot has briefed you thoroughly on your duties?"

"Yes, sir," Lupus replied succinctly, his posture as rigid as his tone, hands clasped behind his back. He stood poised in the center of the room, his military bearing as pronounced as ever. The smile that had briefly graced his features was now replaced by a line of firm, straight lips. Yet, in a soft contrast to his stern demeanor, his tail continued to sway gently behind him.

Hart's gaze held on Lupus for a moment longer before he inquired, "Do you have any questions about your role or responsibilities?" Hart emphasized the second portion of the question to underscore his only interest in the wolf—as his new security guard.

A flicker of uncertainty crossed Lupus's face. After a brief pause, he voiced the concern that had been nagging at him. "Regarding the compensation, sir," he began with caution. The approved salary was significantly higher than what he had anticipated. Rob had suggested that the senator was behind the generous adjustment, prompting Lupus to seek clarification directly.

Hart leaned back, his eyes never leaving Lupus's. "A stag like me, hiring a wolf as a guard," he paused, eyes narrowing slightly as he observed the wolf's reaction. He noted the slight tension in the wolf's shoulders at the comment. "It's bound to stir whispers across Anthroterra," Hart continued, his gaze piercing into the green depths of Lupus's eyes. "I do not wish to contribute to that by undervaluing your expertise."

Lupus swallowed, the pressure in the room almost tangible. Hart's stoic expression was unreadable, his brown eyes cold and detached, a stark contrast to the soft warmth he once saw in them, as Lupus recollected.

"Unless," Hart continued, his tone sharpening like the edge of a knife, "you intended to offer subpar service."

Lupus's eyes widened, taken aback by the blunt question. "No, sir. Not at all," he replied quickly.

Hart's gaze remained unwavering, as if he were attempting to delve into the very depths of Lupus's soul with those piercing, earthy brown eyes. "Does that answer your question, Mr. Greyfang?"

Lupus responded with a slight nod, his voice measured. "Yes. Thank you, sir."

Hart's gaze shifted to the corner of his desk, where stacks of documents awaited his review. He reached for a particularly thick bundle on top, drawing it closer, letting the rustle of the pages fill the brief silence.

"I'll be working late tonight, beyond your shift. You can leave early," Hart said, his eyes not leaving the papers as he spoke. His voice, though steady, carried an undertone of fatigue. "We return to the Capitol early tomorrow. Be ready." His focus remained on the document from the Head of Wilfen Security Department, which requested resources from Anthroterra Central. The attached reports, highlighting a concerning uptick in recent incidents across the district, demanded his full attention.

"Understood, sir," Lupus replied, his gaze heavy with unspoken concern for Hart, sensing the layers of weariness beneath his composed exterior. He wanted to inquire about Hart's relentless work schedule and if he was affording himself any rest. Yet, the clear and cold boundaries set by the senator held him back.

After a moment of tense silence, Lupus spoke with genuine respect, "Thank you for the opportunity to serve, Senator," he said, warmth infusing his voice. His eyes briefly lingered on the faint scars etched into Hart's antlers, noting the healing scratches he had observed during their last encounter.

Hart's jaw clenched for a moment. "Good day," he dismissed curtly, his tone icy, not bothering to look up as Lupus departed.

With the click of the closing door, Hart's composure crumbled. He exhaled deeply as his ears drooped, the weight and anxiety of their encounter lingering in his mind. He kneaded his forehead, trying to stave off the headache that threatened to bloom.

He's just a security guard. Just keep it professional, Hart reminded himself. With a determined sigh, Hart refocused on the resource request, swallowing the lingering emotions lodged in the back of his throat.

The rhythmic lull of the train, with its gentle sways and consistent hums, should have been the perfect backdrop for Hart to focus on his upcoming briefing for the Education and Culture Committee.

Yet, every so often, his concentration wavered, and his eyes would drift towards the pair of alert black ears peeking over the top of the Wilfen Daily he was holding.

Those ears belonged to Greyfang, Hart's newly appointed security guard, seated across the snug train table. The pointy set of ears twitched and rotated at every sound, focusing on the surroundings within the train carriage as it bounced along the tracks.

As a senator, Hart was no stranger to the weight of his responsibilities, nor to the contention he sparked among certain factions of the Greats. The others ranged from indifferent to mildly curious. With Lupus, a wolf security guard, now visibly by his side, Hart pondered whether this would amplify the scrutiny or perhaps act as a deterrent. Doubt gnawed at him. Maybe he should rethink this arrangement, acknowledge the potential misstep, and let the wolf return to Wilfen.

Absorbed in these ruminations, Hart barely noticed the passage of time, until he became aware of Rob's scrutinizing gaze, capturing the unspoken torrent of thoughts that was probably hidden only from Lupus due to the newspaper serving as a barrier.

Hart knew that Rob genuinely worried about his safety, especially being the first herbivore senator. Beyond the district finances she had leveraged against his possible disapproval of hiring a security guard, dismissing Lupus on the sole premise of his species wouldn't sit well with her. This might remain the case until he found someone else and proved that they were better than Lupus—a feat Hart doubted was possible, even with the revised salary they'd negotiated.

As the train neared the Capitol, a knot of anxiety tightened in Hart's chest. He momentarily wondered if he could persuade Rob that the Capitol's existing security detail was sufficient, rendering a personal guard unnecessary.

With a heavy sigh, Hart turned his attention to the window, setting the newspaper aside. In an effort to dispel unproductive thoughts, he focused on the passing scenery, attempting once again to center his attention on the committee briefing.

Just focus, he mentally admonished. Yet, despite his best efforts, he remained acutely aware of the watchful, subtly concerned eyes of his new security guard.

Arion Sterling, the High Chancellor of Anthroterra Central, was a silver fox terrian who had welcomed young Senator Hart Redfern warmly during his initial visit to the Capitol following his election. Known for her sincere commitment to unity among terrians, Hart had admired her since his days at the academy, when she served as a senator for a neighboring district.

With the support of the Advisory Committee, she ensured that the senatorial residence within the Grand Enclave, which historically only served carnivore senators, was adequately modified for Hart's unique stature. The modifications included wider and taller doorways and hallways to accommodate his antlers. Despite the objections of some senators who grumbled about preserving the architectural integrity and its historical value, the Chancellor had insisted on these necessary changes. She recognized that Senator Redfern would not be the last stag senator to walk the halls of the Enclave.

Every time Hart navigated the corridors without his antlers getting ensnared, his gratitude for Chancellor Sterling deepened. The weight of Hart's gratitude was particularly pressed even more at this moment, as he was spared the embarrassment of entangling his antlers in a doorway, particularly with Lupus in attendance.

Rob trailed behind Hart as they stepped into the grandeur of the senatorial residence, pointing out, "Staff quarters are further down the hall."

"I'll be down shortly," said Hart, his gaze sweeping over the familiar grandeur. With a nod to Rob, he began his ascent up the stairs near the entrance.

The room assigned to Lupus was adequately spacious, offering a view of the backyard with a greenhouse full of fresh greens—another special modification the Chancellor had arranged for Hart.

"I'll inform the kitchen about arranging proper meals for you. Do you have a preference? Poultry or fish?" Rob inquired, pulling out her notepad and fountain pen with practiced ease, her ears perked in anticipation of Lupus's response.

"Ms. Longfoot," Lupus began, his voice gentle yet firm, halting her hand mid-air. Her eyes, sharp and attentive, met his. "I don't require meat. Eggs and dairy products will be more than sufficient."

Rob regarded him with a quizzical tilt of her eyebrow, her eyes swirling with curiosity and a hint of skepticism. "Are you sure?" she probed.

Lupus offered a reassuring smile, seeking to put her doubts to rest. "It's a longstanding personal choice, one that doesn't pertain to my duties. I assure you, it won't compromise my performance." He hoped his words would assuage any concerns she might have, though he sensed there was more to her query than just his dietary preferences.

Rob acknowledged his assurance with a small nod, her expression still contemplative. "Very well, Mr. Greyfang." She paused, her tone shifting to a more professional cadence. "The Senator will be heading to his congressional office soon. Once you're settled, we'll reconvene in the dining room." With a nod of acknowledgment from Lupus, she exited the room.

In the fleeting silence of the townhouse, punctuated by faint footsteps overhead that he assumed were Hart's, Lupus looked out at the backyard and surveyed the quarters. It was another stark reminder of what Hart had accomplished.

A wave of nostalgia washed over Lupus, poignant and bittersweet, as he ran his fingers over the contours of a pair of faded metal rings that accompanied his military tag. *They would have been so proud*, he mused, sensing their presence lingering in the serene hush of the room.

The goat terrian joined the table without an invitation, her eyes gleaming with mischief and curiosity. "Tell me, Rob," she began, her voice dripping with intrigue, "was the wolf security guard actually hired by Senator Redfern?" Her question lingered, filling the space between them, as she settled more comfortably in her chair, her ears standing tall and focused on Rob.

A rush of irritation surged through Rob, her patience fraying at the audacity of the question. With deliberate slowness, she placed the fork down, letting the greens and sliced tomato tumble back onto her plate with a muted thud. "What's that supposed to mean?" she countered, her voice edged with a sharpness that matched the intensity of her narrowed gaze, now locked onto the goat's bright yellow eyes that sparkled with the thrill of gossip.

The goat leaned back, a smirk playing on her lips, clearly enjoying the moment. "Oh, come now, Rob," she cooed, the silver ring adorned with the eye emblem of Anthrople twirling between her fingers. "A wolf as a guard for the stag senator? It's rather… unconventional, don't you think? Sounds more like a ploy by the Greats, or, who knows, perhaps *the Shadow Clan*." She paused, her words heavy with implication, suggesting they were more than mere rumors. "Why else would a stag like him hire an old wolf for protection? He's smaller than the senator, past his prime, and unlike herbivore guards, he can't even carry a weapon."

Rob's eyes flashed with annoyance, her fingers curling tighter around her fork. "Nonsense," she snapped, dismissing the goat's insinuations with a flick of her wrist. She turned her attention back to her meal, taking a deliberate bite in an effort to compose herself. The task was becoming increasingly difficult as old memories of their shared academy days resurfaced— memories of Leah and her close friends, unashamedly flaunting their skewed Anthroplist leanings even back then, fueling her growing rage.

Rob had always held Anthrople's teachings close to her heart. The doctrine, which professed that the All Father looked upon every terrian with equal adoration, was a beacon of unity since the early days of the United Districts of Anthroterra.

Each terrian, irrespective of species, was a testament to the All Father's boundless love—a living embodiment of his pure human essence. The faith celebrated the shared human traits among terrians, viewing these commonalities as a divine gift. It called for the recognition of the All Father's diverse beauty in every terrian, to nurture intelligence, and to cultivate empathy, transcending species boundaries.

While the central tenets of Anthrople were universally respected, interpretations varied. Some purists contended that herbivores, with their non-violent diets, were closer to the All Father's pure human essence.

This suggestion of a spiritual hierarchy troubled Rob. She firmly believed that all terrians, regardless of diet or lineage, were equal in the All Father's eyes. Such divisive notions not only contradicted Anthrople's original teachings but also threatened the unity and harmony that Anthroterra had fought so hard to achieve.

"I'd hoped you'd outgrown these conspiracy tales, Leah. Please tell me you're not leaning towards those extremists," Rob spat, barely concealing her rising irritation.

Leah's eyes widened, the weight of Rob's words causing her to momentarily falter. "You mean the Hooves? You can't be serious, Rob." she whispered, disbelief evident in her voice. She reached out, gently tapping on Rob's shoulder in a gesture meant to comfort but also to seek reassurance. "I'm not going to go around vandalizing carnivore-owned stores," the goat continued, her voice a touch softer, casting a wary glance around as if expecting eavesdroppers. "But you have to admit, with almost half of the prison population–"

"Stop," Rob cut in, her voice sharp and commanding. She leaned in, her eyes steely. "There's no 'but' in this, Leah. Be careful reciting what you read from the Hooves' propaganda, especially with the Bureau just a short walk away from the congress building," Rob growled as she furrowed her eyebrows in disdain. "Mr. Greyfang literally saved the Senator's life. Everyone in Anthroterra knows that. Show some respect."

"Yeah, but how do you know if that wasn't a staged act?" Leah persisted, her fingers playfully twirling the ribbon on her polished horns. "The scenario sounds overly convenient, doesn't it? The carnivore war veteran just happened to be present during the senator's time of need."

Rob's fingers tightened around her fork, the metal biting into her skin. She took a deep breath, trying to rein in her rising anger. Slowly placing her fork down, she locked eyes with Leah, her gaze icy and unwavering. "Do you have anything better to talk about other than disrespecting a war veteran who stood up against oppressive carnivores, based on mere rumors and speculation?" Her voice was a controlled whisper, laced with contempt.

Leah visibly flinched, the weight of Rob's words causing her to momentarily falter. The confident facade she had put up earlier crumbled, replaced by a mix of embarrassment and frustration. After a moment, she pushed back her chair, the scraping sound loud in the charged silence. "Alright, Rob," she muttered, her voice laced with defeat. "I'll see you at the staff gathering later today." Without waiting for a response, she turned sharply, her tail flicking in annoyance, and strode away.

Rob's brown gaze lingered on the retreating figure of the goat. She let out a weary sigh, rubbing her temples. The rumors, the whispers, the doubts—they had been a constant presence ever since Hart's election. And now, with Lupus by his side, the murmurs had only grown louder. Regardless, she had faith in her senator to maintain his integrity in his work and prove any critics whispering behind his back wrong about him and Lupus.

In the Shadows

"My parents are doing well, Senator. Thank you for asking," Ms. Whitetine said with a gentle smile, placing her gardening gloves on the counter. "They still run the shop on weekdays. I'm trying to coax them into taking some leisure time, away from work."

"That's good to hear," Hart replied, a smile tinged with relief spreading across his face. The hint of concern that had lingered in his mind dissipated upon learning that the elderly mule deer owners were simply absent from the plant nursery, not unwell.

His gaze wandered lazily around the shop, the earthy smell of soil mingling with the fragrance of various flowers, easing the tension from his shoulders. His eyes were drawn to a collection of small pots, their delicate paintwork standing out among the larger plants, nestled like hidden gems.

Noticing the senator's interest, the doe's smile brightened. "They're from a new pottery shop in River East, handcrafted by a bear family," she explained, her hands cradling a green pot adorned with a delicate white stag. She offered it to the senator. "I stumbled upon them while searching for a gift for my aunt last week and thought they'd make a perfect complement to our smaller plants."

"That must be the Nightfurs. Their attention to detail is among the best in town, in my opinion," Hart commented, his eyes reflecting a depth of thought as he examined the pot. He handed it to Rob, his mind wandering back to his own visit to the pottery shop, where the black bear owner and his playful cubs had greeted him with warmth.

Decades had passed since the end of the war, and with the decline of many carnivore packs and the rise of the herbivore extremist group, tensions between species had been slowly escalating.

Yet, within the Wilfen communities, the unbridled and friendly interspecies interactions had always remained a beacon of hope, steadfast despite the turmoil unfurling across the nation. This enduring harmony filled his heart with profound warmth, kindling a gentle smile that reached all the way to his eyes.

"It's beautiful, Ms. Whitetine," Rob said, her ears perked up in genuine interest as she admired the pot.

"Could you recommend a plant that would pair well with this? I'd like to buy it for the office," Hart inquired, his gaze following Rob as she handed the pot back to Ms. Whitetine.

Her face lit up as she accepted the pot back. "I have the perfect plant in mind for this one," she assured with a smile "Just give me a moment, please. I'll get it ready for you," she said, her voice trailing off as she moved toward the back of the shop.

While Rob busied herself with preparing the payment, Hart's gaze wandered among the plants and flowers. The scent of fresh blooms danced on his nostrils, adding a small contentment in his mind.

His eyes eventually settled on the wolf standing guard outside the shop, his silhouette framed by the expansive shop window. The wolf's ears twitched rhythmically, in tune with the bustling street.

The passersby's curious glances and hushed whispers didn't escape Hart's notice; they were unmistakably drawn to the old wolf, a mysterious war veteran with little to no information, who had become a topic of fervent discussion in Wilfen Daily ever since his first appearance at the Capitol following Hart's recent incident. Lupus, however, appeared unfazed by the attention, his posture rigid and authoritative.

Then, as if sensing Hart's scrutiny, one ear swiveled backward before he turned slightly, his green eye locking with Hart's.

"This is a Croton Petra," the doe's gentle voice pulled Hart from his reverie, nearly startling him into movement. He managed to maintain his composure, betraying his surprise only with a subtle lift of his eyebrows as he turned to see the doe standing beside Rob. The vibrant yellow and lush green of the plant accentuated the pot's color, making it come alive.

"That is gorgeous!" Rob's voice was a blend of surprise and delight, her eyes sparkling as she admired the plant on the counter.

"Thank you so much, Ms. Whitetine," Hart said with a warm smile, as Rob completed the purchase and carefully cradled the plant and pot in her arms before stepping out of the shop. "Please extend my regards to the Whitetines," he added, tipping his head in a farewell as he followed Rob out.

"Oh, wait, Senator," Whitetine called out, hastening after them. "I've got something to share with you. Sorry, it won't take long," she said, her words tumbling out in a rush as she darted back into the store before Hart could respond, leaving him momentarily stunned in her wake.

At that moment, a pair of playful fawns burst around the corner of the building, charging straight towards Hart without regard for their path. Lupus, positioned just outside the store, noticed them immediately. He swiftly stepped in to brace Hart, his firm hands steadying the senator's back, anchoring him firmly as the two fawns collided with their unintended target.

Lupus's sharp gaze met Hart's, searching for the signs of distress—the brief flicker of panic that danced across Hart's eyes, the way his furry ears snapped to attention, and his tail bristled with alarm. Recognizing the senator's momentary vulnerability, Lupus's voice, soft yet unwavering, cut through the chaos in Hart's mind. "It's okay, Senator," he murmured reassuringly, his hand patting Hart's back in a steady, comforting rhythm. His gaze, steadfast and confident, served as an anchor, steadying the senator.

With a deep breath, Hart felt the icy tendrils of shock that had clawed into his mind begin to melt away, replaced by a soothing calm. He offered Lupus a small, appreciative nod, his tail easing its tension, signaling his regained composure.

Having ensured Hart's steadiness, Lupus turned his attention to one of the fawns now seated on the ground after the impact. Lowering his stance to appear less daunting, he asked, "Hey there, are you alright?" His voice, as warm and gentle as his green gaze, was laden with genuine concern toward the fawn. His ears were folded down in an effort to appear less intimidating, while his tail swept the ground in a friendly rhythm. He was concerned that the fawn might be frightened of him, but instead, he was greeted with wide, innocent brown eyes, brimming with curiosity. The purity of that gaze stirred a tender emotion deep within Lupus.

Abruptly, a panicked voice cut through the moment. "Jane! Jimmy!" Ms. Whitetine burst from the store's ornate doorway, her arms laden with a flat wooden box. The sight of her children, especially her daughter mere inches from a wolf, sent a jolt of primal fear through her. Her ears shot up in alarm, and her eyes widened in a dreadful mix of maternal protectiveness and instinctual apprehension.

Sensing her distress, Lupus swiftly took a deliberate step back. An apologetic smile played on his lips, with his tail giving a few friendly wags, signaling his harm-less intentions. The two fawns, sensing their mother's anxiety, quickly scrambled to her side.

Hart, detecting the lingering tension, swiftly redirected the focus to the little doe with a warm smile. "You're quite the runner, Jane," he remarked, crouching slightly to meet the young fawn's gaze. His voice was soft, imbued with a gentle playfulness that aimed to put her at ease.

Jane's large, round eyes flitted between Hart's kind face and the impressive span of his antlers, her curiosity evident. She clutched her mother's skirt, her fingers tangling in the fabric. "I'm sorry…" she whispered, her voice barely audible, the weight of the situation making her words tremble.

Hart's eyes sparkled with a blend of amusement and understanding. "That's alright, but you could have gotten hurt. Just remember to be careful next time, okay? Promise?" He extended his pinky finger, offering a playful pact. Jane hesitated for a moment, looking up at her mother for reassurance. Ms. Whitetine, with her ears relaxed as her earlier fear replaced by a gentle smile, gave a nod of approval. The fawn's ear gave a playful twitch as she let out a giggle and linked her tiny pinky with Hart's.

The senator's chuckle was light and melodic, a sound that seemed to harmonize with the gentle ambiance of the moment. After a gentle tousle of Jane's hair, he straightened up, turning his full attention to Ms. Whitetine with a respectful nod.

"I apologize for the children. Their energy seems bound-less these days," the doe said, her eyes briefly meeting Lupus's in a silent expression of apology. The wolf responded with a reassuring smile, signaling that all was well.

Hart chuckled lightly, remarking, "We all have those years. I still remember mine." Nostalgia swept over him as he recalled faint childhood days spent racing through the old, forgotten corners of his neighborhood, the comforting presence of his parents a constant embrace.

But as quickly as the warmth came, a shadow of melancholy followed. Memories shifted, and it was Lupus's warm laughter that echoed from the depths of his past. A knot of emotions tightened in Hart's chest, stealing his breath for a moment.

"Oh, and this is for you, Senator," Ms. Whitetine said, breaking the fleeting silence as she presented the box she had been cradling. "My mother baked it just a couple of hours ago. I thought you might enjoy some sweets after your long day visiting the town," she added, her voice laced with a homely warmth.

As Hart carefully lifted the lid of the wooden box, the sight that greeted him was a beautifully decorated blueberry pie, its sweet aroma immediately enveloping him. For a split second, his expression wavered, betraying a flicker of vulnerability before he regained his composure, offering a warm smile.

"This looks incredible, Ms. Whitetine. Thank you for sharing such a delightful homemade treat," he said, his voice soft yet composed as he gently closed the box. "I'll share this with our staff today." His tone was steady, masking the brief flicker of vulnerability with the polished veneer of his public persona, a skill he had mastered over the years.

"Thank you always for your hard work, Senator," the doe replied, her eyes crinkling with a genuine smile as she lifted her younger fawn into her arms, affectionately stroking her daughter's head. "Have a wonderful weekend."

"You too, Ms. Whitetine," Hart responded with a nod and a smile, then turned to leave. He brushed past the concerned look on Rob's face, setting off down the street at a brisk pace.

At the end of the block, where the senator's carriage awaited, Hart paused. He turned to face Rob and Lupus, his features settling into a stoic mask, a stark contrast to the genuine warmth he had shown his constituents moments before.

"I believe we've accomplished enough for today, Ms. Longfoot. I need some rest," Hart declared, his tone leaving no room for argument. A weary sigh escaped him as he addressed his guard. "Mr. Greyfang, could you accompany Ms. Longfoot and deliver this to the council building for the staff?" he asked, extending the box to Lupus.

Lupus accepted the box, his reluctance evident, a silent protest to the impending separation from the senator. "Sir, perhaps I should..." he began, his thumbs anxiously sweeping over the wood, his gaze locked on the senator's usual icy expression. But the senator was already boarding the carriage, not sparing a backward glance.

"Enjoy your evening," Hart said, giving a brief nod. His gaze met Lupus's quivering green ones for a fleeting moment before the carriage pulled away.

Lupus stood rooted to the spot, watching the carriage recede into the distance, while Rob flagged down another carriage. "We should head back, Mr. Greyfang," she urged, nudging the wolf out of his reverie before climbing into the carriage, mindful of the small plant she cradled. The wolf soon followed, his heart heavy with thoughts and emotions.

As their carriage rolled toward its destination, Rob observed Lupus closely. His attention was still on the wooden box, his brow furrowed with silent contemplation.

"Lupus," she said gently, drawing his gaze. "Don't fret over him. He…" She hesitated, her mind flickering back to the instances when Hart's demeanor turned cold at the mere mention of blueberry pie. It was one of those peculiar quirks of Hart Redfern that he kept closely guarded; the reason behind it remained a mystery to Rob. "The senator doesn't like blueberry pie," she offered with a casual shrug, trying to lighten the mood. "Who knows why."

Lupus responded with a silent nod, his eyes drifting to the evening scenery racing by the window, his fingers still wrapped firmly around the wooden box.

Rob observed the distress and sorrow seeping out from the wolf, his ears completely drooped. "If you don't mind me asking," she began softly, prompting Lupus to meet her gaze. "How do you know Hart?"

Lupus's jaw slackened slightly, visibly taken aback by the question. "I, uh," he stammered, struggling to find his words. The realization that Rob, despite having been by Hart's side for over a decade, was oblivious to their shared past, sent a fresh wave of pain through his heart. It was perhaps expected, maybe even preferable. His gaze briefly dropped to the wooden box in his hands, as he swallowed down his emotions. "I knew his parents," he finally murmured, managing a forced smile as he met Rob's curious, yet cautious, brown eyes.

Rob knew that his smile was more a polite shield than a genuine expression. "I see," she responded, respecting the boundary he had subtly set, not unlike the barriers surrounding Hart's own heart. The rest of the journey passed in silence, punctuated only by the rhythmic clicking of the carriage wheels and the steady clop of horse hooves.

"Heading home soon, Lupus?" Rob's voice, laced with a hint of playfulness, disrupted the office's stillness. She was tidying her workspace as her workday neared its end, excited to head back home and spend time with her family before their return journey back to the Capitol the next morning.

Seated at his desk adjacent to hers, Lupus looked up from his book, gently removing his glasses. "Probably," he responded softly, with his fluffy tail swayed lazily behind him.

A couple of weeks had passed since Lupus began his tenure as Senator Redfern's bodyguard. Thankfully, there haven't been any significant incidents, and Rob found herself appreciating Lupus's quiet company, especially when Hart was staying in his office for hours, buried in books and documents. Lupus brought a comforting peace to their work environment, a sense of tranquility that went beyond the mere feeling of safety Rob had initially expected. His serene demeanor seemed to fill the room, much like the small green pot with a stag painting, adorned with thriving plants under Lupus's care, that Hart had picked up during a town visit—now a friendly fixture on Lupus's desk.

Despite the physical proximity following Lupus's hire, Rob hadn't noticed any significant interaction between him and Hart. Lupus's unwavering commitment to his role was evident. The soldier's creed, which once bound him to protect all terrians, now seemed to anchor him in his duty to Hart. His actions radiated genuine concern for the senator, always maintaining a respectful distance, his interactions marked by a blend of warmth and professionalism.

Yet, Hart's responses were often limited to brief, silent nods, as if words were an unnecessary luxury between them. The bitter twist to Hart's mouth when Lupus's name came up did not escape Rob's notice. It led her to speculate that their shared past bore some jagged edges that had left their mark on Hart. Considering Lupus's character, which she had come to know, she struggled to envision what kind of wounds he could have inflicted upon Hart.

In the end, their individual history was less relevant than the roles they occupied—a senator and his protector—which they both fulfilled with a level of excellence. While a senator wasn't obligated to share a close bond with his security guard, the latter's genuine concern for his charge was indispensable. The balance they maintained in the office, despite the undercurrents of unspoken emotions and lingering questions, was enough for Rob to continue working amicably alongside them.

Shaking off her introspective reverie, Rob stood up, stretching slightly as she collected her belongings from her organized desk. "Come on, Lupus. Leaving the senator all by himself, who enjoys having you next to him? I bet you stay until he wraps up for the night," she quipped, her voice dripping with playful sarcasm as she shot him a teasing smirk.

She fully anticipated a light-hearted retort from Lupus. It was no secret, even for Lupus at this point, that Hart often worked late, and the towering stack of paperwork on his desk earlier was a clear indicator of another long night ahead.

Moreover, Hart had been explicit about the boundaries of Lupus's contract. Rob could still vividly recall the senator's firm demeanor, ensuring that Lupus's role was strictly limited to official duties and public events. No overtimes, no personal engagements. Given Hart's consistent coldness and his almost tangible efforts to uphold a barrier between himself and Lupus, the very idea of Lupus voluntarily staying late was laughably absurd. It was a jest she was sure even Lupus would appreciate.

To her surprise, however, her amusing comment seemed to have taken him off guard; his furry ears and tail stood on end as if she had discovered a closely guarded secret. The usually composed wolf looked momentarily flustered, a sight that Rob found both surprising and endearing. Her bushy tail twitched in amusement, as her ears perked up, focusing on the wolf.

"Wait," she began, her voice dripping with feigned shock, "you don't actually stay back with him, do you?" She paused, a mischievous glint in her eyes. The icy demeanor of the senator toward Lupus and his attempt to stay as far as possible from his guard, however, lingered in Rob's mind. "Have you somehow persuaded our dear senator to let you accompany him home on these late sessions?"

Lupus's eyes darted around, as if searching for an escape route from the playful interrogation. "No, Rob, it's not like that," he replied, his voice tinged with a hint of embarrassment. He cleared his throat, trying to regain his usual poise. "I leave before he does. It's just... I like the quiet of the office after hours. That's all." The wolf straightened his black tie and mustered a smile to conceal his brief unease.

Rob's eyes twinkled with realization. *So, he does linger until Hart departs*, she mused, attributing his unexpected loyalty to Lupus's military discipline. "Hmm," she hummed teasingly, her eyes dancing with mirth. "Alright, Lupus, I'll take your word for it. But just so you know," she leaned in, her voice dropping to a whisper, "your secret's safe with me." She punctuated her statement with a cheeky wink, her smile broadening in genuine delight. She genuinely enjoyed these light-hearted moments with Lupus, and she had no intention of pushing him too far.

Lupus's shoulders, previously rigid with tension, now eased. A soft chuckle resonated from him, and a subtle rosy hue dusted his cheeks. "Thank you, Rob. I appreciate that," he responded, his tone infused with heartfelt warmth. "Enjoy your evening."

With a buoyant wave, Rob turned to leave, her spirits lifted. Casting a final glance back, she saw the wolf, still slightly abashed but unmistakably content, a sight that filled her with warmth.

⤸⧉⤵

The dim glow of the streetlights barely penetrated the thick curtain of twilight as Lupus made his way to his flat. His covert security patrol, shadowing Hart's every step back to his residence, had been uneventful, yet something felt amiss. An intangible sense of unease clung to the air around the stag senator, setting Lupus's instincts on edge. No overt threats had presented themselves, but it felt as if elusive shadows danced just beyond his line of sight, like whispers of a ghostly presence.

Engulfed in his musings, Lupus's focus was abruptly snapped back to the present as he entered his modest flat. A familiar, yet unsettling scent prickled at his senses, immediately putting him on high alert.

"Snowclaw?" His voice, a mix of surprise and caution, echoed in the dimly lit room. The unexpected presence of the Special Operations Director of the Central Security

Bureau in his personal space was alarming. "What are you doing in Wilfen?"

"Checking on my agent, that's all." Emerging from the shadowy recesses of the room, the white wolf's golden eyes scrutinized Lupus from head to toe, making no effort to veil her dissatisfaction. "Wasn't sure if you were doing your job or just playing the security guard, if you know what I mean."

With a deep sigh, Lupus wiped his weary face, feeling the roughness of his evening stubble against his palm. Hands settling on his hips, he finally met Snowclaw's intense gaze. "I've included every detail in my reports. I've found no evidence to suggest Senator Redfern's involvement with the Hooves. He's dedicated to his role, to his constituents. That's all there is to it."

The white wolf's eyebrow arched, her expression a mix of skepticism and amusement. "And you expect me to believe that a red stag senator, the first ever herbivore to sit at the Senate among the Greats, has no connections to the most notorious herbivore resistance group in Anthroterra?" Folding her arms across her chest, the white wolf clicked her tongue with a scornful gaze. "Do you think I'm a blind idiot?" Snowclaw's growl resonated in the room, her combat boots echoing ominously as she closed the distance between them.

Lupus stood his ground, his voice unwavering. "I've been shadowing him for almost a year, only to find nothing. Now, you've had me act as his direct guard for weeks, and the conclusion remains the same. *He's clean.*" His voice dropped to a growl as he continued, with simmering frustration lacing his voice. "Stop wasting time spying on an innocent terrian."

Snowclaw's smirk took on a chilling edge, her golden eyes narrowing into slits. "You had one job, Greyfang. Observe and report," she hissed, her voice dripping with disdain. She stepped closer, her finger jabbing into his chest with each word, asserting her dominance. "Yet, it was you who chose to play the hero, revealing yourself to the senator, and risking the whole operation. You served the potential leader of the Hooves our investigation on a silver platter."

"That bear was overdosing on Wild, ready to prey on anyone." Lupus shot back, defiance flashing in his eyes. "The kid would have been seriously injured if I hadn't intervened." Memories of the sheer panic he'd felt in that moment resurfaced, a terror that had driven him to act against years of ingrained protocol from his tenure as a covert agent. Letting out a short sigh, Lupus shook his head in an attempt to dispel the dreaded feeling. "Where did that bear get such a potent dose of Wild? Is there any connection to the other feral overdose cases in different districts these past few months?"

Luna leaned in, her proximity almost suffocating. Her golden eyes, sharp and predatory, bore into Lupus's. "That's beyond your operation, agent." With a deliberate slowness, she traced her finger down the rugged scars on his cheek, continuing onto his neck.

Lupus swallowed hard, the proximity of the white wolf both unsettling and familiar. "Snowclaw, please. If this is related to the Shadow Clan…" He paused, the weight of his words settling heavily between them. He met her gaze squarely, determination burning in his eyes. "I need to know," he pleaded with a desperate whisper.

The white wolf huffed out a mocking laughter at his comment. "You know you were told to steer clear of anything related to Wild the day you were inducted into Sector Zero. That is not going to change. Not now, not ever," she whispered, her voice dripping with a mix of mockery and disdain. "Need I refresh your memory?"

"Luna," Lupus implored, his eyes pleading for under-standing, for a glimpse of the bond they once shared. But his words faltered as her expression shifted, a raw vulnerability flashing briefly before being replaced by cold fury.

"Shut your fang, agent," she hissed, venom dripping from each word. "To you, it's Director Snowclaw. I am *not* your fucking friend." With an aggressive jerk, she caught the top button of his shirt, pulling him even closer, their faces inches apart. The button gave way with a sharp pop, but her gaze remained unyielding. "Do NOT test me. My patience with you is wearing thin," she snarled, her fingers tightening threateningly around his throat. The air between them crackled with tension, thick with memories and old wounds.

"Just do your job, unless you'd want another extended assignment in a foreign land for sticking your snout where it doesn't belong," she warned, her ears twitching in clear annoyance. "Make yourself useful. Find something of value." With a forceful shove, she sent Lupus stumbling back against the wall. Without sparing him another glance, Luna strode out, leaving a heavy, suffocating silence in her wake.

Lupus let out a weary sigh, Luna's lingering scent gradually dissipating from the room. He picked up the stray button that had been torn from his shirt during their confrontation. He moved to his bed, lying down but not seeking sleep. Instead, he found himself rolling the button between his fingers, lost in the whirlwind of his thoughts.

The shadows of his past crept into his mind, unbidden. Memories from that fateful night, the one that had thrust him into the secretive world of Sector Zero, surged forward with relentless clarity. Nearly two decades had passed, yet the images remained as sharp and harrowing as if they had been etched into yesterday. They were nightmares of moments he wished to forget but that couldn't be erased, like a permanent burn seared into his soul.

He squeezed his eyes shut, pressing the button into the heel of his hand as if to anchor himself away from the ghosts that haunted him. His jaw clenched in a silent battle to expel the specters of his past. Redirecting his focus, he turned his thoughts to the growing problem of Wild in Anthroterra, hoping to drown out the painful memories with the urgency of the present.

The alarming escalation of incidents involving carnivores under the influence of Wild had evolved from hushed whispers in shadowed alleys to open conversations under the scrutiny of daylight. While most incidents had been confined to brawls among carnivores or rash criminal acts, the Hooves' propaganda was exploiting the situation with disturbing effectiveness. Their incendiary messages, now boldly plastered across major districts like Wilfen, fanned the flames of fear and mistrust. The average citizen, regardless of their species, could sense the growing rift, a tension that threatened to unravel the delicate fabric of interspecies unity that Anthroterra had so painstakingly woven over the years.

It had been years since the Bureau had triumphantly declared the Shadow Clan's defeat, proclaiming the eradication of their Wild trafficking and criminal enterprises from the streets of Anthroterra. However, with each passing year, the looming specter of another malevolent faction seizing control of the Wild trade grew more tangible, casting a shadow of uncertainty over the land.

Among all the unnerving possibilities, if this indicated the potential resurgence of the Shadow Clan, it wouldn't just be about the illicit drug trade. The faint, almost imperceptible aura of unease that clung around Hart, which had been incessantly pricking at Lupus's keen senses, now loomed larger in his thoughts. His close association with Hart—the stag senator unjustly marked as a potential radical by the Greats and the Bureau, solely due to his red deer heritage—could inadvertently draw danger into Hart's life. The sheer injustice of the situation ignited a deep, burning indignation within Lupus.

Snowclaw's stern warning echoed in his mind, but he defiantly brushed it aside. The mere notion of personal danger, of living a life in the shadows and sleeping with one eye open in foreign lands, paled in comparison to the paramount importance of ensuring Hart's safety. He felt a compelling need to trace the roots of this escalating drug menace himself.

Swiftly changing into nondescript clothing, he draped himself in a weathered cloak, its hood casting a shadow over his distinct lupine features. With quiet determination, he ventured out into the depths of the night, hoping to find answers lurking in its shadows.

The Little Fawns

Chancellor Sterling's gaze was drawn irresistibly to the intricate antlerlette adorning Senator Redfern's nearly mature prime antlers. The earthy green-brown tone of the lace blended harmoniously with the soft velvet of the antlers and the deep green of Hart's formal attire, creating an aura of understated elegance.

"Such a stunning piece, Senator Redfern," she remarked, her voice filled with genuine admiration as her fluffy tail swayed gently behind her. The ambient light of the grand hall caught the small gemstones embedded within the antlerlette, making them shimmer and dance. The droplet-shaped gems that adorned the tip of her ears, a match to her wedding ring, chimed softly as she tilted her head to get a better view, captivated by the craftsmanship. "Is this a Verdelian masterpiece?"

Hart's lips curled into a modest smile, the pride in his eyes unmistakable. He had received numerous compliments throughout the evening, but praise from the Chancellor held a special weight. "Thank you, Chancellor Sterling," said Hart, and the elegant sway of his head gave life to the antlerlette, the faux flora and vegetation rustling, making it seem as if a piece of Verdel's lush forests had taken root atop his head. "I was told my mother crafted it. She hailed from Southern Verdel."

As he spoke, his gaze momentarily drifted toward Lupus. The wolf was clad in attire that allowed him to blend seamlessly into the background, a stark contrast to the extravagant outfit of other male terrians in the grand hall. He maintained a deliberate distance, close enough to act if the situation demanded, yet distant enough to respect the senator's privacy. His sharp green eyes scanned the bustling grand hall, as ears twitched and pivoted to catch every sound.

A flood of memories washed over him—the warmth of a crackling fireplace, the comforting aroma of burning wood, and the deep, resonant voice of the wolf recounting tales of his parents. The dim, ambient lighting, combined with the gentle haze of the evening's libations, seemed to soften the scars and lines on Lupus's face, momentarily sending Hart to a time when laughter flowed freely between them, a time when they were a family beyond blood.

That was nothing but a pathetic illusion in your head, a cold, cynical whisper hissed from the recesses of Hart's mind, its icy tendrils wrapping around his heart, wrenching him from the warmth of those cherished memories. The bitter truth was that to Lupus, their time together had always been a matter of duty, a responsibility entrusted to him by Hart's father. Hart had been a charge, a poor little fawn to be looked after, and a burden to be released once he matured into a stag.

The passage of time hadn't dulled the sting of this re-alization. No matter how much Hart tried to suppress it, the pain of feeling abandoned by Lupus, coupled with the guilt of being a shackle during the wolf's prime years, persisted. It was a dagger lodged within his heart, its blade twisting with every memory that brought Lupus to the forefront of Hart's mind.

The Chancellor's voice, rich with emotion and under-standing, broke through Hart's reverie. "I'm certain she watches over you with immense pride," she said, her amber eyes shimmering with genuine warmth and empathy. The sincerity in her voice acted as an anchor, gently pulling Hart back from the precipice of his emotions, grounding him in the present moment.

The corners of her lips lifted in a tender smile as she continued, "I hope the rigors of the Annual Senate Assembly this week haven't dimmed your enthusiasm," she added with a playful lilt, her ears giving a teasing flick, and her eyes dancing with a hint of mischief. "To her, and her invaluable gift she bestowed upon our nation," she proposed, lifting her glass in a heartfelt toast.

A rush of emotions welled up within Hart by her genuine gesture, almost making him forget about the fatigue and stress that had been crushing his body and mind the entire week. "Your words mean more than I can express," he replied, his voice thick with gratitude. Raising his glass to meet hers, he echoed, "To her loving spirit, and to the enduring unity of Anthroterra."

The crystalline chime of their glasses meeting rang out, a melodious note amidst the ambient hum of the gathering. The effervescence of the champagne danced on Hart's palate, its light buzz amplifying the warmth of the moment.

The Chancellor's red fox aide, who had been in a lively conversation with a group of senators just a few steps away, gracefully extricated himself and quietly approached Hart and the silver fox. "Good evening, Senator Redfern," he greeted, his voice smooth and warm, the corners of his eyes crinkling into a genuine smile.

Hart, recognizing the familiar face, responded with a gracious nod and a smile that reached his eyes. "A pleasure, as always, Mr. Bush."

The fox's gaze then shifted to the Chancellor, his posture subtly straightening. With a respectful nod, he acknowledged her, "Chancellor." The Chancellor returned his nod with a slight tilt of her head, her eyes reflecting her approval.

Turning her attention back to Hart, the Chancellor's voice softened, taking on a maternal warmth. "Enjoy the evening, Senator. You've earned it." Her hand reached out, giving Hart a reassuring pat on the shoulder.

Feeling a rush of gratitude, Hart's eyes sparkled with appreciation. "Thank you, Chancellor. I wish you a delightful evening as well," he responded, his voice tinged with emotion.

As the chancellor and her aide turned around and stepped away, Hart took a final sip from his glass, the sparkling liquid leaving a pleasant tingle on his tongue. An attentive sheep servant approached with a tray, noticing the gentle tilt of the majestic antlers. The servant gestured to exchange Hart's empty glass for a freshly poured one.

Hart felt a flush creeping up on his cheeks, fleetingly considering rejecting another glass. But as his gaze inadvertently wandered to Lupus, he saw the wolf engaged in a light-hearted exchange with Rob. The gentle sway of Lupus's tail and the warmth radiating from his smile momentarily caught Hart off guard, another wave of bittersweet memories digging its sharp edge in his heart.

With a swift, internal shake, he redirected his gaze, his face settling into a practiced, neutral expression. He gave a gracious nod to the servant, who had been waiting patiently, and accepted the offered glass with a soft, "Thank you."

Hart's brown, slightly sluggish gaze sweep across the grand hall, taking in the myriad expressions directed his way. The warm, approving eyes of fellow herbivore dignitaries contrasted sharply with the cold, calculating glances from certain senators and their close confidants. The low hum of whispered conversations filled the air, many undoubtedly discussing the first stag senator in Anthroterra's history.

The weight of the week's relentless schedule, combined with the emotional ups and downs of the evening, left Hart feeling drained. He sought solace in the champagne, letting the bubbles tickle down his throat. As he sipped, his attention was momentarily captured by the red deer doe singer on stage. Her voice, rich and melodic, harmonized beautifully with the instruments, creating a soothing backdrop to the evening's events.

Rob, her cheeks flushed with a warm glow, approached Hart. Her smile radiated genuine warmth. "I believe you have greeted everyone present, Senator," she remarked, her fingers deftly adjusting the decorative ribbons and vibrant flowers that adorned her furry ears. Noticing the lines of fatigue marring Hart's face, she gently steered him towards a quieter corner of the hall.

Hart's gaze shifted from the mesmerizing performance on stage to the rabbit beside him. He nodded in acknowledgment, taking another sip of his drink. "You're taking the night train back home, correct?" Hart asked, glancing at his wristwatch, trying to recall her travel schedule.

Rob chuckled, her eyes twinkling with mischief. "Can't wait another half a day to find out what chaos my bunnies or my lovely husband managed to create again," she jested. After her mocked enthusiasm, Rob's expression softened at the thought of her sweet home and her family, likely all the bunnies clustered atop her husband, awaiting her return.

Hart adjusted his stance, recognizing Rob's intention to head back to her quarters. "Perhaps Mr. Greyfang could escort you to the station," he suggested, his mind briefly recalling the sizable bag she had with her, nearly half her size, meticulously packed for the various events at the assembly.

Lupus, momentarily taken aback by the unexpected suggestion, stepped forward, his eyebrows raised in mild surprise. Wanting to counter any concern the guard might have about leaving him in public, Hart added, "I won't be far behind. I plan to retire to the enclave shortly."

Sensing Hart's unspoken insistence and considering the well-secured perimeter of the hotel and its grand hall,

Lupus nodded in silent agreement. He then turned to Rob, his eyes softening with genuine concern. "I remember you had quite a substantial travel bag with you this week. Allow me to assist," he offered, extending his forearm with a gentle, reassuring smile.

"Thank you, Mr. Greyfang," Rob responded with a chuckle, gracefully accepting Lupus's arm. "Have a restful weekend, Senator. I'll see you next week."

"You too. Enjoy your time with your family," Hart replied, his smile mirroring the warmth in his words. His gaze lingering on them as they made their way toward the door. The wolf briefly met Hart's gaze for a fleeting moment, before they vanished into the night outside the grand hall.

Despite what he had mentioned to Lupus, Hart lingered in the grand hall long after Rob and Lupus had left, indulging in the beautiful song that filled the building. Lost in a whirlpool of personal contemplations and senatorial responsibilities, an eruption of applause drew Hart's attention back toward the stage.

The performance had reached its end, and the singer descended from the stage with graceful steps. She paused to exchange polite greetings with a few admirers before she began heading in his direction. The muted light from the ornate lamps and chandelier played upon the sleek fabric of her evening gown, making it shimmer like a starlit night as she glided effortlessly across the room.

"Senator Redfern," she began, her voice a gentle caress, "it is an honor to finally meet you." Her eyes, deep pools of emotion, sparkled with genuine warmth.

Recognizing the enchanting red deer terrian before him as Stellar, Anthroterra's renowned singers, Hart responded with a gracious nod. "The honor is mine, Ms. Stellar," he replied, the low timbre of his voice reflecting his genuine admiration. "Your performance was nothing short of mesmerizing, as always."

A melodious chuckle, as enchanting as her singing, escaped Stellar's lips, causing the gemstones on her ears to dance in delight. "Thank you, Senator. But please, just Stellar will suffice," she responded, her tone a blend of playfulness and sincerity. Accepting a flute of champagne from a passing servant and continued, "I'm truly pleased you enjoyed the performance. I accepted the invitation to perform tonight in your honor." Her gaze, tender yet piercing, traveled from the intricate design on Hart's antlerlette to meet his own. The fingers of her free hand tapped rhythmically against her glass, mirroring the soft beats of the music from the band. "Your antlerlette is truly a work of art. It complements your impressive set splendidly," she observed, her voice filled with genuine admiration as she gracefully bridged the gap between them. "It's a rare pleasure to see a fellow red deer adorned with such prime antlers."

Caught slightly off-guard by the compliment, a warm blush tinted Hart's cheeks as his tail pleasantly fluffed up at her comment. The genuine interest in her deep brown eyes, the closeness of their proximity, and the faint, intoxicating hint of her perfume left him feeling unexpectedly vulnerable. The subtle heat of the alcohol coursing through him only heightened this sensation. He lightly brushed his mustache to compose himself, before meeting her gaze with a smile that reached his eyes.

For many stags, especially those in the majority of professions that demanded practicality over aesthetics, maintaining a full set of prime antlers was a luxury they couldn't afford. The primal allure of such a display, coupled with the associated status and prestige, never failed to draw the lingering gaze of fellow deer terrians.

Usually, Hart would deflect such attention, especially since his antlers hadn't emerged from their velvet. But tonight, with Stellar's genuine interest and the warmth radiating from her, he found himself embracing the attention, allowing himself to bask in the glow of her admiration.

"Your words are truly kind, Stellar. I'm honored," Hart replied, warmth evident in his eyes. In a gesture of deep respect and appreciation, he leaned in, delicately cradling her hand and pressing a gentle kiss to her knuckles.

With a bit of a blushed smile, Stellar gestured for a whisper, beckoning Hart to draw closer. "I've got a favor to ask, Senator, if it's not too much trouble," she whispered as her lips brushed against his ear, her voice a sultry murmur. By the gentle drag of her fingers against his jacket's chest pocket, the intention seemed pretty clear, if not by the following suggestion, "Might we discuss it... in private?"

As Hart entered his residence, his arms encircling Stellar's slender yet muscular waist, and their closeness becoming more intimate, a realization began to dawn on him. The warmth of their touch and the softness of their shared breath couldn't mask the underlying truth. The 'favor' Stellar had alluded to earlier was not what he had initially imagined. The tremor in her cold fingertips and the distant look in her eyes painted a picture that was hard to ignore. It was evident that her closeness was a *price* she was paying, a transactional act for some undisclosed favor he was yet to comprehend.

The weight of this understanding began to penetrate the alcohol-fueled fog and the haze of lust that had previously clouded his judgment. A heavy sigh involuntarily escaped Hart's lips, his grip on her tightening in a reflex before he consciously eased his hold. He paused, taking measured breaths to calm his racing heart and to collect his scattered thoughts.

Drawing a deep breath, he carefully stepped back, maintaining a respectful distance as Stellar perched on the edge of the bed. He then reached out to light a lamp on the bedside table. The soft, golden light from the flame bathed the room, momentarily dispelling the encroaching shadows and revealing the tension that hung heavily in the air.

Stellar's voice, a soft whisper, broke the silence. "I'd prefer the darkness," she confessed, her voice quivering with a vulnerability she sought to disguise with a hint of seduction. "But a dim light would be fine, if that's to your liking." Her fingers, hesitant yet seeking, reached out to gently cradle Hart's hand.

However, before their fingers could intertwine, Hart deftly withdrew his hand, creating a deliberate distance between them. He turned his back to her, his steps muted against the plush carpet as he approached the ornate dressing mirror.

"There seems to be a misunderstanding, Ms. Stellar," he stated, his tone frigid and deliberate. The mirror reflected his intent gaze, now locked on the doe who appeared both bewildered and exposed. With meticulous care, he adjusted his suit and combed his hair back into place, each movement precise, each detail meticulously attended to.

He made his way to his desk, pulling out a chair with calculated precision. He positioned it to face Stellar, taking a moment to observe her. The doe's ears lay flat against her head, a clear sign of her growing apprehension. With a final, measured motion, Hart seated himself, crossing his legs and resting his arms on the armrests, his hands clasped in front of him. This created an atmosphere of cold formality, a stark contrast to the earlier warmth.

After a moment of heavy silence, Hart broke the silence, his voice cold and firm. "I'm not particularly fond of being manipulated," he began, with his eyes, sharp and unyielding, locking onto Stellar's. The dim glow from the oil lamp painted a haunting silhouette of the stag on the wall, the shadow of his majestic antlers seeming to sway with a life of its own. "Even less so, deceived." The subtle rumble in his tone made Stellar's throat tighten. After a deliberate pause, the stag continued, "What is the favor you wish to request of me?"

Stellar took a deep, steadying breath for a moment. "Okay, Senator. I'll be straight with you," she said, her voice shaky yet determined. She rose and paced they room as she nervously adjusted her gown with trembling hands, gathering her thoughts and formulating her forthcoming confession. As she leaned against the wall not too far from the door, distancing herself from the phantom of Hart's gently undulating shadow, Stellar finally broke her silence. "I need your help finding out which feral devourant preyed on my brother."

Hart's eyebrow quirked in surprise, his stern facade momentarily faltering. Giving her an opportunity to elaborate, he stayed quiet, observing her clenched jaw before she proceeded.

Swallowing hard, Stellar pressed on, "My brother, Owen Deerfield, was brutally murdered, *devoured* by a carnivore, but the Bureau covered his death and paid my family to stay quiet, and to move away from our hometown."

Hart's posture shifted subtly, his back straightening and arms folding across his chest. His gaze, previously sharp and direct, now took on a distant, introspective quality as he processed Stellar's words, requesting information related to the Central Security Bureau.

He recalled recent senatorial discussions led by the Special Operations Director Snowclaw, notably concerning the Wild's ongoing investigations. It brought back the brief moment when a jaguar senator obliquely mentioned the increasing disturbances caused by the Hooves in his district, casting a pointed look towards Hart. Amid a ripple of disapproving murmurs, along with a few chuckles and sidelong glances, many clearly directed at the lone herbivore present, the senator's question was swiftly brushed aside. Director Snowclaw had stated that while they responded to all relevant reports, there were no significant developments that warranted the Bureau's proactive attention.

Snapped back to the present, Hart scrutinized Stellar, a steely resolve forming in his eyes. He felt his stomach twist with simmering fury.

Unaware of the storm brewing within Hart, Stellar continued, her voice thick with emotion. "Seventeen years ago, a Bureau agent stood at our doorstep, delivering the grim news of his death. They said he was caught in the crossfire of an operation. No further explanation was given. They wouldn't even allow us to see his remains." Her voice began to waver as she grappled with a torrent of emotions. Her eyes, filled with unshed tears and brimming with emotion, seeking some sign of empathy from Hart for what she had gone through. "I had to see him, Senator. I had to see his last moment with my own eyes, or else I could never accept that he was truly gone. I sneaked into the morgue, and..." The haunting imagery rapidly overwhelmed her mind; her once vibrant and boundlessly tender brother, now cold and torn, devoured like an animal. The chilling atmosphere of the morgue, the cold touch of the stone, and the overpowering scent of death flooded her senses.

Hart rose from his seat, his back momentarily turned to Stellar as his eyes drifted to the window. After a moment of contemplation, he spoke in a flat, emotionless tone. "Any information or specifics related to the

Bureau's operations is classified as top secret. Releasing any portion of it, no matter how old or insignificant it might be, is considered a threat to national security. Not to mention it is an act of treason," he stated, the gravity of his words hanging heavily in the air.

He turned to face Stellar, his gaze sharp with simmering rage. With his ears pinned back, Hart advanced slowly, his tall stature looming over her without a trace of sympathy to her evident emotional turmoil. "The mere fact that you still walk freely leads me to believe that you've never approached any other senators with this request," he growled, his low rumble laced with a hint of accusation. His jaw clenched, and his eyes darkened with a mix of anger and frustration. "Did you presume I'd help because I'm of your kind?" In a sudden, swift motion, his hand slammed against the wall beside her, effectively trapping her. "*Answer me!*" The intensity of his gaze bore into her, as the threatening sound of his teeth gritting and heavy breathing pressed down on the doe.

Yet, defiance and desperation blazed in Stellar's eyes. Even as tears brimmed, she held Hart's gaze, her chin raised in a show of unwavering determination. "Because I don't trust the carnivores, *the Greats.* They're all nothing but beasts," she retorted, her voice quivering but resolute, echoing the tumultuous emotions churning within her.

Hart's nostrils flared, his tail bristling with barely contained rage. The weight of every sneer, every whispered insult, every belittling of his devotion and efforts, everything he had endured as the stag senator came crashing down upon him. The alcohol coursing through his veins only served to amplify his emotions, stripping away the layers of restraint he'd cultivated over the years. The raw pain of past humiliations, combined with Stellar's insults against the Greats, seemed to wrench him away from his position, igniting a firestorm of anger within him.

"Who do you think you are, assuming you can dare to spew such bigotry in my presence?" he hissed, his voice dripping with venom. His fingers curled into a tight fist, knuckles white with tension. "Did you actually believe you could belittle my position and question my loyalty to this nation without facing consequences?" In a swift, aggressive motion, he seized her arm. "I'll personally hand you over to the Bureau. Right now." With a forceful tug, he began to drag her as he stormed out of the room.

"Let go of me, you spineless traitor!" Mustering unexpected strength, Stellar viciously yanked at his tail, forcing him to release her arm as he uttered a pained hiss. Tears stained her flushed face as she furiously wiped them away, her ears pinned back in rage. "I can't believe I was foolish enough to think I could trust you, when it was so obvious. I even felt pity for you, being paraded around by the Greats with that damned wolf leashed to your side." With a few determined strides, Stellar jabbed a finger into Hart's chest, her sudden fiery demeanor momentarily stunning him. "You're nothing but a carnivore admirer, desperate for their approval."

"Watch your fucking mouth," Hart shot back sharply, his voice carrying a dangerous edge. He quickly ensnared her pointing hand, squeezing her fingers with an unyielding grip before flinging it aside. The force of his action made the doe stagger.

Unfazed by his rage, Stellar continued her tirade. "Do it, then," she challenged, her voice dripping with contempt. "March me to the Bureau. Tell them how I dared to blaspheme the mighty fucking Greats in your esteemed presence." With a burst of strength, she pushed him, forcing him to stagger back, down the stairs toward the front door. Spreading her arms wide in open defiance, she taunted, "Better yet, tell them you suspect I'm part of the Hooves. I'm sure they'll pat you on the head for dragging in a defenseless deer, parading me around as their latest 'rebellion' trophy, then they'd put their disgusting meat-smeared nose on every corner of me and my family in a desperate hunt for even a hint of a connection." Her voice was venomous, her scornful gaze piercing. "What a disgrace you are. *A senator?* You're more interested in flexing your power than seeking true justice, ready to denounce a fellow terrian for mere dissent. You revel in your authority, just like those carnivores you so admire."

She stepped closer, the dim lights casting ominous shadows behind her, causing Hart to retreat further down the stairs. The darkness seemed to haunt him, choking his throat. "You've got no morals, no concern for anything beyond your pathetic ego, hiding behind that *unworthy title* you've earned by deceiving your constituents."

Hart's retort died in his throat. Her words sliced deep, laying bare the insecurities he had long tried to conceal. His brown eyes swelled with unshed tears, a tumultuous mix of doubt and self-loathing flickering within them. They were a reflection of the inner turmoil he'd battled throughout his life, further amplified by his intoxication.

With a look of utmost disdain, she spat on his cheek, sneering, "You are a *fucking joke*, Redfern." Without another word, she pushed past him, flinging open the front door and stormed out into the night.

The distant conversation beyond the closed door barely registered in Hart's consciousness, and neither did the seemingly unending passage of minutes. He stood as if petrified, a statue on the staircase, his breath trapped within the confines of his chest. He couldn't dare to move, breathe, or even think. The sensation was akin to standing on the edge of a precipice, the ground crumbling beneath him, the vast expanse of darkness beckoning him to plunge into its depths.

The echo of familiar voice, laced with deep concern, eventually perforated the fog encasing his senses. "Senator? Is everything okay?"

Hart turned slowly, his gaze meeting Lupus's, who had approached cautiously. The wolf's expression contorted with a mix of confusion and concern as his gaze fell upon the degrading trail of spit clinging to Hart's beard. Taking out his handkerchief, Lupus carefully wiped away the remnant from the stag's beard and his suit. His intense green gaze never left the stag, to understand the storm raging behind Hart's vacant stare. Yet, Hart remained unresponsive, his expression hollow.

Lupus's voice, usually so steady and composed, wavered with an undercurrent of raw concern. "Senator Redfern, *Hart*, talk to me. What happened? What did she do?" His eyes darted over Hart's form, searching for any sign of physical harm, even though the air was devoid of the metallic tang of blood. When his gaze locked onto Hart's eyes, now glistening with unshed tears, the depth of the stag's emotional torment was laid bare. Shaky breaths betrayed Hart's efforts to hold himself together, as he felt the world around him crumble.

"I..." The word was barely a whisper, fragile and trembling. His vision grew hazy, the world around him blurring as tears threatened to spill from his eyes, pooling on the edges of his long lashes. "I've tried," he murmured, his voice quaking with the weight of suppressed emotions. Slowly, he began to sink down onto the stairs, overwhelmed by the burden of his feelings and years of silent suffering. The constant struggle to prove his worth, to battle against the prejudices and expectations of others, now converged into a tidal wave of despair. "I swear, I've tried to be better, to prove myself. I have…" His voice faded into a breath, his thoughts drowning in an overwhelming tide of emotions.

Without any words, Lupus enfolded him in a comforting embrace, pulling him close and gently rubbing his back. It was a gesture reminiscent of times long past, when Hart was but a little fawn seeking warmth from his only family, the pillar of his world. The embrace, warm and protective, served as a temporary shield from the relentless judgments and expectations that had battered Hart throughout his life.

"I know, Hart. I know," Lupus murmured soothingly, his voice laden with a raw emotion that hinted at shared pain, as if he too bore the weight of Hart's struggles. The warmth of the wolf seeped through Hart's defenses, reaching his broken heart, reminding him of the unconditional support he once found in Lupus's presence. "It's okay. Let it out. I'm here for you."

As Lupus's words washed over him, a dam broke within Hart. Decades of suppressed anger, frustration, and longing surged forth, overwhelming him. Desperately gripping the fabric of Lupus's cloak, Hart sought refuge in the familiar scent and strength of the wolf, allowing himself to completely unravel, to be the vulnerable little fawn once more.

"Get your filthy paws off me!" Stellar's voice rang out sharp and clear as she slapped away the hand offered to help her up. The unexpected encounter with the wolf, especially on the heels of her tumultuous exit from the residence, had thrown her off balance.

"Ms. Stellar?" The voice, laced with genuine concern and a hint of confusion, made her heart skip a beat as she regained her footing. "What were you doing here? Did Senator Redfern invite you?"

"Mind your own business, meat-eater." Stellar hissed, her voice dripping with disdain. But as she attempted to storm off, a strong grip encircled her wrist, anchoring her in place. Panic and anger surged within her as she tugged, trying to free herself from the iron grasp.

"This *is* my business, Ms. Stellar," the wolf guard retorted, his voice cold and firm, his piercing gaze never wavering from Stellar's fiery brown eyes.

"I'm leaving. Let me go!" With a sudden burst of strength, Stellar wrenched her arm free, immediately cradling the reddened area where his fingers had left their mark. She looked at him with a mix of disdain and challenge, her eyes raking over his form in a deliberate, dismissive manner. "Why don't you go tuck your precious stag into bed and kiss him good night," she taunted, her voice dripping with sarcasm.

The wolf's entire demeanor shifted in an instant. The once stoic guard now radiated a dangerous aura of anger. His ears stood erect, tail stiffened, and his narrowed eyes bore into her with a predatory intensity. "Show your respect, Ms. Stellar," he warned, his voice no longer carrying its earlier civility. Instead, it was a deep, menacing growl that seemed to echo from the depths of his soul. "Senator Redfern holds a position of honor and respect in the Anthroterra Central Senate."

The sight of his glinting fangs, gleaming ominously under the dim streetlight, combined with the predatory gleam in his piercing green eyes rooted Stellar to the spot, freezing her. The raw aggression she saw, an intensity she had never faced before, sent a chill down her spine. She was trembling, paralyzed by a fear that was both primal and instinctual.

It was the distant chatter of voices, drawing nearer to the Enclave, that finally jolted her back to reality. The chilly night air burned her lungs, reminding her to breathe. Without a backward glance, she darted away, instinctively feeling the weight of the wolf's feral stare still lingering on her from behind.

The moment Stellar's body touched the plush interior of her waiting carriage, she felt the weight of the evening's events pressing down on her. The lingering threat of the wolf's predatory gaze was slowly being overshadowed by the tumultuous confrontation with Senator Redfern. She exhaled deeply, her hand trembling as it gripped the carriage's metal handle with a vice-like intensity.

"Rough night?"

The deep, velvety voice pierced the silence, causing Stellar's heart to skip a beat, eliciting a sharp gasp as her furry ears shot up in alarm. However, upon recognizing the shadowed figure seated opposite her, a sigh of relief flowed through her. Her advisor had a penchant for slipping into dimly lit carriages unannounced, maintaining the secrecy of their clandestine meetings.

"Moonlight! You almost stopped my heart," Stellar exclaimed, her voice a mix of relief and playful annoyance, her heart still racing from the unexpected presence. Her nerves started settling as she accepted the soft gloved hand extended to her. A faint brush of a mustache met the back of her hand in a comforting gesture as Moonlight gently put his lips on her knuckles. It was both a tender greeting and a silent apology.

"Rough night, indeed. I was being reckless," she admitted, her voice barely above a whisper, the weight of her actions evident in her words. Holding onto his hand, she sought solace in the concealed warmth beneath the silk. "Thought I could get closer to the truth behind Owen's death." Her voice cracked slightly, the pain of her brother's memory still raw. "The stag senator has already been tainted by those filthy animals." Moonlight's thumb gently traced the back of her hand, a soothing gesture that momentarily eased the tight knot of anxiety in her chest.

"He was ready to hand me over to the Bureau, you know," she continued, her voice laced with disbelief and a hint of anger. "I had to push him, challenge his convictions." As she bit her lip, a rueful smirk played on her face, hinting at her self-derision for the dangerous gamble she'd taken, one that could have compromised everything.

Moonlight's grip on her hand tightened, anchoring her to the present moment. He slightly leaned in, releasing her lip from its captive bite with a gentle touch. "Stellar, you must know I would never let anything happen to you," he murmured, his voice a soft caress.

Even with the enigmatic shadows cast by the deep black hood of his signature cloak, the intensity of his amber gaze pierced through, reaching the depths of her soul. It was a look she had come to rely on, one that was both a challenge and a promise, making her feel vulnerable yet fiercely protected. "I know you wouldn't, M," she whispered, as she leaned into the hand that now tenderly cradled her chin and let out a weary sigh tinged with deep regret. "I'm sorry. I should've consulted you before doing something that risky."

"Just glad to see you safe, Starlight," he comforted her, his voice tinged with warmth and lingering worry. His fingers began a gentle exploration, tracing the contours of her face, then cascading down her neck, and finally dancing along her sides, tracing delicate patterns on her dress. "The Hooves would be nothing without your leadership," he whispered, his hands coming to rest just above her pelvis, where the emblematic tattoo of the Hooves lay hidden beneath the delicate fabric.

Anchored by his touch, a soft, contented hum escaped Stellar's lips, resonating with the warmth that spread through her, as she rested her hand atop his. "Only with your guidance and support, M," she whispered, her eyes, deep pools of brown, shimmered with a mix of gratitude and an affection she no longer tried to hide.

She gently pushed her fingers sneaking beneath his shirt cuffs, seeking the warmth of his skin. "I can't wait for the day you can step into the light without fear, when our land is free from the shadow of those monsters, and you no longer have to cloak your true beliefs from the prying eyes of the Greats." With gentle caution, Stellar leaned in and reached beneath his hood, tracing the familiar lines of his face, feeling the soft tickle of his mustache as she brushed against the curve of his lips.

"Our dawn is on the horizon, S. I promise you." Moonlight's voice, a soft whisper, sent shivers down her spine, from the thrill of their proximity.

Yet, as they reveled in their shared moment, a familiar, elusive scent wafted to Stellar, momentarily distracting her. "Moonlight," she began, her voice tinged with curiosity, "were you at the ball tonight?"

He evaded her question, but not her touch. "You know I can't tell you that, love," he whispered, a note of regret lacing his words.

A playful, yet genuine blush painted Stellar's cheeks, her heart fluttering at the thought. "I know, but I just wondered… if you saw me on the stage." The tantalizing thought that Moonlight, the enigmatic herbivore who had unwaveringly supported and guided her for years in the formation of the Hooves, might have been present during her performance was intoxicating.

However, their intimate exchange was abruptly halted as the carriage began to decelerate, signaling their arrival. After swiftly peering out of the window, Moonlight reached into his cloak, producing a meticulously folded note. "I've arranged another safe house, complete with a large letterpress printer suitable for our needs. It's located near the Unity Foundation's meat distribution facility, by the east train yard."

"Thank you, M. You always leave me indebted," she replied, her voice laden with warmth and gratitude, as he gently pushed open the carriage door.

As she stepped out, Moonlight's hand was there, steady and reassuring, guiding her descent. Once they were on solid ground, he spun her around, tightening his strong arms around her waist from behind. With her back pressed against his chest, he leaned down, his breath warm against her ear, the shadow of his hood enveloping them both. "You looked breathtaking on stage tonight," he began, the hint of a playful tease in his voice. The faint tickle of his mustache against the shell of her human ear, as the low rumble of his voice ignited a blaze within her heart, and his embrace tightened possessively. "or so I'd imagine... if I had been there."

His words lingered in the air as he released her into the night. Before she could weave words into a response, the carriage lurched forward, the clang of the wheels and the thuds of the horses' hooves echoing in the night. She was left standing alone, the image of his enigmatic smile, illuminated by a lone streetlight, etched into her memory as he disappeared into the shadows.

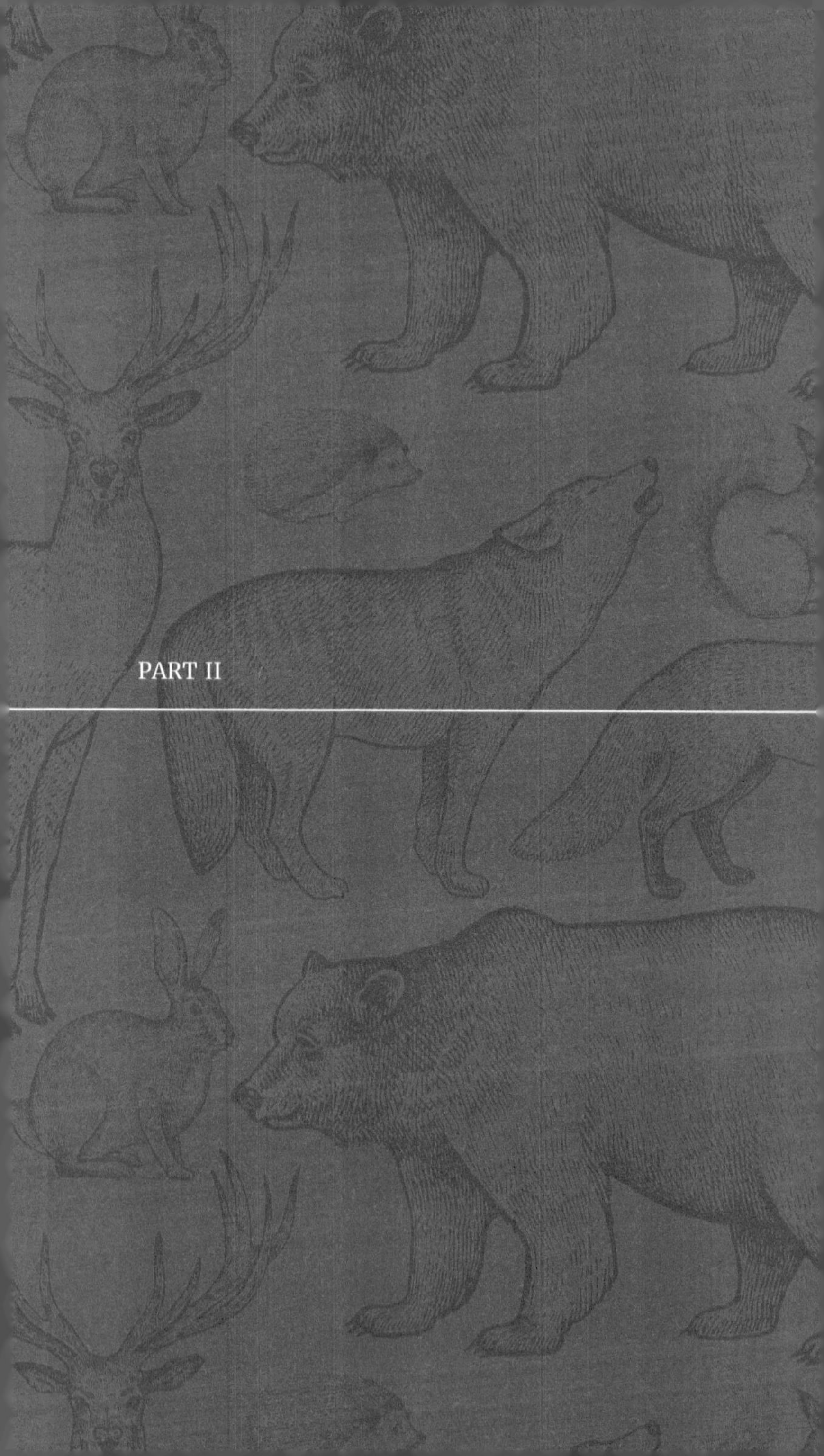

PART II

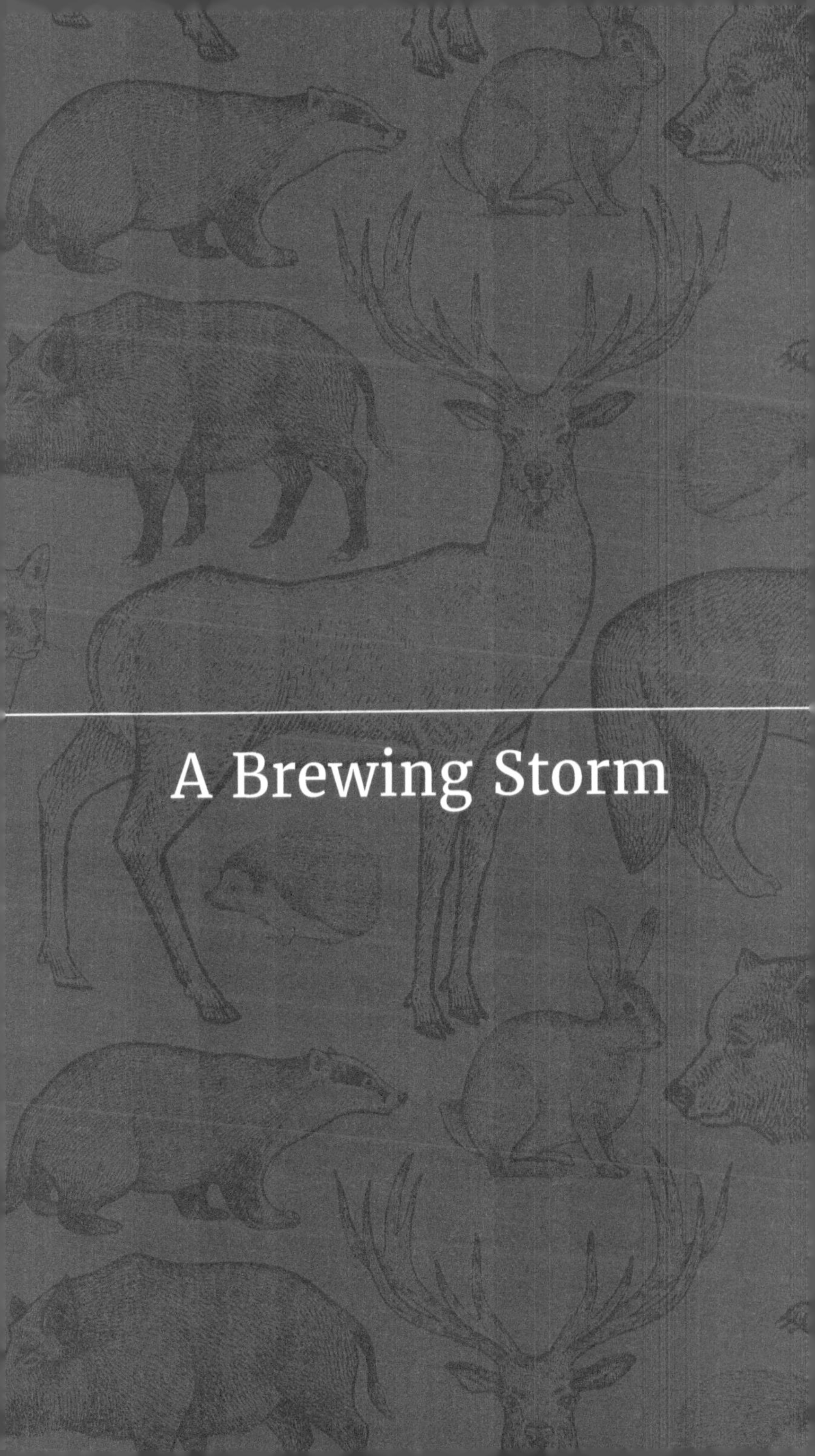

A Brewing Storm

A Wild World

Exiting the main hall after the monthly district budget planning meeting, Senator Redfern and his aide proceeded down the corridor. Lupus, a few steps behind, observed with slight concern the uncharacteristic frustration in the senator's strides. Each step down the ornate corridor seemed to amplify his irritation, evident in his brisk pace and the tight set of his jaw.

The senator, usually the embodiment of grace and patience, was clearly ruffled. The senator's usual slow pace, always considerate of his aide's shorter stature, was noticeably absent. Instead, Rob was practically marching alongside him, her own face a mask of displeasure, her heels clicking in rhythm with her determination.

As they entered the senator's office, Rob broke the tense silence. "I can't say I agree with Councilor Brew's counterpoint on the welfare budget reallocation," she said, maintaining professionalism despite the palpable irritation in her voice. "It's clear that the Unity Foundation's community initiatives could counter the Hooves' slanderous leaflets, especially with the Phennelion just a couple of months away."

She recalled the misleading leaflet she had torn down from her community board that morning. The leaflet depicted a distorted image of herbivores feeding an obese bear—a blatant reference to the high unemployment rates among carnivores. It was a stark reminder of the societal divides, conveniently ignoring the post-war support systems for herbivores and the unspoken biases carnivores faced in the job market.

Rob's hands moved almost mechanically, organizing the meeting minutes with precision, a task that did little to distract her from the whirlpool of frustration swirling within her. "Councilor Brew's attempts to undermine the Unity Foundation seem petty. He's been pulling these stunts ever since he lost the election to you, Senator. And I can't help but feel it's personal. Your longstanding association with the Foundation, the countless hours you've dedicated as a volunteer—it's no secret. Perhaps he sees it as a vulnerability, a point to exploit."

Hart, who had been standing with an air of restrained patience by her desk, accepted the minutes she handed him. His eyes quickly absorbed the text, but then his pace slowed, his gaze fixing on a particular section. The silence stretched between them, filled only with the soft rustle of paper. After a moment, his gaze returned to Rob as he responded with a practiced diplomacy. "Councilor Brew represents Downtown Wilfen, Ms. Longfoot. Every concern should be taken seriously." His tone was firm, but a subtle edge in his voice hinted at his own lingering frustrations.

Councilor Nicholas Brew, a formidable figure from the Great Bears, had become a recurring thorn in Hart's side throughout his relatively short tenure as a senator. While Hart held a genuine respect for the councilor's vast political experience, that didn't mean he wasn't growing tired of the consistent opposition he faced on nearly every decision he made as a district senator. Such continual resistance not only extended project timelines but also, on occasion, cast doubt on Hart's credibility.

Hart swallowed his frustration and weariness, like he had done numerous times before. He was the Senator of Wilfen, entrusted by the people to execute his duties effectively. Navigating these intricate political dynamics, no matter how unjust they seemed, was an inherent part of his role. It was a burden, yes, but it was also a privilege he wore with pride, much like the majestic antlers that crowned his head.

Drawing a deep, steadying breath, Hart continued, "I might have to cancel or reschedule the district visit planned for tomorrow. We'll need to plan residential surveys in collaboration with fellow councilors and the heads of both the Estate and Commerce Departments." As ideas and action points swirled through his mind, Hart began making annotations on the minutes. Every so often, in a moment of contemplation, he'd absent-mindedly scratch the base of his antler with the cap of his pen.

Picking up on the subtle shift in Hart's demeanor, Rob promptly responded. "Certainly, Senator. I'll rearrange the district visit and inform the security department about the changes to your schedule. A meeting for tomorrow morning will also be arranged," she assured, her voice steady and efficient.

Hart offered her a fleeting smile, its edges tinged with genuine gratitude. "Thank you, Ms. Longfoot," he acknowledged, appreciating her unwavering professionalism.

As he began to move towards his private office, his fingers, almost instinctively, sought out the burr on his antler, trying to soothe the itchiness from the sensitive velvet that was soon to be shed. However, his motion was interrupted when his eyes met Lupus's. The wolf's warm, understanding gaze made Hart acutely aware of his unconscious action.

As if he'd been caught in a private moment, Hart's hand jerked away from his antler. He hastily tried to cover it up by clearing his throat and pretending to scratch his beard. A warmth of embarrassment crept up his neck, the reddening evident even beneath his meticulously groomed beard.

Lupus remarked, his tone gentle yet tinged with amusement, "Guess it's about time for a blossom?"

Caught off guard, Hart nodded, his voice a touch higher than usual. "Yes," he cleared his throat again, trying to regain his composure as he fumbled slightly with his pen, attempting to tuck it into his pocket. "They should be fully grown in a few weeks." Offering a fleeting smile to deflect his embarrassment, Hart swiftly retreated into his office, softly closing the door behind him.

Despite the recent conversation between Hart and Rob centered around pressing political matters, Lupus couldn't help but let his thoughts drift to a time when Hart was younger. He fondly remembered Hart as a gangly, irritable teenager, grappling with the itching and discomfort of his first antler blossom, his two-tined juvenile antlers a constant annoyance. The discomfort of the antlers, coupled with the multitude of changes brought on by puberty, certainly hadn't made things any easier.

Having grown up without the guidance of his own parents, Lupus often felt overwhelmed by the challenge of supporting the tempestuous moods of the young stag. Yet, despite the slammed doors and biting words, that tumultuous period in Hart's life was dear to Lupus, igniting a warmth deep within his soul whenever he recalled those memories. They were raw, filled with growing pains for both of them. But it was during those times that Lupus truly grew into his role as Hart's guardian, understanding the depth and breadth of what it meant to support a young red deer stag transitioning into adulthood, beyond just the protective cocoon he had provided for the fawn.

Now, watching Hart from his side, the once restless young stag now matured into a deeply dedicated senator, stirred a profound sense of pride in Lupus. The senator, with his unwavering commitment to his constituents and devotion toward the value of unity, was a testament to his growth and resilience.

Yet, intertwined with that warmth was a pang of sorrow. There were moments, crucial junctures in Hart's life, that Lupus had missed while their lives were apart. Periods of growth and pain that Hart had faced and endured alone, times that Lupus could never reclaim or be a part of. The weight of those missed moments tugged at his heartstrings.

Pushing aside the bittersweet nostalgia, Lupus anchored himself in the present. He deeply valued the trust Hart had placed in him on that eventful night at the Enclave, allowing him to stay by his side during a vulnerable moment. Despite Hart's consistently cold demeanor towards Lupus, suggesting he might have preferred anyone else's company, Lupus felt relieved to have been there for him in his time of need. Fortunately for Lupus, since that night, he had noticed a subtle warmth in Hart's brown gaze during their exchanges—a glimmer hinting at the promise and potential of their evolving bond.

Rob, noticing the closing emotional chasm between Hart and Lupus lately, cast a playful glance towards Lupus, who appeared lost in thought. The gentle curve of Lupus's smile and the rhythmic sway of his bushy tail painted a picture of contentment. It was a stark contrast to the usual hustle and bustle of their political world, and Rob cherished these fleeting moments of tranquility.

As her gaze lingered on Lupus, he seemed to sense her attention. Meeting her eyes with a gentle smile and a nod, the wolf reached for his reading glass. With practiced ease, he unfolded his newspaper, immersing himself in the day's headlines.

Rob soon turned her attention to the task at hand as well. She pulled out a fresh stack of papers, ready to draft the necessary meeting requests and notifications for the upcoming changes in the senator's schedule.

"Senator Redfern, would you care to present your reports?" Councilor Brew intoned, his voice gentle but carrying an undercurrent of challenge. His searching gaze bore into Hart, making the senator feel like a specimen under a magnifying glass.

Hart's gaze instinctively dropped to his desk, expecting to find the comfort of his meticulously prepared documents. Instead, the polished wood stared back, devoid of any evidence. A cold dread began to snake its way up his spine, its icy fingers tightening around his throat.

"It's, um," he stammered, voice wavering. Panic clouded his eyes as they darted frantically, hoping to find the missing documents among the sea of faces. This presentation wasn't just about the reports; it was a testament to his capability as a senator. Each passing second made his heart race faster, its beat echoing loudly in his ears. The oppressive weight of the council's collective gaze made him feel trapped, like a timid fawn caught in the glare of predators. The once authoritative senator now felt vulnerable, every ragged breath amplifying his insecurity.

Suddenly, the council chamber's solid ground morphed into a treacherous path. Sinister sketches from the Hooves' leaflets started spreading like shadowy tendrils, ensnaring his feet. As he tried to flee, the world around him transformed into a misty, ominous forest.

Stumbling, his feet tangled in unseen roots, Hart found himself face-down in the cold, damp ground.

A prickling sensation on the back of his neck prompted him to glance over his shoulder. Emerging from the shadows, the predatory eyes of a monstrous bear locked onto his vulnerable body, glowing with a malevolent red hue.

As Hart struggled against the oppressive weight of his own limbs to crawl away, a vice-like grip clamped onto his antler, pulling his head back. "*A Senator?* You are a fucking joke, Redfern," sneered a chillingly familiar voice, dripping with venomous contempt.

The world seemed to tilt as Hart felt the sickening snap of his antler breaking followed by a disheartening thud on the forest floor. The pain, though distant, was overshadowed by the humiliation and vulnerability he felt. Warm rivulets of blood streamed down his face, coloring his vision crimson with his perceived failure.

His attempts to call out for help were stifled, emerging as pitiful, muffled cries. The sensation of being dragged was jarring, the rough forest floor scraping against his skin. The massive hand around his ankle belonged to none other than the monstrous bear, its intentions clear in its predatory grip.

A hot steam of bear's breath landed on the back of his neck, sending shivers of terror down his spine. As he tried to pull away, his eyes caught sight of polished dress shoes, incongruously pristine amidst the chaos. With a glimmer of hope, Hart lifted his gaze, and found Lupus looking down on him, with his usual composed posture.

But these weren't the warm, protective gaze he had come to rely on. Instead, they were cold, distant, and filled with a depth of disappointment that felt like a dagger to Hart's heart.

Lupus's gaze shifted from Hart's pleading eyes to the antlers on the ground. "You don't need me around anymore," Lupus remarked coldly, his voice devoid of emotion. With a final, dismissive glance, the wolf turned away, leaving Hart to the mercy of the looming predator.

Desperation surged within Hart as he clawed at the ground, trying to escape the impending doom. But it was too late. The sharp, agonizing pressure of the bear's jaws closed around his neck.

Jolted awake, Hart's breath came in ragged gasps, the chilling tendrils of the nightmare still wrapping around him. Cold sweat clung to his skin, making the sheets stick uncomfortably to his bare back. With trembling hands, he instinctively reached for his neck, half-expecting to feel the cruel bite marks. Finding only smooth skin, his fingers then traveled upwards, tracing the sturdy burr of his antlers, ensuring they remained attached to his head. *It was just a dream*, he tried to convince himself, though the weight of the terror still pressed heavily on his chest.

Taking deep, deliberate breaths, he tried to ground himself, letting the familiar scents of his room anchor him back to reality. He exhaled slowly, his fingers rubbing his eyelids as he tried to dispel the haunting images that threatened to pull him back into the abyss.

Yet, as he sought solace in the familiarity of his surroundings, an unsettling silence enveloped him. The gentle, rhythmic ticking of the floor clock was conspicuously absent. A spike of panic shot through him. That clock, with its intricate deer carvings, had been a fixture in the house before he could remember. Its rhythmic ticking, akin to the house's heartbeat, had always been a source of comfort for Hart, especially since he became the sole occupant of the house.

In the oppressive darkness, Hart fumbled for the lamp on his bedside table. His fingers, still trembling from the remnants of the nightmare, struggled to strike a match. Each failed attempt, marked by the snap of a broken matchstick, only heightened his anxiety.

By the fourth attempt, the match finally caught, casting a feeble glow that pushed back the encroaching shadows. But the small circle of light, though comforting, did little to quell the storm of anxiety and dread overwhelming him.

Roughly donning his gown and tightly clutching it around his shuddering frame, Hart made his way downstairs. Each step was hesitant, the weight of the dream still pressing heavily on his chest. The house, usually a sanctuary, now felt foreign and unwelcoming, corridors and stairs seemingly stretching under his feet.

Reaching the foot of the stairs, the sight of the silent clock intensified his distress. He distinctly remembered winding it upon his return to Wilfen, a ritual he never missed. With trembling fingers, he gently nudged the pendulum, breathing a sigh of relief as it resumed its familiar oscillations. Hart found himself entranced by its steady motion, allowing the clock's reassuring heartbeat to drown out the lingering echoes of his nightmare.

"*AHH!* I'M SORRY!! PLEA–"

Lupus lunged forward, pinning the bear to the cold cobblestones of the alley with a swift, decisive movement. He clamped a hand over the bear's mouth, effectively muffling any further outbursts that might draw unwanted attention. "Hey, buddy, listen," Lupus panted, his voice a low, urgent whisper, his lungs burning from the relentless chase. "I'm not trying to hurt you. I just want to talk. I'll let you go, but you have to promise not to run or scream. Got it?"

The bear, breathing frantically through his nose, nodded with equal urgency. His trembling hands were raised beside his head, and his furry ears lay flat against his skull in fear. Sensing the bear's compliance, Lupus cautiously loosened his grip. He pushed himself off the bear's back and extended a hand to help him up.

As they both rose to their feet, Lupus worked to calm his racing heart. He maintained a firm but not overly tight grip on Teddy's hand, ensuring he maintained control. "Theodore Brown, right? The one who attacked Senator Redfern?" Lupus's tone was firm yet not unkind, his eyes searching Teddy's for answers.

The subtle twitch in Teddy's muscles didn't go unnoticed by Lupus, prompting a slight tightening of his grip. Teddy's ears remained flat, his broad shoulders hunched as his brown eyes darted around the nearly deserted alley, searching for an escape or perhaps reassurance. "Y-yes, sir. I am Theodore Brown," he began hesitantly, his voice quivering with emotion. "I swear, I never meant any harm to anyone. Senator Redfern was kind enough to help me reduce my charges, so I've been doing my community service at United Foundation every week." The young bear's voice trembled, his eyes shimmering with unshed tears as he continued, "I've never been near the damned drug ever since, I swear on All Father. Please, don't send me back to prison."

Lupus, sensing the genuine remorse in Teddy's voice, softened his stance. "Teddy, hey, it's okay," he said gently, trying to convey understanding, "I believe you didn't mean to. Let's sit down and talk this through."

Guiding the visibly shaken bear to a nearby staircase, Lupus took a seat beside him. With a comforting hand, he gently massaged the tense muscles at the base of Teddy's neck, attempting to soothe the young bear's frayed nerves as he locked eyes with Teddy's tear-filled ones. Drawing comfort from the touch and the genuine concern in Lupus' eyes, Teddy took a moment to gather himself, inhaling deep, steadying breaths.

Theodore Brown, infamously known as the bear who assaulted Senator Redfern, seemed an unlikely candidate for a Wild overdose. He wasn't a vagrant or a habitual offender; he held a sporadic part-time job and had a roof over his head, albeit in a humble flat nestled in one of Wilfen's less prosperous neighborhoods. The idea that Teddy would impulsively overdose on Wild during a lunch break, leading to such a violent outburst, struck Lupus as an anomaly.

The district security office had hastily labeled him an addict, overdosed on Wild, citing his admission of drug use and the small amount of the substance found in his possession. This was despite the absence of a thorough investigation or an official medical assessment.

However, Senator Redfern's response was notably more compassionate. Touched by a heartfelt apology letter from Teddy, the senator chose not to press any personal charges. Furthermore, the senator not only hired but also paid for Teddy's defense attorney. This attorney adeptly protected Teddy from the more severe charges of attempted devouring levied by the Bureau, in light of his cooperation during the investigation and his evident remorse. Acknowledging these factors, the court converted most of his sentence to community service, following a brief mandatory prison term for possessing the illicit substance. This leniency came with a stern condition: any future possession of Wild would result in Teddy serving his full prison term.

While Hart hadn't delved into the specifics of Teddy's letter, he did mention to Rob, after securing legal representation for Teddy, that Teddy wasn't the type to repeat his mistake. He believed that imprisoning Teddy for attempted devouring would only condemn him to a life marred by societal rejection, making it nearly impossible for him to find employment or housing again.

Leaning forward slightly, Lupus initiated the conversation with a tone of genuine curiosity, "Do you recall the events of that day? You don't strike me as someone who'd recklessly overdose, especially during work hours."

Teddy hesitated for a moment, taking a deep, shaky breath before speaking, "I never intended to… you know, get high or anything," he began, his voice barely above a whisper. "It had been a rough week after starting a night shift. That lunch was the first proper meal I had in a couple of days, and I was just trying to make it taste a bit better… I've sworn off it now, truly." He quickly added, and Lupus simply nodded, his face devoid of judgment, encouraging him to continue.

"You know the smoked fish and poultry sausages that the United Foundation distributes? With most of my earnings going towards rent and savings, those hand-outs are often the only meat I can afford. I'm genu-inely grateful for it, I really am. But sometimes…" He trailed off, his ears drooping in shame. "The sausage is so… bland. It's dry, almost tasteless." He hesitated, guilt evident in his eyes as he grappled with the idea of criticizing a meal that, despite its flaws, kept him from going hungry.

"I don't know if you've ever done it… The Wild," he ventured, his gaze searching Lupus's face for any sign of judgment. The bear sighed, trying to compose his thoughts on how to describe the drug to someone who seemed to have never done anything illegal. "The Wild—it completely transforms the meal. I swear, you can almost taste the various fish meats mixed in the sausage, as if freshly caught from a crystal-clear stream," he explained, his voice tinged with a mix of nostalgia and regret.

Teddy hesitated for a fleeting moment. The wolf's calm-ing and patient presence stirred a small urge within him to spill his story, for the first time ever. Fumbling nervously with his thumb, he finally found the courage to open up. "After... I ran away from the foster home, determined to prove them all wrong, I found myself alone and cold, taking shelter beneath a bridge. I was naive to think the world would be kinder outside. But without a pack, without a family, I was just an unstable, dangerous carnivore, an outcast in a world that didn't want me. I was nothing more than a useless mouth to feed, *a failure*—just like how I was labeled in that foster home, even after escaping it." His voice broke slightly as he echoed the harsh words from his past. A wry smile tugged at the corners of his mouth, a stark contrast to the pain in his eyes, as he recalled the suffocating darkness that had almost consumed him. "I couldn't see any reason to keep living, enduring such pain every day, when I already felt dead inside."

His eyes, glistening with unshed tears, looked far away, lost in the memories. "One day, a volunteer from the Foundation approached me, offering a small fold of Wild. And that... That was the first time I truly felt alive." A bittersweet chuckle escaped his lips as he wiped away a tear. "Funny, isn't it? The very thing I was warned would destroy me was what breathed life back into me. It gave me a flicker of hope, a desire to live and not just merely exist in the shadows."

He swallowed hard, the weight of his next words pressing down on him. "I was aware of the dangers of overdosing, how it could turn some carnivores feral and make them lose control. I never imagined it would be me, that I would be the one to harm another."

Lupus watched the young bear, beyond the rugged facade. Beneath the exterior of a young adult bear was a fragile spirit, scarred and seeking for understanding and a touch of kindness. With a gentle gesture, Lupus reached out, resting a comforting hand on Teddy's broad shoulder, silently conveying understanding and compassion.

Gathering himself, Teddy continued, "That day, the fold I had was different—way too potent, almost like a different drug. I hid in the alley behind the shop, fearing my manager would see me high," he recalled, his fingers rubbing the back of his neck, the ghostly memory of the euphoric pleasure from the Wild rushing through his veins making his skin prickle. "I–I'd never gotten that high with Wild before. The feeling and the sensation... It was too much. I started panicking, thinking I was having a heart attack. I remember sensing someone passing by. I tried to ask for help, but she..." His voice faltered, choked by the resurgence of fear that had overwhelmed him then. The memory of the rabbit terrian's eyes—wide with primal dread as she ran past him—crushed his soul anew. "She just ran past me. I knew how I must have looked to her, and I understood it, I swear. But something inside me felt so sad, so frustrated. It was starving for something, anything. It wanted to *live*," he murmured, his voice barely a whisper as he wiped away tears clinging to his lashes. "I remember seeing the senator's antler across the road, on the other side of the alley. And then…" He trailed off, the weight of the realization hitting him anew. The chilling memory of awakening in a cold cell, confronted with the horrifying reality of his actions he was oblivious to, momentarily overwhelming him. He inhaled deeply, a desperate attempt to banish the haunting images that threatened to consume him.

Drawing strength and pulling himself out of the self-despair, Teddy turned his gaze to look at the wolf next to him. "It was you, wasn't it? You stepped in that day." In Lupus's deep green gaze, Teddy didn't find pity, but a profound understanding of the challenges he'd faced, and he was deeply grateful for that. "I can't thank you enough. I never had the chance to express how relieved I was that the senator, or anyone else, wasn't gravely hurt because of me. I could never have lived with that guilt."

Lupus looked deep into Teddy's eyes, seeing the raw pain and vulnerability that lay beneath. "You're welcome, Teddy," he replied softly with a gentle smile, his voice imbued with genuine compassion. He tightened his hand on Teddy's shoulder, feeling the tremors that ran through the young bear's frame, grounding him with the warmth of his touch. "I know it's hard, but trust me, you'll get through this. Senator Redfern sees that potential in you, and so do I."

Teddy's eyes shimmered with unshed tears, deeply moved by Lupus's words. "Thank… Thank you, sir," he whispered, his voice choked with profound gratitude. For the first time in his life, he felt truly heard and understood. Drawing his knees to his chest, he buried his face between them, surrendering to the torrent of emotions he'd held back for so long.

As sobs wracked his frame, Lupus remained a steadfast presence at his side, gently pulling the bear into a comforting embrace. Hesitantly, Teddy's hand clung to Lupus, his face buried in the nape of the wolf's neck. The gentle, rhythmic pats on his shoulder were a tangible reminder that he wasn't alone, that someone genuinely cared. This reassurance continued until the last of his tears had been shed.

After a few heartbeats, Teddy slowly pulled back, his eyes red-rimmed and puffy from crying. He took a shaky breath, trying to regain some semblance of composure. With the back of his hand, he wiped away the remaining tears, a faint blush of embarrassment coloring his cheeks.

"I'm sorry. I didn't mean to…" he murmured, his voice still thick with emotion. He met Lupus's gaze, his brown eyes, though wet, now held a spark of gratitude. He chuckled softly, a self-deprecating smile playing on his lips as he rubbed the back of his neck.

Lupus, his tail gently swaying in a comforting rhythm behind him, returned the smile with warmth. "No need to be sorry, Teddy. We all need one of those days."

"Thank you," the bear smiled. Taking another deep breath, Teddy nodded. "Right. So..." Clearing his throat, he continued, "After all that, my memories blur. The next thing I remember is waking up in the holding cell."

"Do you remember where you got the Wild from? Are they still around?" Lupus inquired gently, maintaining a comforting rub on the bear's back.

Teddy's eyes clouded with uncertainty, his brow furrowing. "There was this new dealer who started showing up like once or twice a month, dealing exclusively in Wild, and in quite large quantities, which was odd." Lupus tilted his head slightly, curiosity evident in his voice. "Why was that?"

"Considering how hard the Bureau cracks down on Wild? Other dealers usually have just a fold or two, if any. It's not easy to come by. Well, it wasn't, until she showed up. This dealer was obviously inexperienced, but she had plenty of good stuff." Teddy huffed out a laugh, shaking his head. A wry smile formed as he recalled the awkward image of the amateur dealer, clearly unnerved by his size, who struggled to maintain eye contact even during the exchange. "It wasn't my business to wonder where or how she got them," he murmured, shrugging. "The potency of her folds was inconsistent, but mostly on the weaker side. So that day, I, uh, I used a bit more than usual, thinking it wouldn't hit as hard." Teddy rubbed the back of his neck, the weight of remorse still evident in his posture. "I've heard there are a couple of new dealers around, and one of them shows up near Memorial Park. Of course, that's just what I've heard, not sure if it's true," he added quickly, a hint of defensiveness in his tone.

Lupus gave a thoughtful nod, his eyes reflecting genuine appreciation. "Thank you, Teddy. That helps." He gave Teddy's shoulder a comforting squeeze before rising to his feet. Teddy followed suit, brushing off the dirt from his pants and wiping away any lingering traces of tears.

From within the depths of his cloak, Lupus retrieved a ribbon-tied roll of villent notes, extending it towards Teddy. "For your time and trouble, including tackling you on the ground earlier," he said, the corners of his mouth lifting in a rueful smile, recalling their earlier scuffle.

Teddy's eyes widened as he registered the generous thickness of the roll, uncertainty apparent in his gaze. "Sir, this... this is far too much. I can't possibly accept it."

Lupus, with a gentle firmness, guided Teddy's big hand and pressed the notes into his palm. "A few blocks south from here, there's a store marked with a fish drawing on its door. I've heard they receive a fresh batch of salmon every weekend from Velton. And for a little extra, they'll prepare it with spices in their brick oven, served with a side of warm honey butter bread rolls." Lupus's smile grew warmer as he saw Teddy's eyes light up, the bear clearly visualizing the mouthwatering meal. "Do me a favor and give them a visit. Would you?" Lupus added, his voice softening, his hand resting on Teddy's shoulder, feeling the tremors of emotion beneath.

Just as he was about to leave in pursuit of the new Wild dealer Teddy had mentioned, he was momentarily halted by a sudden, heartfelt embrace from Teddy. The young bear's arms, strong yet gentle, encircled Lupus's smaller frame, the wolf almost disappearing within the bear's embrace.

"Thank you. Thank you so much..." Teddy whispered, his voice thick with emotion, muffled by Lupus's cloak. Overwhelmed by the weight of the moment, the warmth of the hug, and the dampness of Teddy's grateful tears seeping through the fabric, Lupus responded instinctively, wrapping his arms around Teddy, patting his back in a comforting rhythm.

 # Lost into the Night 

The remnants of a turbulent night were evident in Hart's weary face. Dark circles under his eyes and a pallor to his skin betrayed the turmoil that had plagued his dreams. As he tried to focus on the meeting's agenda scheduled in a few hours, he felt the weight of his antlers pulling him down into the depths of his fatigue, seemingly heavier than they'd ever been. There was a moment, a brief lapse in his concentration, when he nearly collided with his desk, the tips of his brow tines brushing dangerously close to the polished wood as his consciousness momentarily slipped into oblivion.

It was undeniable that the clock was broken. The pendulum would come to a standstill within a couple of hours of being set in motion. Hart couldn't bear the silence of the house—a deafening quiet that underscored the solitude he'd been both evading and confronting. This undercurrent of unease repeatedly yanked him from sleep, leaving him gasping for breath and drenched in cold sweat.

As dawn's pale light seeped into his room, a fleeting thought of escaping to the Enclave passed his mind. The idea of hopping on the first train was tempting, but the day's commitments bound him to Wilfen. Besides, the prospect of spending a solitary weekend in the bustling Capitol, amidst unfamiliar faces and sounds, brought its own set of anxieties.

Hart tried to coax his weary body into action. *Perhaps a short walk could help*, Hart persuaded his weary body as he rose from his seat, gathering a few signed documents that Rob had left on his desk earlier.

Watching the senator unexpectedly appearing from his private office, Rob couldn't help but to notice the unusual disarray in his appearance. A stray curl, having broken free from its usual restraint, rested defiantly on his temple, drawing attention to the deepening lines of fatigue. The morning's shadows, which she had initially dismissed as a result of an early start, now seemed more pronounced. "Is everything alright, Senator?" Rob asked, concern evident in her voice as she took the stack of papers from his hands.

"The clock in my house stopped. Couldn't sleep much," Hart confessed, yawning into his palm before he could stifle it. The mask of stoicism he wore so well was slipping, revealing a rare glimpse of vulnerability. The effort to maintain his usual facade, in his current state, felt like an insurmountable task.

Rob's eyebrows knitted together, a mix of concern and curiosity. "A clock?" she echoed, intrigued by this unexpected insight into Hart's private life.

He nodded, his voice tinged with weariness. "Just an old floor clock. I don't know what's gone wrong with it," Hart replied with a weary sigh. Without realizing, he found himself leaning heavily on Rob's desk, his fingers pinching the bridge of his nose and pressing into his eyelids, as if trying to massage away the stinging sensation of fatigue-induced tears.

Lupus, who had been observing Hart with a growing sense of concern, finally broke his silence. "Senator," he began, his voice tinged with hesitancy. His furry ears drooped, mirroring his uncertainty. "I could perhaps take a look at the clock," he offered, pausing to gauge the reactions of both Hart and Rob, who had turned their attention to him. "That is, if you're okay with it." His fingers unconsciously played with the corner of his book, his tail tensing slightly. Beneath his offer, driven by his genuine concern for Hart, lay a whirlpool of apprehensions—the prospect of Hart perceiving this as an overreach, the risk of rupturing the bond they'd been fostering, and the potential for a cold response.

Rob, sensing the tension in Lupus's demeanor, chimed in with a playful tone, "Didn't realize you were a clock-smith on the side." A teasing smile played on her lips, lightening the mood.

Lupus' eyes crinkled at the corners with a soft smile, the anxiety that had briefly gripped him now replaced by a gentle wave of nostalgia. "Given my age, it shouldn't surprise you that I could fix a thing or two," he replied, a wistful tone creeping into his voice, as fond memories seeped into his mind. Back when Lupus was still a part of Hart's family, he used to spend hours tinkering with various household items alongside a younger Hart. Yet, the floor clock had always stood apart, a majestic piece that required only their collective attention for its weekly winding ritual.

Hart felt a rush of words, unbidden, rising to his throat. "Could you… maybe drop by after work today?" The words tumbled out, and as they did, he was met with Lupus's wide-eyed surprise—a reflection of Hart's own internal astonishment at his sudden invitation.

"It's, uh, I think…" he stammered, voice faltering. He cleared his throat, trying to find the right words, all the while avoiding Rob's inquisitive gaze and Lupus's stunned expression. A flush of embarrassment crept up his neck, and he found himself rubbing it in a futile attempt to dispel the warmth. "A good night's sleep would be… beneficial, given tasks at hand," Hart elaborated, the words sounding more like a desperate plea than a logical explanation. A dark, cynical voice berated him—*Making a fool of yourself again, are you?*—even as another part of him clung to the hope of a peaceful night, free from the torment of nightmares and the oppressive silence of his home.

Lupus, momentarily disarmed by the sudden request, took a beat to process Hart's words. With a gentle nod and a wider smile, he responded, "I'd be more than happy to help." While his voice remained calm and steady, the lively wag of his tail betrayed eagerness. Memories of a younger Hart, from the grumpy fawn refusing to wake up after stubbornly staying up to witness a meteor shower, to the young stag who nearly smashed the toast into his nose due to sleep deprivation on an exam day, danced in Lupus' mind, warming his heart with the realization that, in some ways, the senator remained unchanged.

"Thank you, Mr. Greyfang." Hart murmured, his voice carrying a hint of fatigue but underscored by genuine gratitude. A faint smile, tinged with weariness, tugged at the corners of his lips. He pivoted, abandoning his initial idea of a refreshing walk, and instead made his way back to the sanctuary of his private office.

Upon reaching his desk, Hart eased into his chair with a heavy exhale, fingers massaging his temples, trying to marshal his scattered thoughts. The haunting remnants of the nightmare, combined with the physical toll of sleep deprivation, loomed large, casting a shadow over his usually resilient spirit.

Yet, amidst this haze, memories of shared moments with Lupus in their once-shared home began to seep through the cracks in his guarded heart. The thought of the older wolf's impending visit, with its promise of familiarity and comfort that he painfully spent years trying to bury in the darkest corners of his mind, stirred his mind with a swirl of emotions. Hart's usually stoic exterior, a mask he wore with practiced ease, now bore the unmistakable signs of weariness and vulnerability.

Concentration was already a challenge, and this added layer of emotional turmoil didn't make it any easier. *Stop whining and get back to work, already,* Hart scolded himself, clenching his jaw as he pushed away fatigues and emotions.

He grabbed the next stack of documents awaiting the senator's attention, deliberately moving to stand by the window, hoping the soft daylight might dispel his encroaching drowsiness.

He gave his furry ears a brisk shake, trying to dispel the fluttering anticipation that, for a fleeting moment, overshadowed his fatigue.

As twilight bathed the office in fiery red hues and stretched shadows across the walls, Hart meticulously sorted through the last of the planning documents. He was determined to ensure that his growing fatigue hadn't led to any oversight. Each page he reviewed carried the weight of collective thoughts and discussions from that day's meetings with fellow councilors and department heads, serving as a tangible reminder of the day's achievements.

Emerging from his office, Hart was startled to find Lupus still stationed at his desk, the soft glow of the lamp illuminating the pages of the book he was engrossed in. The subtle twitch of Lupus's ears, finely attuned to Hart's presence, prompted him to glance up. Closing his book, the wolf's eyes crinkled in a warm smile, and his tail swayed in a gentle rhythm. "Evening, Senator," he greeted in a soft voice. Setting his reading glasses aside, Lupus stood up gracefully. "Shall we head home now?"

Hart blinked, the realization dawning on him. "The clock," he quietly exclaimed, a touch of embarrassment coloring his human ears. "My apologies, Mr. Greyfang. I completely lost track of time." He had initially relegated Lupus's offer to the back of his mind to maintain focus, only for it to be buried beneath the avalanche of meetings and documents.

Lupus offered a gentle smile, his green eyes radiating warmth and patience. "Not a problem, sir," he assured, his tail maintaining its soft swaying behind him.

The absence of Rob's familiar presence suddenly struck Hart, casting a shadow over his already fatigued mind. He swallowed the weight of their shared history and the day's emotional tumult pressing heavily on his chest. With a nod, more to himself than to Lupus, he took a hesitant step forward, his legs feeling oddly detached. Lupus followed closely behind, still maintaining his usual respectful distance.

The walk to the house was enveloped in a contemplative silence. As they navigated the dimly lit corridors and emerged from the building, the soft hum of the evening greeted them. They exchanged courteous nods with the security officers, who were engaged in a light-hearted conversation, their laughter echoing faintly in the twilight.

While Hart's demeanor had taken on a shade of warmth, the boundaries of their professional relationship remained solid. Lupus pondered their current situation, wondering if this invitation was merely an extension of their professional relationship or a tentative step towards rekindling a personal bond. Opting to play it safe, he chose to withhold any forward comments, allowing the evening's ambiance to fill the spaces between them.

The gentle caress of the evening breeze, carrying with it the faint scent of the Wilfen River, was invigorating. Families and couples were out, sharing tales of their day with happy smiles. Chuckles of small children tugged at Lupus's heartstrings. He hadn't felt the ominous sense of danger around Hart recently, although he couldn't be certain if that was for better or worse. Yet, in this moment, he found solace in Hart's silent companionship.

The tree-lined street leading to Hart's residence seemed to stretch endlessly, each step amplifying the anxiety gnawing at Hart's already weary soul. The haunting specters of his nightmares, where he grappled with feelings of insignificance and profound loneliness, cast long shadows over his thoughts. Inviting Lupus into a home steeped in shared memories was, in retrospect, perhaps a hasty decision. As Hart's fingers nervously fiddled with the familiar contours of his house key, he stole a fleeting glance at his security guard, whose furry ears were busy capturing their surroundings.

But before he could delve further into his thoughts, they were at the front gate of his home. The journey, it seemed, had passed in a blur, with Hart ensnared in the labyrinth of his own thoughts.

"Thank you again for offering to help," Hart said, breaking the prolonged silence as he unlocked the decade-old lock on the front door.

Lupus noticed Hart's fluffy tail giving a brief quiver. A tender smile emerged on his face, recalling how that had been a sign of Hart's nervousness when he was younger. "My pleasure, anytime," Lupus responded sincerely as he stepped into the house he once called home.

Stepping into the house, Lupus was immediately enveloped by a familiar scent, one that transcended the passage of time. While the subtle notes of the senator's signature cologne lingered in the air, it was the earthy, verdant aroma of the house that truly stirred Lupus's soul. Despite everything that had happened and the years that had passed, he felt like he was truly home.

His fingers, almost instinctively, traced the small dent near the front door. It bore an uncanny resemblance to a tiny wolf, or so a young Hart had once playfully declared. That innocent observation, made during a time of shared laughter and joy, was a memory Lupus had clung to during the years of their separation.

His gaze swept across the interior, bathed in the soft glow of ambient lighting, each corner evoking a cherished memory. While the house retained its pristine elegance, there were subtle shifts in its character. The decor was more restrained, perhaps a reflection of Hart's evolving tastes or a conscious choice to minimize distractions. The impeccable cleanliness hinted at the diligent work of house staff, their presence evident even in their absence.

The gentle undertone of a woody soup scent took Lupus back to a time when he had prepared clover pesto soup himself, a remedy associated with the blossom of his antlers. The blossom, or the shedding of the velvet to reveal the majestic bone structure beneath, was always a sensitive time for every stag. It necessitated specific meals to soothe the irritation and provide essential nutrition. Lupus surmised that the house staff might have prepared a similar comforting meal in anticipation of the upcoming blossom.

Hart's steps echoed softly on the wooden floor, each step heavy with the weight of memories he was desperately trying to keep at bay. The delicate balance of the present and the past of the house, that Hart had mastered over the years, seemed to be threatened to tip off at the presence of its previous occupant. With practiced efficiency, he placed his briefcase and shed his jacket by the door, a routine that momentarily anchored him to the present.

"The clock," he began, his voice slightly strained, "It's… right over there." He gestured toward the quiet floor clock as he gently lifted the lit oil lamp, illuminating the room with a soft glow. He couldn't help but wonder if Lupus still remembered the intricate details of the house they once shared.

Lupus, momentarily lost in the flood of memories, was jolted back to the present by Hart's words. "Right, the clock, of course," he stammered, as he placed his belongings beside Hart's. A warmth fluttered in his chest as he found himself instinctively falling back into routines from a bygone era, without hesitation.

Approaching the clock, which stood regally in its familiar spot, Lupus felt a comforting sense of familiarity. The intricate details of the timepiece, unchanged by the passage of time, evoked a rush of tender memories. The gentle curve of his lips, as he observed the cherished timepiece for a moment in awe, spoke volumes of the affectionate memories it evoked.

The clock was in excellent condition, similar to the rest of the house, not even a speck of dust atop it. Lupus carefully probed its inner workings, closely observing the pendulum's swing while his twitching ears focused on the mechanical clicks.

After several moments of careful observation, punctuated only by the soft clicks of the clock's mechanism, Lupus beckoned Hart over with a hushed whisper, "Come take a look, Hart." With his eyes focused on the pendulum swing, Lupus subtly made a bit of space for Hart to stand close next to him.

Mindful of the expansive span of his antlers, Hart positioned himself slightly behind the wolf, leaning in to get a better view of the pendulum's path. "The pendulum," Lupus began, his finger tracing the air in sync with its swing. He outlined a narrow elliptical path rather than a straight line. "It's swinging at an angle, not in a straight line. Do you see?"

Hart's eyes followed the movement of Lupus's hand, then the pendulum for a moment, observing and analyzing its movement closely. "Yes," he responded, his brow furrowing in thought. "Could that suggest imbalance at the suspension point?"

Lupus nodded thoughtfully. "That's my suspicion," the wolf agreed, momentarily lost in contemplation. "Help me turn the clock around, kid," he requested, carefully grabbing the corner of the clock.

Hart promptly set the lamp aside, joining Lupus in rotating it, revealing a small opening accessing the mechanism on the other side of the clock. Hart, long immersed in a world of inks and papers, found himself momentarily captivated by the rhythmic mechanics. His brown eyes widened with childlike wonder, and his ears leaned forward, attuned to the delicate and precise movements of each part.

After observing the pendulum's movement near its suspension point, Lupus identified a minor crack in the suspension spring. "Seems like this little part has a small crack where it gets bent, which I'm guessing could be the issue," he ventured, as he carefully un-hinged the pendulum and suspension spring then held it up to the lamp's light for a closer inspection.

"I'll check with the clockmaker tonight or tomorrow," Lupus suggested, the light revealing the hairline fracture in the metal. "Maybe we can get it fixed before our return to the Capitol." He passed the spring to Hart, who held it gingerly, his eyes reflecting a mix of fascination and concern.

The room, once filled with the comforting rhythm of the clock for a while, now lay in profound silence. Lupus's furry ears drooped slightly, his concern deepening as he recalled Hart's remarks about struggling to sleep without the clock's ticking. "I'm sorry, Hart," he began, his voice filled with genuine regret, "but until we get this fixed, the clock will remain silent," Lupus murmured, his gaze studying Hart's serious expression, trying to gauge the depth of his disappointment amidst the shadows cast by the lamp's flickering flame.

However, to Lupus's surprise, Hart's usually stoic face melted into a gentle smile, his eyes, deep pools of brown, shimmering with gratitude. "Lupus," he began, his voice tender, a timbre Lupus hadn't heard in what felt like lifetimes, "there's no need for apologies. Just understanding the problem and knowing it could be fixed is comforting," he assured as he handed the delicate clock piece back to Lupus.

Lupus's tails began to wag gently, the corners of his eyes crinkling, revealing the depth of his relief. "I hope that's enough to help you sleep, Hart." As he pocketed the metallic part, he playfully tapped Hart's arm, a friendly gesture reminiscent of their past.

While returning the clock to its original position with the help of Hart, this time without need for a request, a realization washed over Lupus. Hart had addressed him by his first name, just like the old times. He wondered if it was a slip or a conscious choice. Reflecting on their interaction, Lupus recognized that he too had reverted to old habits, even affectionately referring to Hart as 'kid' without a second thought. The lack of resistance or correction from Hart to this familiarity filled Lupus with a warm nostalgia, as if he had never left; as if they were still a family—*a pack*. Lupus's soul fluttered at the thought.

"Well..." Lupus hesitated for a fleeting moment, taking in the view of the clock for the last time. Slowly, he lifted his eyes, locking onto Hart's gentle brown ones. "I suppose that's all for now. I should be heading home." Lupus's tail slowly wagged as he made his way to the entrance.

Hart trailed behind, the lamp's soft glow casting a warm light that pushed back the encroaching evening shadows. As Lupus donned his jacket and collected his briefcase, a subtle tension hung in the air. Lupus silently hoped that Hart hadn't picked up on the slight informality in his tone or, ideally, didn't mind it.

"Sleep well," Lupus said, warmth evident in his smile as he stood at the threshold. He hesitated for a moment, deliberating between addressing Hart formally or using his first name, but ultimately chose neither, allowing the moment's sentiment to speak for itself.

"You as well. Thank you again." Hart replied with a small, yet gentle smile. He stood framed in the doorway, watching the figure of Lupus retreat into the night, as a whirlpool of emotions played across his features. Only when the familiar silhouette had completely vanished did Hart gently close the door, sealing away the memories of the evening.

That night, Hart basked in a deep, uninterrupted slumber. The worries and distressing dreams that haunted him just the night before faded, and he found serenity, even in the absence of the clock's familiar tick.

A comforting dream filled with protective whispers and a warm embrace cradled him, though the details of the dream quickly evaporated as he woke up to the bright sunlight warming up his bedroom.

Lupus's eyes widened slightly, a mix of disbelief and surprise evident. "10? For a fold?" His eyebrow quirked upwards, questioning the quoted price.

Even with the shadows from her hood, the younger terrian's agitation was evident as she retorted, "Fine, 8 vil then. But not a vil less, old-timer."

That was the opposite of Lupus's surprise; just days ago in the Capitol, a paper fold of Wild would fetch over 50 villent. Even accounting for the economic gap and the distance between the Capitol and Wilfen, the disparity was staggering.

Shaking his head slightly, as if to clear his thoughts, Lupus remarked with a nonchalant air, "I've been out of the loop here in Wilfen." He handed over a few notes to the young seller, adding, "You can keep the change."

"Yeah, well, not many are interested in Wild past couple weeks," she remarked with a shrug, her fingers stretching out to grasp the notes. "You know, after what happened at..." Her words trailed off abruptly as Lupus's hand shot out, firmly encircling her wrist and preventing her from taking the payment.

She shot him a glare, her eyes flashing with a mix of defiance and irritation. "Oh, fuck off." She sighed exasperatedly, her body going slack under Lupus's grasp, looking more annoyed than frightened. "First that bison yesterday, now you? I don't know where you guys heard it, I don't do *that*. Whatever you pervs are into," she spat, her fangs catching the dim light, her voice dripping with disgust and disdain.

Lupus blinked, taken aback by her vehement reaction. His brow creased in genuine confusion. "Do what?" he asked, genuinely puzzled.

"That," she spat out, jerking her chin towards Lupus's exposed wrist. "I sell Wild. That's it."

Glancing down, Lupus noticed the smattering of bruises and scrapes encircling his own wrist. Caught off guard, he murmured, "Oh." It dawned on him how his marks from handcuffs—remnants of nightly precautions taken at the senatorial residence, where he shared space with two herbivores—could be misunderstood.

"This is not... You've misunderstood. That's not what I'm..." he stammered, awkwardness evident in his voice. He cleared his throat, trying to regain some semblance of composure, and hastily adjusted his cuff to cover the marks. Yet, he maintained a firm grip on the terrian, ensuring she couldn't escape. "I just have a few questions." he clarified, his voice carrying a mix of authority and a hint of embarrassment.

Her gaze blazed with disdain as she narrowed her eyes. "And what makes you think I'd answer any of your stupid questions, pervert?" she retorted, her tone defiant as she struggled against his grasp.

"Because I could easily escort you to my desk at the Bureau," Lupus replied with an unwavering stare, choosing to ignore her insult. The mere mention of the Central Security Bureau seemed to do the trick, as the terrian's resistance waned, replaced by a wary apprehension. "Now, are you ready to talk?" Lupus inquired, sensing her blend of resentment and anxiety.

She huffed, her gaze darting around nervously. "Depends on the questions," she muttered begrudgingly. Lupus's attention was drawn to her bushy tail, protectively tucked between her legs and tipped with white fur—a clear sign she was a fox terrian.

Lupus drew her closer by the wrist, his gaze intensifying. "Who are you working for?" he whispered, his voice carrying a chilling edge. His piercing green eyes locked onto hers, unyielding.

Her cloak hood was swept back by his sudden movement, revealing her defiant expression. She met his stare with a sneer. "What are you talking about?" Yet, the subtle quiver in her stance, her pointy ears pinned down, and her tail curled protectively around her legs betrayed her words. "I just sell to make a living," the fox retorted, her smirk slightly faltering as her eyes trembled, revealing a hint of vulnerability.

Lupus's expression darkened, his voice dropping to a dangerous timbre. "Are you with the Shadow Clan?" The mere thought of the Shadow Clan's involvement made Lupus's grip tighten, his fangs peeking out from beneath his lips. "Answer me!" His demand was edged with impatience, his guttural growl sending a shiver

down the fox's spine, her defensive demeanor inter-
preted as an admission of guilt.

The depth of Lupus's predatory menace became palpable,
causing the fox's defiance to waver. She whimpered
in anxiety, her eyes wide with fear, darting around
in search of an escape. "I, I swear, I don't know anything about any clan," she pleaded, her voice quaking
with desperation. As she tried to pull away, Lupus's
grip became almost vice-like, his snarl growing more
pronounced.

"I'm not an idiot, fox," Lupus snarled, irritation seeping into his low voice. He grabbed the front of her
weathered cloak with his other hand, pulling her face
closer. His ragged breaths landed heavily on the fox's
shivering face. "Do not test my patience."

Taking a shaky breath, she seemed to crumble under his
intense scrutiny. "It's…" she began, her voice barely
above a whisper, each word heavy with the weight of
her confession. "Some bison terrians approached me.
They were armed, knew about my past dealings. They
threatened to ruin my sister's tailor shop if I didn't
comply and stay silent about it."

Lupus's eyes widened in surprise. "Armed bisons?" he
echoed, releasing her cloak as he stepped back, taken
aback. Memories of national herbivore factions involved
in illicit activities, closely monitored by the Bureau,
flashed through his mind. Yet, to his knowledge, none

had ever dabbled in the distribution of Wild, especially given its niche appeal and the inherent dangers for non-carnivore distributors.

As the revelation shifted his focus away from the Clan, Lupus suddenly became aware of the intensity of his grip. He noticed the young fox's wrist, pale under the pressure of his fingers, and the evident fear in her trembling amber eyes and flattened ears. Hoping she wouldn't take advantage of the moment to flee, he gently released her.

Cradling her wrist, the fox shot him a wary glance. Lupus, sensing the need to bridge the chasm of mistrust he had inadvertently created, Lupus softened his voice, asking, "Why didn't you ask for help from the security office? Or the Bureau?"

"Seriously? You're joking, right?" the fox spat back, her regained defiance evident in her disdainful look. "Go to the officers, tearfully claiming a bunch of herbivores forced me into Wild peddling? All while risking the chance that those bisons could wreck the shop my sister spent a decade dreaming about?" She gave a sarcastic smirk, which soon dissolved into a bitter grimace. "They'd probably throw me into a holding cell, assuming I was high on Wild, rather than offering help."

She crossed her arms, hesitating for a moment, reluctant to divulge more details. Yet, there was something about the wolf's softened green gaze, his ears attentively focused on her, that compelled her fatigued soul to share the burden—a burden she could never have shared with anyone else. Maybe his mention of the Bureau gave her a thread of hope that he might be able to help, though she wasn't sure.

After scrutinizing Lupus for a moment, she opened up. "I have to sell them in Downtown Wilfen and hand over the required amount. They drop new batches at the start of every week. They stash them in some abandoned building and give me a note with the location when they come to collect the money." She let out a deep sigh, rubbing her temples as she tried to ward off a looming headache. A mix of frustration and fatigue evident in her voice as she continued. "At least the money they demanded isn't even that much. I just want to offload this stash without getting caught." she murmured, swallowing down the thick emotion lodged in her throat.

Wiping her weary face, she sighed. "I promised my sister I won't do this shit again," she whispered, almost to herself, clenching her jaw to push aside the stinging sensations in her nostrils. The thought of shattering her sister's trust, and imagining her beloved tailor shop in ruins, pressed heavily on her heart. "That's my pathetic life you wanted to hear. Are you happy now?" she snapped, her voice a raw blend of anger and vulnerability, as her amber eyes bore into Lupus with a fiery intensity.

The warmth in Lupus's green eyes was evident, a deep well of empathy reflecting back at her. "I'm... sorry for what you've been through," he said, his voice a soft whisper that seemed to carry the weight of her burden. She responded with nothing more than a shrug, the gesture laden with exhaustion and resignation.

With a careful balance of respect and curiosity, Lupus gently probed further, "The bisons, did anything about them stand out?" His inquiry was gentle, giving her space to recall without pressure.

She shook her head, a flicker of frustration crossing her features. "No. Nothing I can think of, really. I was busy trying not to get shot, alright?" Her words were tinged with a raw edge, the dread of facing down a barrel crawling back into her mind.

"Understood," Lupus replied, nodding in acknowledgement. He reached into the depths of his cloak, his hand emerging with a roll of notes. "This is for the risk you've taken in sharing what you know," he explained, his movements smooth as he tossed the roll to her. It cut through the air in a perfect trajectory, landing effortlessly in the fox's startled grip. "Dispose of the rest of the batch. Same deal next week. Meet me here. I'll buy the entire batch."

Her trembling eyes, wide with a complex mix of disbelief and cautious relief, locked onto his, searching for any deception or trick. "Are you... are you serious?"

A soft, melancholic smile graced Lupus's lips, a gentle curvature that held a bittersweet edge. His green eyes deepened with a hint of sorrow, reflecting the inner turmoil that shadowed her life. It pained him to see such wariness etched into her youthful features, a clear testament to the hardships she had endured.

"Just stay safe, kid. I'll see you next weekend," he assured her, his voice carrying the weight of a promise, offering her a small nod as his silent pact of their agreement.

Turning his back, Lupus felt the weight of her gaze on his back. As he slowly walked away from the stunned fox, he wished he could offer assistance, if his position at the Bureau weren't so limited. Director Snowclaw's stern warnings echoed in his mind, a grim reminder that his rogue investigation delving into the world of Wild was a dangerous gambit that threatened immediate exile to distant shores.

His hand slipped into his pocket, fingers brushing against the cold metal spring of the clock, a stark reminder of what was at stake—Hart's safety. The mere thought of the Shadow Clan's ominous presence in Anthroterra sent a shiver down his spine, solidifying his resolve. He couldn't *afford* to leave the country. Not now, not when so much remained uncertain.

Lupus paused, casting a glance over his shoulder. The fox, her silhouette now a small, hooded figure preparing to vanish into the darkness of the night, seemed to carry the weight of the world on her slender shoulders.

"Hey, kid!" His voice cut through the distance, halting her in her tracks. With a flick of his wrist, he sent another roll of notes arcing through the air. They spun gracefully before landing in her adept grasp.

"Get yourself and your sister some fresh meat," he called back, his voice laced with a hint of remorse for the force he had exerted upon her, the memory of her fragile wrist in his unyielding grip gnawing at his conscience. "I'm sorry I almost broke your wrist."

The young fox stayed silent for a moment. before her amber gaze lifted from the roll up to Lupus. A silent nod, a subtle acknowledgment of his apology, was all she offered before she vanished into the dim labyrinth of the town, leaving Lupus with his heavy thoughts.

The Ugly Edges

Lupus was pushing the clock. The Enclave awaited his return, and with each passing minute, the window for his clandestine activities was rapidly closing. Patience was essential, yet challenging, as he waited for the shadowy figure, whom he had been tracking near the Wild dealers, to emerge from its den.

Infiltrating the building on the outskirts of the Capitol required caution, but time was a luxury Lupus couldn't afford. Hart would soon begin his morning routine, earlier than his official schedule, as was his habit. After managing only one or two hours of sleep the previous night, barely returning to his quarters through the window moments before hearing Hart descend the stairs, Lupus couldn't risk his nightly absence being discovered.

His mission was clear: infiltrate, gather intelligence, and exit without detection.

Inside the seemingly abandoned building, Lupus detected the faint scent of Wild emanating from behind one of the locked doors. The lock gave way under his skilled fingers with a satisfying click, allowing him entry into a nondescript room. As he suspected, boxes of Wild and its mixers were stacked atop a desk, confirming his suspicion about the figure's involvement in the Wild distribution network. However, it was the wall that immediately seized Lupus's attention.

Covered in notes, sketches and interconnected threads, it provided a murky window into a complex web of connections. The flickering light of his lighter cast an ominous glow on the materials, highlighting the centerpiece of this extensive collage. It was an illustration of a hare terrian who had mysteriously vanished near the academy just a few weeks earlier. Clearly, the room's occupant was more than a mere distributor in the Capitol's Wild dealings.

A unique, familiar scent halted Lupus in his tracks just as he was about to defend against the figure behind him. "Didn't expect to see you here, old-timer." The voice was unmistakably playful, even as the cold touch of a revolver pressed harder against the back of Lupus's head. The subtle sound of the squirrel's tail twitching and quivering tickled his lupin ears. A light chuckle escaped Lupus. "Not bad, Nutterson," he complimented, raising his hands and feeling grateful for his instincts that had prevented a lethal mistake. "You almost had me… if I was truly alone."

Nutterson's momentary distraction, indicated by a slight shift in the revolver's pressure, was all Lupus needed. In a fluid motion, he spun around, seizing control of the weapon as his lighter flew straight toward Nutterson's face. Within moments, he was pointing the revolver at its former owner, who narrowly caught the metal lighter before it could strike his face.

"You knew I was alone. Trust your instinct," Lupus chided gently, his grin teasing as he relaxed his posture. "It's been a while since I trained you. You've clearly honed your skills," Lupus praised, his voice warm with genuine pride and a touch of nostalgia. With a nod of respect for Nutterson's improved skills, he extended the revolver back to its owner, handle first.

The squirrel's bushy tail continued its agitated dance with the adrenaline coursing through him. A soft chuckle escaped him as he absentmindedly scratched behind his furry ear. "Thanks, Greyfang," he murmured, tossing Lupus's lighter back. Lupus caught it effortlessly in mid-air. "Your voice, I swear, it's always so convincing. Might be some leftover trauma from our training days, I reckon," Nutterson quipped, the corner of his mouth lifting in a half-smirk. Accepting the revolver, he holstered it with practiced ease.

Lupus returned the smile, as he lit the oil lamp on the desk. He stepped closer to the wall that had caught his attention earlier. "Impressive work, Nutterson," he mused, fingers brushing over his stubble chin, his ears pitched forward in keen interest. His tail moved in a slow, measured sweep behind him. Then, with a piercing gaze, he fixed his attention on the squirrel. "Yet, your investigation room doesn't seem… official, to say the least."

Nutterson reclined in a chair beside the desk laden with boxes of Wild, his tail swaying idly. "You followed me spying on those Wild dealers, didn't you?" he shot back with a playful glint in his eye. "I have a feeling the director didn't sign off on your side investigation into Wild trafficking."

Turning slightly, Lupus met his gaze squarely, a smirk tugging a corner of his lip. "Seems like we both have secrets to keep," he replied, the lightness in his tone belying the seriousness of his words, as he turned his attention back to the wall.

The notes, connected by threads, sprawled across the wall, but it was a peculiar symbol that caught Lupus's eye—an eye with two pointy peaks on top and twin dots below. The emblem tugged at the fringes of his faint memories. "Is that…" Lupus's brow creased, glancing over at Nutterson. "That symbol, is that a deer hoof print merged with an eye?"

"Huh," Nutterson's expression shifted to one of respect, his eyebrow arching in surprise. "Took me days to decipher that," he admitted. A wry smile played on Lupus's lips as he pushed down on an old memory. "Call it a lucky guess," he quipped.

Nodding towards the symbol, Nutterson elaborated, "That is the Hooves' secret symbol." Rising from his seat, he approached the wall adorned with papers and threads. Pointing at a crumpled paper pinned on the wall, he continued, "This symbol was on a discarded note from Mr. Cloverfield's trash. It contains an address in the Capitol. The place was empty when I checked, but this," he gestured to a piece of a newspaper ad in the same section, "was in a month-old newspaper, before he went missing." The circled ad, containing the same address, read: 'Verdelian literature club – Every weekend evening at the exclusive herbivore lounge.'

Adjacent to it was another newspaper clipping, featuring a similar ad for the Verdelian literature club. "I found that ad last week, in a different newspaper. I attended their meeting a few days ago. It was unmistakably a Hooves' recruitment event, disguised as a literature club on the surface." Nutterson's tail quivered, and his face involuntarily grimaced as he recalled the evening, filled with old Northern Verdelian poems that glorified herbivores while disparaging carnivores. "I tracked some of the main organizers. One led me to Wild dealers," said the squirrel, turning to face Lupus. "And that's what brought you here tonight, obviously."

Lupus's ears perked up, his focus sharpening on Nutterson's investigation trail. His eyes widened, reflecting the gravity of the revelation. "Wait, so the Hooves are distributing Wild?" he echoed, the weight of the implication dawning on him. His recent findings about the unusual involvement of herbivores in the distribution suddenly clicked into place in his mind.

Nutterson pointed towards an expansive map of Anthroterra, adorned with red and blue pins. His finger hovered over clusters of pins in major towns. "These red pins represent Hooves activity—from posters and leaflets to vandalism against carnivore-owned shops and, in some cases, outright assaults on carnivore terrians. And these blue pins," he began, pausing briefly to ensure Lupus was fully engaged, "represent Wild-related incidents—from minor offenses like theft and aggravated assault committed by carnivores, to severe cases of Wild overdosing and possession. Over 95% of these incidents occurred in the same towns, even the same blocks, where the Hooves are active, if we adjust for a year-to-year average."

He turned, arms crossed, one hand tapping his chin thoughtfully. "The details about this new wave of Wild that I've gathered, like a novice herbivore dealer making a mistake mixing Wild and filler, or batches ruined by humidity during the rainy season and found abandoned—the scale of distribution doesn't align with these amateur mistakes. It's too organized, too widespread." His pondering brown gaze lifted from the ground, meeting Lupus's attentive green eyes. "It starts to make sense when you consider the Hooves are behind the distribution."

He gestured towards a note above Cloverfield's illustration: *I'll see the end of this.* "That was the last entry in his journal, found by the river bank after he went missing. The Bureau leaned towards theories of voluntary disappearance or suicide, rather than foul play. But I believe he stumbled upon something about the Hooves and tried to investigate on his own, leading to his disappearance. So, here I am," Nutterson concluded, gesturing expansively to their modest surroundings with open arms.

"Nutterson, this is a significant discovery," Lupus remarked, his tone laced with awe and confusion. "Why haven't you shared this with the Bureau?"

Nutterson stood firmly, arms defensively folded, the earlier playful twinkle in his eyes now replaced by steely determination. His ears gave a nervous flick, and his tail quivered with evident apprehension. "I'm unsure of who's really on our side anymore," he confided, his eyes lingering on Lupus's face, seeking to gauge his reaction.

Choosing his words carefully and speaking in a hushed tone, Lupus ventured, "Do you think there's a leak in the Bureau?"

"Considering the questionable origins of the drug, the sophistication behind its distribution, and how all of this has managed to evade the Bureau's surveillance," the squirrel paused briefly, his voice dropping to a whisper, "it suggests support that goes beyond a mere informant."

Lupus regarded Nutterson with a penetrating gaze. "You've withheld this from the Bureau, suspecting deeper involvement," Lupus deduced, his tone sharpening.

A tumult of emotions flickered across Nutterson's face, his affirmation coming with a heavy nod. He hesitated, the next words seeming to weigh on his tongue. "I believe…" His voice wavered, and the erratic swish of his tail betrayed his escalating anxiety. Sensing the gravity of what was to come, Lupus tensed. "The Greats, or at least a faction within them, might be orchestrating the Hooves and steering the Bureau's investigation," Nutterson finally revealed, his bold theory hanging in the air.

A ripple of shock passed over Lupus's features, prompting Nutterson to quickly lay out his reasoning. "It's speculative, of course. However, " Nutterson began, pacing back and forth, his thoughts spilling out in a rush, "the quality and purity of the Wild that the Hooves receive from their supplier is top-notch." He picked up a wooden box from the desk, shook it gently, then set it back down. "How would those herbivores get their hands on high-quality batches of a drug known to be produced exclusively by carnivores in foreign countries? It's also the one drug under the strictest surveillance, where possessing even a small amount can lead to imprisonment. And in such quantities that it flooded the country? It's hard to imagine it's purely an internal operation within the Hooves without the help of a more influential player."

Deep in thought, Lupus countered, "But their propaganda—the posters, the leaflets. The Hooves are vehemently against all carnivores, including the Greats."

"True, but that rarely interferes with them, unlike it does for other carnivores, much like their policies," Nutterson replied, leaning against the desk and crossing his arms. A hint of dissatisfaction crept into his features as he continued, "the Greats—they've manipulated the narrative for decades since the end of the war, casting lower-class carnivores as pawns to appeal to other species for reparation of what happened in Furrocia. They maintain their pristine position with those discriminatory, populist policies, feigning 'sacrifices' for some perceived greater good. Would the Greats ever be affected by the housing act that made landlords prefer herbivore tenants?" the squirrel scoffed. "But it's evident that many terrians have grown skeptical of the Greats' leadership. Can you believe we have a stag as a senator now? A mere decade ago, such a thought would've been laughable."

So engrossed in his analysis, Nutterson failed to notice a brief flicker of irritation on Lupus's face nor the perked up ears. He carried on, "They're likely feeling threatened, searching for a catalyst as impactful as the war," Nutterson mused, pausing to lock eyes with Lupus, where echoes of those wars glinted in his deep green stare and faded battle scars. "My theory is that they are intentionally agitating carnivores using the Hooves, anticipating a rise in carnivore aggression, maybe even an uprising by carnivore extremist groups. They can then position themselves as saviors, defending the nation and its powerless terrians from these 'uneducated and dangerous' carnivores. It's a power play of their dominance, reminding everyone of their predatory prowess without baring a single fang, while keeping their seat at the high table with grace. Whether it breeds loyalty or fear, they come out on top."

As the weight of Nutterson's words sank in, Lupus hardly noticed the squirrel advancing until he was right in front of him. Nutterson's brown eyes burned with intensity. "I'm sharing this with you because, well, besides the fact that you found my hideout during your own rogue operation," he said, a hint of humor in his voice, a nervous laugh punctuating the tension. "Out of everyone in the Bureau, I trust you the most." With a surge of emotion, he firmly grasped Lupus's shoulder, his hand betraying a slight tremor. "Fortune favored me today, having you on my trail."

A solemn warmth spread across Lupus's features. He returned the gesture, gripping the squirrel's shoulder firmly. "Thank you for entrusting me with this, Nutterson." The squirrel's affirming nod echoed the depth of trust shared between them.

The distant bell of the congressional building chimed, signaling the top of the hour. It severed the weighty silence, grounding them back in the present. With a resolute look, Lupus met the other agent's eyes. "I'm constrained by my obligations, Nutterson, but know that I'll do all in my power to uncover the truth."

As Lupus made his way to the door, Nutterson's voice, soft but impassioned, halted his departure. "I genuinely believe in Senator Redfern, Greyfang. He's the leader Anthroterra needs." A beat of silence, then with heightened intensity, he continued, "Please keep him safe."

Lupus cast a final, unwavering glance over his shoulder, his nod resolute as a silent vow. "Stay safe, Nutterson." he cautioned before briskly exiting, consumed by the weight of their discussion and the uncertain future of Anthroterra.

Every step back to the Enclave was hastened by Lupus's swirling thoughts. The theories, speculative yet deeply unsettling, gnawed at his mind with relentless persistence. Director Snowclaw's directive echoed—*Make yourself useful. Find something of value.* They'd stationed him as Hart's shadow, monitoring every move since the senatorial election, based solely on speculations from the Greats. Despite Lupus's consistent assurances of Hart's integrity, his reports were summarily dismissed.

What if their hidden agenda was to twist Lupus's findings, manipulating them to portray Hart as the mastermind behind the Hooves? They might seek to disgracefully remove him from his position, branding him a radical traitor to the nation. The mere idea of the Greats tarnishing Hart's integrity and recklessly manipulating public sentiment lit a fierce fire in Lupus. A low growl rumbled from his throat, his teeth bared in silent fury.

By the time he reached his quarters, dawn's first light was breaking. Even so, it took him some time to quell the rage evoked by the hypothetical scenario. It remained, no matter how convincing, a speculation lacking solid evidence. He needed to tread cautiously as he focused on gathering further intelligence about the Hooves.

As it was evident he wouldn't be able to sleep at his agitated mind, Lupus freed his wrist from the hand-cuff that leashed him to the bed frame. He hoped that the steady stream of water from a shower might wash away some of the turmoil before he resumed his duty guarding Senator Redfern.

The usual, quiet morning at Senator Redfern's residence was abruptly interrupted by heavy footsteps rapidly approaching. Lupus's sensitive ears perked up, instinctively tuning into the noise. His muscles tensed as he looked toward the front door. Shortly after, there was an insistent rapping. With a swift gesture, he cautioned Hart and Rob to maintain their distance as he advanced towards the entrance.

"My apologies for the intrusion at this hour, Mr. Grey-fang," the flustered security guard of the Enclave began, dabbing at the sweat forming on his brow. "There's a hare terrian from Wilfen at the gates. He's adamant about speaking with Senator Redfern. Claims it's a matter of great urgency."

"A hare?" Lupus's voice wavered as his brows knitted in confusion, his instincts sending a ripple of unease through him. As he was about to suggest checking with the senator, Hart's voice came from behind him, firm and decisive, "Let him in, please. I'll speak with him."

"Yes, sir," the guard responded with a brisk nod and retreated towards the estate's threshold. Moments later, a lanky hare, escorted by two guards, appeared at their door.

"Senator Redfern, please pardon my intrusion at such an hour, but we didn't know where else to turn," the hare intoned, his voice strained as he struggled to maintain composure. His long ears lay flat against his head, and his hand, quivering, gripped a handkerchief tightly, betraying his barely contained agitation.

"Mr. Redtail," Hart responded, a flicker of recognition lighting up his features as he recalled their previous encounter. It was during one of his early weekend visits to the Wilfen towns, shortly after being elected senator. Mr. Redtail, along with his fox wife, had opened a quaint tailor shop in the town of River North. "Please, come in." Sensing the urgency in Mr. Redtail's demeanor, Hart ushered him into the living room. Rob promptly offered a glass of water, which the hare accepted with a nod of appreciation.

"Last night, my fox sister-in-law, Freya Redtail, was shot in the leg," he began, his voice quivering with emotion. As he spoke, his facade of composure began to crumble. "Though the doctors are optimistic about her survival, she might need a cane for the rest of her life. But the security district officers—they treated her like a criminal," the hare growled, his hands clenching into fists upon his lap, quaking with anger. "They've accused her of Wild overdose and an attempted devouring. They shackled her to her hospital bed, and even put a locked muzzle as if she'd gone feral," he recounted, his voice wavering. Tears glistened in his eyes as he sought understanding from the senator seated opposite him.

"Mr. Redtail, I'm deeply sorry for what has befallen your family," said Hart, his brown eyes reflecting genuine concern, but his tone was calm and composed. "How is Lyria holding up?" He recalled a joyful fox who had greeted him with fervor on his visit to their shop, sharing her excitement about the shop's opening and offering heartfelt congratulations on Hart's election as senator.

"She's devastated," the hare responded, his voice unsteady. "She's at the hospital with her sister." He wiped his face with a crumpled handkerchief, pausing to gather his strength. "Freya confided in me. The bison who shot her, he tried to… to claim her against her will. In her struggle to escape, she bit him. Then, as she ran, he shot her from behind." The words caught in his throat, the image of Freya post-surgery, convulsing from the ill-suited herbivore anesthesia due to the lack of proper carnivore medication at the hospital, burned into his memory. He could still feel Freya's desperate grip on his hand, sweating and trembling as she was telling him about what had happened, swallowing down her cries of agony.

"I've tried reasoning with the officers, but they wouldn't hear me or Freya," the hare continued, frustration coloring his voice. "They waved us off, claiming Freya was feral because she bit him, and that the bison was justified in shooting her. How can they justify it based on his word alone? Just because she's a fox? They couldn't even conduct proper medical tests to prove their claim due to her severe blood loss!" Anger colored his features as his ears pulled back, his grip on the handkerchief white-knuckled. "Freya had a past with drugs, but that was ages ago. I'm not excusing her past actions, but she was trying to make ends meet—keeping a roof over their heads and food on the table so Lyria could focus on her apprenticeship at my father's tailor shop."

He paused, his words catching in his throat as his gaze dropped to the handkerchief. It was the first gift from Lyria, given on the night she confessed she couldn't continue her apprenticeship. After his desperate and persistent inquiries, she had revealed her sister's sacrifices to support her financially, expressing guilt for not realizing the burden she had placed on Freya while she pursued her dream.

Her heart-wrenchingly painful smile had followed as she poured out her heart, confessing her admiration and love for him, without a fear of him doubting her intentions now that she was leaving the tailor shop. It was that smile that had compelled him to hold her tightly, confessing his own discreet love for the beautiful fox who never lost her warm smile despite the judging eyes and biting insults she faced as a female fox at one of the most renowned tailor shops in the country. He had vowed then to keep her happy for the rest of her life, a promise made less than a month after that fateful night.

Swallowing down waves of emotion, he steeled himself for the sake of both foxes, vowing to find a way to fix everything that had gone wrong. His blurry gaze lifted to meet the senator's serious expression. "I swear by the All Father, Senator, Freya is not an addict. She swore she'd never used them—not then, not now. My wife and I trust her with our own lives," he declared, his gaze unwavering.

Quietly standing behind the senator, Lupus grappled with his own rising emotions, his jaw clenched tight in an effort to maintain composure. It was evident that Freya was the same one he'd spoken to just a week prior. The image of the young fox, her delicate wrist within his grip and the mingled look of gratitude and sadness in her eyes, haunted him. The thought of her struggling against a formidable bison, enduring a gunshot, and then being treated like a feral overdosing on Wild, stroke a fire within him. The realization that he was perhaps the only one who could have spared her this suffering, and that he had failed to act due to fear of the consequences, tore at his heart. His fingers curled into his palms, determined to stay composed despite the overwhelming surge of emotions.

"Mr. Redtail," Hart began, his deep concern evident in every aspect of his demeanor. Every line on his face, the tilt of his ear, and each subtle gesture showed he was completely attuned to the hare's words and emotions. "I understand the depth of your desperation and the profound distress that has propelled you to seek me out at this hour. I can assist in securing a defense attorney, but the manner in which the Wilfen Security Department handles the case is beyond my direct influence. However, I will personally ensure the department treats every piece of evidence with the utmost diligence, free from any shadow of bias."

"Thank you, Senator. Your assistance means the world to my family." Gratitude washed over the hare, visibly easing the tension in his frame. "I won't take up more of your precious time. Thank you again for your kindness." He rose, his eyes sparkling with gratitude, a stark contrast to the lingering fatigue etched deep in his features. "May the All Father enlighten your way." Lupus swiftly moved to escort the hare, whose jaw was tightened with lingering emotions and the weight of the situation, as he turned toward the front door.

Yet, it was the senator's voice that halted their steps. "Mr. Redtail," Hart called out, approaching the distressed hare. He gently yet firmly placed a comforting hand on the hare's shoulder and continued, "Stay strong. I'll pray for your family, and for Freya's recovery."

Locking eyes with the senator, the hare saw genuine compassion that nearly shattered his composure he had so fiercely clung to. The barriers he had erected to hold back his tears wavered. In a voice choked with emotion, he whispered, "I can't thank you enough, Senator Redfern."

Without hesitation, Hart drew him into a comforting embrace. The hare, allowing his strong front he had maintained for the sake of his family to crumble for a fleeting moment, leaned into the refuge of the genuine warmth. Hart, sensing the hare's rigid guard dissolve, offered a gentle reassurance with a pat, offering solace.

After sharing a moment of silent understanding, the hare gently pulled away, wiping his tears and conveying heartfelt gratitude with a smile. With a nod that carried the weight of a thousand thanks, he stepped back into the world, a little steadier than before.

# *The Greater Good* 

The muted hum of conversation and the peaceful strains of a string quintet surrounded Hart, the ambient glow from a small chandelier lending the bar an intimate, warm feel. He sat on a plush stool, his attention captured by the refracted light in his glass, playing within the amber liquid. The subtle pattern etched onto the glass created a delicate dance of light and shadow as he tilted it ever so slightly.

Noticing the warmth on his fingers from the shortened cigarette between them, Hart took a final deep drag before extinguishing it in the delicate ashtray, which already held a couple of his crushed cigarette butts. Closing his eyes, he savored the fleeting buzz of smoky intoxication rushing from his lungs through his veins, before exhaling a deep sigh tinged with faint smoke.

"It's impossible to miss those monstrous antlers of yours," a voice rumbled, laced with familiarity and warmth. The sound pulled Hart from his reverie. He turned his gaze to meet the soft, brown eyes of a bear approaching with a casual, unhurried gait.

Hart's face broke into a genuine smile. "Bradford," he greeted, rising to meet his old friend with a heartfelt embrace.

With his rounded furry ears flickering briefly, Bradford laughed heartily, his deep voice softly echoing around them. "Can you believe it's been more than a decade since graduation?" He settled onto the stool next to Hart, eyeing him with a look that danced between jest and admiration. There was a playful glint in his eye as he added, "After my old man conceded the senatorial seat to you, I wasn't sure our path would cross again." Without warning, he delivered a light jab to Hart's arm, his smirk growing wider. "What's the protocol here? Do I address you as Senator Redfern now?"

A playful scoff escaped Hart's lips as he shot back, "Oh, shut your fang, Bradford." With feigned annoyance, he gave a light smack to Bradford's expansive chest, prompting a deeper, more joyful laugh from the bear. "How's your wife and cubs?"

"Thriving," the bear replied with a warm smile, and then added, "And with another cub on the way, you can only imagine my apprehension about accepting an invitation from an old academy friend to come all the way out to the Capitol." Bradford winked mischievously, drawing a hearty smile from Hart.

As a bartender slid a drink toward Bradford, Hart chimed in, "This one's on me, for your growing family." He casually laid a couple of crisp notes on the polished surface of the bar, a silent nod for Bradford to holster his wallet.

Bradford's response came with a half-smile, his lips curling in a knowing smirk. "Well, if the senator's offering, who am I to turn down a free drink?" His large hand wrapped effortlessly around the glass as he raised the glass in a toast, the clink of their glasses a soft punctuation in the bar's low hum. The liquid shimmered briefly as it caught the low light of the bar, a fleeting sparkle before they each took a sip.

Leaning back, Bradford set his glass down, his playful demeanor shifted subtly. His deep brown eyes, now more focused and keen, met Hart's. "Alright, Hart. We might have shared a dormitory years ago, I have a feeling our meeting in the Capitol isn't just for old times' sake. And it surely isn't about rescuing me from the, let's say, 'frustrated' paws of my lovely wife."

Hart, feeling the weight of the matter pressing in, met the bear's gaze squarely. There was a hint of gravitas in his voice as he replied, "I think you know why, Chief Detective Brew."

A heavy exhale escaped Bradford, the weight of his breath seeming to thicken the air between them. He took a deliberate draught from his glass, savoring it before speaking. "The feral fox case, isn't it?" he posited, his voice a low rumble.

Hart leaned forward slightly, his voice steady, "How can you be so sure she went feral? I went through the reports myself. The officer who escorted her to the hospital was adamant that she didn't show signs of overdosing."

Bradford placed his glass down, his finger tapping on the glass with evident irritation. "That's the report after she was neutralized. Unless there's irrefutable evidence suggesting she was not feral at the moment of the altercation when she bit the bison, she *was* feral, capable of taking down and devouring any prey. This is the second feral carnivore case just within a month. The Wilfen Security Department needs to set a precedent. We need to demonstrate the consequences of reckless Wild indulgences before someone really gets hurt."

Hart's eyes flashed with a mix of frustration and disbelief. The weight of the topic, combined with the alcohol coursing through his veins, lending a fiery edge to his words. "What was she supposed to do, just take whatever the bison was going to do to her, because she is a fox?" He challenged, voice rising. "That bison was twice her size, and he shot her from behind as she fled!"

Bradford's response was a cold, calculated dismissal. "Good. She could've devoured someone else that night if he hadn't." He sneered, his voice dripping with contempt.

"Bradford," Hart growled, his voice laden with warning as he fixed Bradford with a fierce glare and slammed down his glass. His fingers whitened around the curve, threatening to shatter it. The jarring clang captured the attention of nearby patrons momentarily. The lounge's gentle string music, now a stark contrast, played on, seemingly out of place amidst the escalating tension between the two.

Bradford remained unyielding, undeterred by Hart's displeased display. He slowly drained his drink, savoring every drop, his gaze locked intensely with Hart's. Only after the surrounding patrons' attention had drifted back to their own affairs did he respond. His voice was low but sharp, cutting through the hum of the lounge. "Why are you so soft on those Wild addicts?" He shifted his massive frame to face Hart squarely, his round ears flicking with visible annoyance. "Don't think I've forgotten about that feral bear—the one who nearly took your life. You helped him walk free."

Hart shook his head slowly, a gesture of both denial and an attempt to steady his swirling emotions. "Mr. Brown isn't roaming free. He's being watched. And besides," he continued, his voice softening slightly as if the edge of his anger was dulling, "I've heard good things about him from the United Foundation locations where he's serving his community service."

"Does that suppose to make him less dangerous the next time he turns feral?" Bradford's voice, usually deep and calm, now carried an edge of warning, slicing through the air and cutting off whatever rebuttal Hart was formulating. "You were fortunate when he lunged at you, Redfern. Don't bank on everyone having your kind of luck."

For a fleeting second, Hart's gaze dipped to his glass. However, he failed to notice the amber liquid's undulating dance, reflecting muted light and shadow. The profound gravity of Bradford's words pressed hard on his mind, rendering the world around him momentarily insignificant.

Meanwhile, Bradford's eyes shifted, catching the piercing stare of a cloaked figure in the dimly lit corner of the lounge. A prickly sensation crawled up his spine as he felt the weight of that predatory gaze, which had been lingering ever since he approached Hart. Almost instinctively, he recognized it as belonging to Hart's infamous wolf guard.

Drawing in a deep breath, Bradford softened his tone, attempting to bridge the gap with his old friend. "Look, I get it. You've always been empathetic to all. Those weekends at the Foundation facilities, your pursuit of political studies at the academy—it's all been in service to a higher ideal. But that's all it is—an ideal. You know it's different in the real world where we live and breathe." He paused, a hint of bitterness creeping into his voice. "Defending these *uneducated ferals* does nothing but undermine carnivores like me, who actually know how to control ourselves."

The intensity flared back into Hart's eyes as they snapped up to meet Bradford's, but the bear pressed on. "No matter how much you want to believe that all terrians should be treated equally, some are simply born this way. The primal, savage instinct is seared into our souls, woven into the fabric of what makes us *carnivores*. You might not understand it, but you need to face that reality. Your role isn't to be lost amidst the fallen leaves on the forest floor. You're not some volunteer at the Foundation anymore, Senator Redfern. You have to see the forest, focus on what's best for *the greater good*."

After a brief moment of tense silence, Bradford rose to his full, towering height. His silhouette loomed over Hart, casting a long shadow that seemed to declare the end of their exchange. "Thanks for the drink. I'll savor it, knowing it was from Hart, my friend, not the Senator." With a brief, almost affectionate gesture, he tapped Hart's shoulder. Recognizing the finality in Bradford's posture, Hart offered a quiet nod in response. With deliberate strides, Bradford exited, leaving behind the weight of their charged conversation.

Hart let out a weary exhale and pressed his fingers against the bridge of his nose, the cool glass still tight in his other hand. The rigidity of Bradford's beliefs, aligned with the majority of the scholars and the academy's broad-brush labeling of carnivores, always left a gnawing discomfort within him. The percentages, the politics of majorities, they held no sway over his belief. To him, every terrian deserved equality, regardless of species, just as the All Father had crafted each soul with boundless affection and blessing.

But doubts lingered. Had his principles blinded him? Was he compromising public safety in his desperate attempt to demonstrate that one's birth species shouldn't predetermine their worth or fate? To prove that *he* was more than merely a stag?

He drained his glass in a long gulp, savoring the scorching trail it carved down his throat, then dropped a few more notes onto the dimly lit bar top. He knew he was pushing it, staying out late on a weekday, and that more alcohol would only amplify his regret come morning. Yet, he yearned for a relief, anything to blunt the sharp edges of reality. His fingertips, slightly numbed by the alcohol, brushed against his beard and the trace of stubble as he exhaled deeply.

Bradford wasn't wrong—he had indeed been lucky when Lupus intervened in his dangerous encounter with Mr. Brown. Waves of bittersweet nostalgia swept over him, recalling moments of warmth and safety in Lupus's presence. He should be grateful that at least *Senator Redfern* is deemed worthy of Lupus's protection.

Scoffing at his own pathetic self-pity, Hart bitterly downed the glass of liquor, attempting to drown the old, yet sharp, emotions clawing their way to the surface. The burning path of the alcohol seemed to mirror the ache in his heart.

His vision blurred, whether from the strength of the drink or the tears he fought to hold back. The weight of his antlers grew, each strand of velvet feeling more irritating than usual, the numbness from the alcohol providing little respite. *Damn these fucking antlers*, he silently cursed, rubbing near their burr in a futile attempt to ease the discomfort. The world swayed a little as he dug into his coat, searching for more notes, his fingers unsteady and uncooperative.

"Senator." Lupus's whisper, both firm and gentle, sliced through the ambient hum of the lounge. His hand clasped Hart's wrist, halting it mid-air just as Hart was about to signal the bartender for another drink. Hart's face, flushed with drink and etched with inner conflict, tilted to a side, his eyes locking with the deep greens of Lupus's, which were filled with a mix of concern and admonition. "You've had enough. Let's get you back to the Enclave."

"Mr. Greyfang," Hart murmured, his voice a soft slurry. Momentarily dazed, his eyelids fluttered in a slow blink before he recovered with a mischievous smirk. "I wasn't expecting you. I thought you had the night off and wouldn't return until sunrise."

Lupus's breath caught with a surprise. How long had Hart noticed his nightly leaves? He had always ensured that both Rob and Hart were sound asleep, thanks to the subtle squeak of the floorboard and his keen ears, before embarking on his rogue investigations.

Hart's discerning gaze fell on Lupus's ears, now pressed back in a defensive posture, and to the usually steady green eyes that now flickered with the vulnerability of being caught off guard. Amused by Lupus's discomfort, Hart watched Lupus stammer, attempting to form an explanation. With a dismissive chuckle, he said, "Save your excuses. It's not my concern what you do off the clock." A sudden lurch nearly toppled Hart as he violently freed his wrist from Lupus's loosened hold. "So, why not extend me the same courtesy and leave me be when I'm off duty, huh?"

Undeterred by Hart's dismissive and defensive posture, Lupus persisted. "Hart," he said, drawing closer, his voice softening yet retaining a firm undercurrent. The smoky sting of cigarette and liquor on Hart's breath pressed harder on Lupus's heart, deepening his concern and worry for the internal turmoil Hart was shouldering. "You know you can't allow yourself to be this vulnerable in public." The wolf's eyes were deep wells of genuine care, devoid of judgment, reaching out to the sliver of rationality still flickering within Hart.

A rumble of indignation and pain vibrated in Hart's voice as he growled back, "Why, am I not performing the senator role to your standards? Do I seem that *pathetic* in your eyes as well?" Emotions surged, a few stray tears escaping to trace wet paths down his cheeks. His ears pinned back in distress, accentuating his agitation.

"You know that's not what I mean," Lupus countered, holding Hart's gaze with an intensity that was both comforting and commanding.

Taking a moment, Lupus took a deliberate breath, keeping his tone steady, reminiscent of how he used to calm a younger Hart. He carefully chose his words, trying not to exacerbate Hart's distress. "It's about the regret you'll feel in the morning." His unwavering gaze offered an anchor in Hart's turbulent mind. "Come on, Hart. Let's head back."

For a moment, Hart stared back, allowing Lupus's words to pierce the haze shrouding his judgment. And in those steadfast green eyes, he found a glimmer of understanding, an unspoken recognition of the bitterness that Hart had harbored for so long.

Deep down, despite their past, and despite the countless nights spent resenting the wolf who left him, Hart
yearned to believe that Lupus was by his side as family,
not merely as a security guard. This fragile hope began
to dispel the shadows clouding his judgment.

With a shaky exhale, Hart pushed himself to stand.
Lupus swiftly slid under Hart's arm, draping his own
around Hart's waist to provide both support and guidance. With Lupus's gentle murmurs soothing him, they
slowly exited the lounge to flag down a carriage, which
would take them to the Enclave, away from the cold,
judging eyes that lingered on the stag senator.

The ride home was enveloped in silence, each lost in
their own thoughts. Upon their arrival, the grandeur
of their residence stood silent and imposing against
the night sky. Hart's unsteady footsteps, laden with
the weight of his physical and emotional burdens,
echoed in the corridor. He leaned heavily on Lupus's
steadfast support, his arm draped around the wolf's
strong shoulder, trusting that Lupus wouldn't let him
stumble and fall.

With Lupus's assistance, Hart managed to sit down
on his bed without even a scratch on his antlers. As
Lupus carefully removed Hart's coat, the events of

the day seemed to converge upon the senator with a crushing force.

Drowning in a sea of introspection, Hart's voice broke through, faint and laden with fatigue. "I thought I understood what was right and wrong," Hart murmured, dragging a hand down his weary face, his ears drooped. "I'm not so sure anymore." Letting out a weary sigh tinged with the remnants of alcohol and smoke, Hart buried his face in his hands. The weight of his antlers felt like a heavy crown, threatening to press his head down under the strain of doubts.

The warm pressure on his shoulder and the slight dip of the bed beside him prompted Hart to lift his head from the depths of his self-despair.

"I know it's hard, but you are doing great, Hart. I believe in you, and I know I'm just one of many who does. You just have to trust yourself." It was a familiar piece of advice Lupus had given to Hart numerous times, whenever he felt like he was stuck in bad situations. Hart clenched his jaw, fighting back the surge of emotions, and gave Lupus a nod of acknowledgment.

Lupus responded with a gentle smile and a soft pat on Hart's shoulder. "Get some rest. I'll see you in the morning."

Hart's nod came slowly, his movements still muddled by the alcohol. His eyes, misty yet sincere, locked with Lupus's. "Thank you, Lupus, for everything."

"Always, Hart," Lupus returned with equal sincerity, giving Hart's shoulder a final squeeze before he moved toward the door, pausing to cast a protective glance back at Hart before leaving.

Hart lay back, the familiar embrace of his plush pillows gently cradling his head and antlers. The room seemed to spin around him, a combination of his intoxication and the swirling tempest of his thoughts. But as the minutes ticked by, the soothing lull of sleep began to envelop him, offering respite and a hope for clarity come dawn.

As Lupus stepped into the dimly lit room, the figure tied to the chair immediately caught his eye.

He recognized the blindfold bison with two sturdy black horns, trussed up, each restraint causing his posture to slump forward awkwardly. Before Lupus could unleash his fury, he felt a firm grip on his arm. His fangs were already bared in a low growl, the rage in his eyes un-mistakable. He was a breath away from lunging at the bound bison, his intentions clear—a single, forceful punch might have broken the bison's neck.

Nutterson's voice, a razor-sharp whisper, sliced through Lupus's wrath. "Keep it to yourself, Greyfang." he hissed, his tail flicking with irritation as he struggled to maintain his grip on Lupus. "Do you have any idea how difficult it was to discreetly transport a drugged bison on a train to the Capitol? I wish to bring *the package* back intact. We don't have much time to spare until the freight train back to Wilfen departs." Seeing the anger still smoldering in Lupus's eyes, Nutterson added with an urgent tone, "He's under the impression that we're allies from the Hooves, trying to save his ass."

Lupus took a moment to rein in his emotions, then let out a deep breath. "Alright." He mustered a shaky reply and clapped Nutterson on the back in a gesture of gratitude. "Great job, Nutterson." The squirrel acknowledged with a nod.

Nutterson squared his shoulders, brimming with determination as he approached the restrained bison. He drew a chair to face the prisoner and, with a swift, measured slap, jolting the bison from his dazed state. Lupus watched intently from the doorway, every muscle taut, his fists clenched tight.

The bison jerked upright, his voice quivering with confusion. "Wh-what's going on?" In a futile effort, he tried to peer through his blindfold and struggle out of his bindings. His labored breaths were punctuated with fear.

Nutterson leaned forward, firmly grasping the bison's chin. "Easy there," he soothed with a veneer of sympathy. "You're in a safe house now. We're free to talk here."

"Oh." A flicker of realization touched the bison's voice as he pieced together fragments of a conversation he'd had with an elusive Hooves agent, one that ended with a stinging sensation on his neck.

"Pardon my rudeness," Nutterson said with a sardonic smile, his voice thick with sarcasm. "Hope you can understand our frustration. It's just that cleaning up your mess out there left us a tad... irritated." Despite his smaller stature, the squirrel exuded a threatening air. The bison, a young terrian with a sizable frame and in the prime of his early 20s, grew tense, a hard swallow betraying his anxiety. He nodded, a mute gesture of recognition.

"Here's how this is going to play out," Nutterson began, shaking the bison's face gently. "You'll tell us what you did and what you disclosed to the authorities. We need to brief our informants and legal team accordingly. And don't even think about lying—it won't end well for either of us." He paused, tapping the bison's cheek to emphasize his words. "Is that clear, Mr. Grounder?"

"Y-yes, sir," the bison stammered, his voice shaking.

A satisfied twitch of Nutterson's tail betrayed his pleasure at the bison's acquiescence. "Good. Now, enlighten me, Grounder. What went down?" Pushing away from the chair, the squirrel fetched a notepad from a nearby desk and leaned against it.

"I had some argument with the fox," the bison began, his voice halting. "She'd probably had too much Wild. She bit me, and then she bolted, so I fired at her." He stopped, his furry ears twitching as he relived the echo of the gunshot. "I think the gunshot might've done something to my hearing."

"And what have you told the officials?" the squirrel asked, disregarding the bison's complaint and obvious discomfort.

"I told them the fox, who seemed a bit off, approached me asking for money. I refused, then she lunged and bit my hand when I tried to defend myself. I said that she started running away, so I shot her to prevent further attacks," the bison recounted, an ugly smirk playing on his face as he recalled the impressed looks on the officers' faces, one even unofficially thanking him for protecting others.

Lupus, maintaining a composed tone despite his clenched fists, pressed further. "What was the argument about?" The bison jerked slightly, only now realizing he wasn't alone with Nutterson.

After a beat, he continued. "She's a dealer under my management. I was there for a weekly exchange. Alone, this time, since other members were assigned to different operations that night. There were directives from the inner circle; they wanted to boost our finances for an upcoming operation. So I increased the supply."

He paused, annoyance evident in his tone. "She didn't take it well—refused to push the extra batch, or whatever," the bison said, shrugging nonchalantly. "I didn't mention anything about Wild to the officials. I doubt anyone would believe her even if she says anything about me and Wild."

Nutterson glanced at his wristwatch, his impatience evident. "So you decided to increase funding, and she didn't 'take it well.' What happened next?"

"I, um," Grounder stammered, blushing with shame as he recalled the impulsive action he hadn't expected to confess. "I thought I'd teach her a lesson. I mean, she's nobody, an uneducated meat-eater. Who cares?" he said with a dismissive sneer.

At this, Nutterson shot a wary glance at Lupus, sensing the wolf's simmering anger. Lupus's body language screamed tension, from the rigid posture of his ears to the taut swish of his tail. He drew in a deep breath, steadying himself, then signaled to Nutterson with a nod, reassuring him that he wouldn't let his emotions sabotage their current objective. Nutterson, jotting down a few quick notes, pursued the line of questioning, "And was it during this 'lesson' that she bit you? Had she gone feral?"

A shiver passed through the bison, the memory of the fox's bite vividly replaying in his mind. "Yes, she bit me, if it wasn't evident already," he said, a hint of bitterness in his voice as his tail lashed nervously. "Had her fangs been just a fraction larger, I'd have lost my fingers entirely."

Lupus subtly tried to catch Nutterson's attention, but the squirrel seemed preoccupied, glancing at his wristwatch once more. Eventually, he refocused on the bison. "The Wild and your gun—what did you do with them?"

With a self-satisfied smirk, the bison boasted, "The fox was caught with the note detailing the Wild's stash spots. The officers found those soon after the arrest, and they were convinced it was hers." He leaned back slightly as he continued, a hint of arrogance creeping into his voice. "As for the gun, I got rid of it—tossed it into the Wilfen River, right under the main bridge. They'll never trace it back to me. I told the officers I borrowed it for self-defense and refused to disclose the lender. The Hooves can fabricate the backstory, just like we were trained."

Jotting the details down, Nutterson grinned. "Smart move. We'll retrieve the gun and have someone testify to back up your weapon possession." He shot another glance at his watch, then gave Lupus a confirming nod. Reaching into a leather pouch on the desk, he pulled out a syringe filled with a clear liquid.

"Time's up," Nutterson said, his voice cold as he loomed over the captive. "Do me a favor, and try to keep your fucking bull stick in your pants, and don't embarrass us any more." With that, he delivered a stinging backhand across the bison's cheek—the other side this time. Then, with a swift motion, he grabbed the bison's hair, yanking his stunned head to the side, and injected the contents of the syringe into his neck before any retort could be made.

"After his court appearance in Wilfen concerning the incident with Ms. Redtail, he'll be transferred to the Bureau for possession and usage of a weapon since he was never registered to own any." Nutterson whispered, his tone dripping with satisfaction. He watched closely as Lupus gently laid the unconscious bison onto a freight train, preparing to leave the station. "Once we recover the gun and confirm it's an unregistered firearm, I bet he'll throw the Hooves under the carriage during the official questioning to save his own skin."

Wiping a bead of sweat from his forehead, Lupus took a deep breath before replying, "Besides, that idiot clearly has no idea what true feral state behavior looks like. When the predatory animal within takes over, there's no All Father's blessing left in them. They don't en-gage in conversations, just primal growls. If we can get a witness to vouch that they had a verbal dispute, his whole narrative falls apart." A grin of satisfaction spread across Lupus's face, and he gave Nutterson a playful slap on the back. "You've really outdone your-self, Nutterson. Have I ever mentioned you were my favorite student at the Bureau?"

"Oh, shut it, Greyfang," Nutterson retorted with a light-hearted laugh, his eyes gleaming in the low light. "At this rate, I'll be the one lecturing you before long."

"Sign me up when you do. I'm serious," Lupus quipped, his tail wagging with a mixture of jest and genuine fondness.

The distant tolling of the congressional building's bell echoed through the night. As the train began to chug away, Lupus called out, "Take care of our 'cargo'!" He raised his hand in a mock salute. Nutterson returned the gesture, his figure a diminishing shadow against the backdrop of the departing train.

"Grounder won't be held up at the Bureau too long," the goat assured, setting down the stacks of reports he had brought for the inner circle to review. "Once the district court rules in his favor, even the Bureau will have to acknowledge the necessity of his actions. His action is seen as laudable, given what I've heard from the officers and the Bureau insiders. We'll prepare one of the bisons with the weapon permit to testify that Grounder borrowed his weapon." The footsteps and murmurs of the audience, along with the peaceful piano welcoming guests in the theater above, filled the subtle silence of the hidden underground room.

"I've been warning about the risks of handling illicit substances, especially the Wild," the caribou stated as she readjusted her simple yet elegant metal antler-lette. Her impressive bony antlers stood tall, her ears flickering with displeasure. "This Wild operation is too dangerous, for both field operators and us. And isn't it suspiciously convenient how we've been receiving such large shipments for months, without a single hitch? I'm not alone in my concern about the Hooves' noble cause being tainted by dealings with the Wild." She paused, her voice dropping to a whisper. "You know, before Cloverfield—"

"Maintaining resources and keeping them hidden from authorities is neither easy nor cheap," Stellar inter-rupted sharply, her arms folded as she stood behind the delicate and opaque stained glass room divider, maintaining her anonymity from the rest of the inner circle. Her voice, though lowered, carried a sharp edge of irritation. "You pledged to our cause of liberating herbivores, regardless of the cost. Maybe you should reconsider your seat if your concern lies elsewhere, not with the disastrous state of our country infested with dangerous and disgusting meat-eaters," she spat, her voice dripping with disdain. Sensing the rising tension beyond the barrier, she continued without waiting for a reply. "Beyond bolstering our budget, the impact of the substance is undeniable. It strips away their masks, exposing their true nature. To shatter this country's unjust equilibrium, we must remind the public who they are really sleeping next to every night."

Stellar sat at her chair and crossed her long legs with deliberate grace, her voice tinged with pride. "As I have mentioned before, I personally vouch for the supplier. He's been a trustworthy ally, deeply committed to our cause since our inception." She leaned back, her fingertips tapping the armrest with a slight annoyance, "Instead of questioning our methods supporting our goal, focus on the feral fox case in Wilfen," she sneered. "Who knows how the stag senator will spin the story to favor the predator."

"Look, Starlight," the caribou retorted, leaning in, her voice taking on a defensive edge. "I know your thoughts about that senator, but it's a stretch to think he'd cover for that feral fox, especially when it was so obvious the fox was a danger," she said, shaking her head slightly in a dismissive manner. Her metal antlerlette chimed softly with the movement. "His tenure is too short to make any real difference. Give him a break. Big changes never happen overnight."

"He would've acted if he had even a shred of the dignity and pride we possess to serve the greater good. He's nothing more than a fancy herbivore puppet for the Greats," Stellar growled, her voice dripping with disdain. Memories of her confrontation with the stag senator flashed in her mind, fueling her anger. "I bet he might even try to twist the story to keep the bison in the Bureau's custody, long enough to make him spill anything if he sniffs a hint of the Hooves from him. Just to please the mighty Greats and keep his seat at the high table to play their favorite herbivore."

The caribou didn't reply immediately. Her posture, arms crossed tightly, was a silent testament to her disagreement. She sighed, a long, weary exhalation that seemed to carry the weight of their predicament. Rubbing her forehead as if to ease a headache, she looked away momentarily, her gaze settling on a couple of other inner circle members, their expressions mirroring her discomfort. She was clearly tired of the ongoing discussion around Senator Redfern, which had dominated their major meetings for the past couple of weeks. She had no desire to hear more disrespectful spouts from their leader.

"Anyhow," she finally spoke, her voice steady but tinged with fatigue, "I think we should put a hold on all Wild operations until the situation with Grounder is resolved. We can't risk having the Bureau on our tail."

"Phennelion is just around the corner. We need more budget for our operation, not less," Stellar countered, rising gracefully from her seat. Her gaze drifted to the decorated wall clock, calculating the time left for their discussion. "We'll put a hold on the Wild operation within Wilfen while increasing our presence in other districts. It's crucial to keep our field operators well-trained and ensure they never act alone from now on."

As the caribou stood to refute Stellar's decision, a series of clean bell chimes rang through the main hall above their room, signaling the start of the performance. Excited murmurs, laughter, and the shuffling footsteps of the guests shortly followed, filling the tense air in the room with a contrasting sense of anticipation.

"That'll be all," Stellar said, her voice authoritative and final. "May All Father enlighten our way." With those words, she turned and exited the room, the door slamming shut behind her with a resounding thud.

Her heels clicked against the stone ground, each step echoing her simmering frustration and barely contained rage as she paced toward her waiting room. She tried to ignore the lingering murmurs of the inner circle members that clung to her thoughts, their doubts and disagreements swirling in her mind. Instead, she focused on the performance ahead and the audience that awaited her, a mask of composure settling over her features as she prepared to face them.

The Traitor

❝ It would've made a front-page headline if it turned out Freya was feral," Rob remarked, sliding Wilfen Daily to Lupus across the breakfast table. "But kudos to the Security District for their discernment. They acted swiftly to recognize she wasn't feral when she bit the bison, after the testimonial about their argument supported by the official medical reports on rare Wild overdosing cases that turned terrians feral. That's no small feat."

Hart took a slow sip of his tea, savoring the robust flavor complemented by a sweet, floral note that enriched his senses, before placing the cup back on the saucer with a quiet clink. "It's fortunate Ms. Bushtail found a reliable witness to shed light on the situation."

Rob, leaning back, tilted her head with a grin. "This is another win for her, isn't it? After the Mr. Brown case?" She watched as Hart's eyes skimmed the Capitol Press, the corners of his mouth curling into a faint smile. She could practically feel the mood in the room lightening, a stark contrast to the recent tense days. "Perhaps a bouquet to express our appreciation?"

"That would be lovely," Hart looked up, warmth evident in his brown gaze. "And maybe another bouquet for the Redtail family."

Rob smiled softly, grabbing her notepad and making a quick note. "Two bouquets it is." Out of the corner of her eye, she caught Lupus's contented expression, easily imagining his tail reflecting the same sentiment.

Lupus neatly folded the newspaper and set his reading glasses on top, then began to clear away the breakfast dishes, including those before Hart and Rob. Hart lowered his paper, his eyes meeting Lupus's with a warm "Thank you" as his plate was taken. Rob, too, shared a silent nod with Lupus, her appreciation for his thoughtfulness evident without words.

"As for today," Rob began, her voice adopting a professional cadence as she perused Hart's schedule on her notepad, "we have the survey analysis review, followed by the Phennelion Preparation board meeting at the

Wilfen council. With the district-level competitions wrapping up next week, the Culture and Recreation Department head will present the final plans and budget for our finalists traveling to the Capitol." She looked up, her eyes twinkling with a playful light. "It's a rather light agenda. You could, in theory, cut out early," she suggested with a teasing smile.

Lupus returned to the table, his tail swaying gently. "I did get the new parts for the floor clock, by the way. If you head home early today, we could tackle that repair," he suggested softly. His gaze momentarily lingered on the sunlight catching the velvet of Hart's antlers, before settling on the deep warmth in Hart's eyes.

Hart carefully aligned the folded newspaper beside his teacup, his full attention shifting to Lupus. "That would be great. Can't wait to hear the clock ticking again." A wistful smile, small but sincere, tugged at his lips. "Thank you, Mr. Greyfang, for taking care of it."

Lupus couldn't help but notice the delicate curves of Hart's eyes and the playful twitch of his furry ears— subtle signs of contentment. Such expressions, absent for too long in his life, made Lupus's heart swell with genuine happiness.

The middle-aged skunk terrian's eyes widened with surprise as Hart entered the house, his arrival notably earlier than usual, and accompanied by a guest. "Mr. Redfern!" she exclaimed, her striped tail giving a slight twitch of delight. "I thought I'd never see you again ever since you were elected," she teased, a playful glint in her eyes.

"Good afternoon, Ms. Whites," Hart greeted, his tone imbued with a warmth that matched his smile. "It has indeed been too long since I last saw you. Thank you always for your service." He handed her the purse she had left by the door.

"Always a joy to serve," the skunk replied, her warm smile lighting up her features. She accepted her bag with a nod of gratitude, then turned her attention to Lupus. "And you must be Mr. Greyfang," she greeted, her hand extended in a gesture of welcome. "I'm Brenda Whites, part of the support staff here for Senator Redfern."

"It's a pleasure, Ms. Whites," Lupus replied, his voice carrying a respectful timbre as he gently shook her hand. Drawing a slow breath, he remarked, "Is that a clover pesto soup I'm smelling?" His nose twitched, identifying the familiar, comforting scent wafting from the kitchen, which made his tail sway.

Brenda's eyebrows lifted in amazement. "You do have a sharp nose. Most terrians wouldn't pinpoint it that easily," she remarked. She then glanced toward Hart, who was in the process of placing his coat on the rack, her eyes twinkling with a mix of respect and amusement. "The senator mentioned his fondness for the soup a few weeks back."

Hart rubbed the back of his neck, noticing an affectionate gaze from Lupus. "It's been particularly comforting for the velvet. Your culinary skills have been a real blessing," he admitted, his ears turning a delicate shade of pink as he adjusted his suit vest in a futile attempt to appear nonchalant.

Brenda's gaze settled warmly on his magnificent antlers. "Anything to assist in maintaining their beauty, Mr. Redfern," she responded, her voice softening. As she spoke, her attention briefly drifted to the window where the familiar silhouette of her husband waited, holding a bundle of flowers in his hand, ready for their evening stroll—a cherished daily ritual marking the end of her workday.

"Much as I'd love to linger and chat," she remarked, a hint of wistfulness in her voice, "I shouldn't keep him waiting." With a flick of her tail, radiant with joy, she signaled to her husband, ensuring he caught her gesture. "Wishing you both a delightful evening," she warmly intoned, gracefully making her exit.

"Enjoy your evening, Ms. Whites." Hart called out gently, his eyes lingering on her retreating form, and with a respectful nod to Mr. Whites beyond the gate. Once assured of her safe departure, his attention redirected to the wolf, his demeanor both courteous and familiar. "May I take your coat, Lupus?"

The casual use of his name caught Lupus momentarily off balance, a flicker of warmth igniting in his chest as he met Hart's gaze. "Oh, thank you." He began to remove his coat, with a slight assist from Hart. Despite his attempts at maintaining his well-practiced poise, the playful wagging of his tail gave away the mix of surprise and flustered pleasure from the unexpected proximity.

After placing Lupus's coat neatly on a hanger, Hart approached the stately floor clock which had been quiet for the past couple of weeks. Lupus followed shortly after fetching the clock parts from his briefcase. Hart turned the clock around, without needing any instruction from Lupus, granting them easy access to its inner mechanism.

Lupus held up a newly crafted metal piece, a glint of pride in his eyes. "The clockmaker was quite proud about his handiwork duplicating the suspension spring." His enthusiasm was infectious, pulling an earnest smile from Hart's lips, as he continued with a wide grin. "They look identical to me. Let's hope our clock is as convinced."

Hart stepped back, making room for Lupus to begin the repair. However, a gentle touch upon his arm coaxed him to pause. Lupus, with a guiding hand, offered the delicate clock part to Hart. "Why don't you put the parts back, Hart?" he suggested, a soft encouragement in his voice.

Carefully taking the parts from Lupus, Hart murmured, "You want me to do it?" The flash of incredulity on Hart's face swiftly transformed into that childlike excitement he often wore as a fawn, with his furry ears perked up in delight. With the wolf's wide smile and a nod, Hart returned a playful smirk. "Alright. I'll give it a try."

As Hart prepared to assemble the spring, recalling his memory, Lupus's soft voice became his guide. "Just there, see? Start with the top part in the center, al-lowing the rod to rest in the groove." As Hart's long fingers moved with precision with his guidance, the spring nestled perfectly within the clock's interior.

"Now, lift the pendulum rod, align the holes, and in-sert the connecting rod." Lupus continued, his tone a calm cadence in the quiet room. Hart's hands obeyed, his brow furrowed in concentration as he connected the rod to the spring with a precision that belied his initial hesitation.

"Nicely done." Lupus complimented, his chuckle deep and genuine. He reached out, a supportive hand resting briefly on Hart's back, his green eyes meeting the soft brown of Hart's. "Now let's turn the clock back and see if that did the trick."

Hart gave an affirmative nod. "Sounds good." Carefully, he shifted the floor clock to its original position. With practiced hands, he wound it up. "The moment of truth," he quipped, casting a playful glance at Lupus as he set the pendulum in motion.

The rhythmic ticking swiftly enveloped the house, a sound both familiar and comforting. Hart kept his eyes sharp, looking at the movement of the pendulum closely.

"How does it look?" Lupus inquired, a twinge of excitement evident in his voice. He observed Hart's gaze, unwaveringly locked on the pendulum's movements.

Taking a deep breath for dramatic effect, Hart furrowed his brow, his visage displaying profound concern. "It looks…" The brief pause earned him a fleeting, anxious glance from Lupus, whose ears were pitched forward, ready to catch every nuance, every inflection.

But then, with a sly tone, Hart declared, "…like it's fixed now." His voice, now teasing, danced with mirth as he shared a playful laugh with Lupus, whose ears had relaxed in relief, flopping gently against his head. The weight lifted from Lupus's chest was mirrored in the lightness of his laughter. "You almost had me there, kid." He gave Hart's shoulder a gentle nudge, his tail flicking lightly in amusement.

Stifling more chuckles, Hart motioned for Lupus to take a closer look. "It's moving perfectly now. I doubt it'll cause any issues anytime soon," he noted, the remnants of his laughter still coloring his voice.

Lupus studied the clock's rhythmic movements for a moment before nodding in agreement with a satisfied smile. "It sure is. Let's hope it stays this course for years to come." His green eyes, glimmering with contentment, met Hart's, savoring the comforting companionship for a fleeting moment. With a final, gentle pat on Hart's arm, Lupus signaled his departure. "I should leave you to enjoy the evening. I'm sure that'll help," he said, walking towards the door, with his tail swaying with content.

But as he reached for his coat by the door, Hart's voice, rich with an unexpected warmth, halted him. "Lupus." Hart's hand rested gently on Lupus's shoulder, turning him around.

Lupus faced Hart, only to be pulled into a heartfelt embrace. Hart's arms were strong, yet they conveyed a vulnerability that he seldom showed. In the tightening of his hold, Lupus could feel the cascade of unspoken words, the emotions Hart grappled with in silence. Words climbed to the back of Hart's throat, yet none seemed right to voice; instead, he simply held the wolf tighter.

Lupus embraced Hart tight as well, offering solace for the vulnerabilities he had only glimpsed in the past months. "I'm proud of you, Hart. I know your parents would be too," he whispered, each word imbued with genuine admiration and pride.

A heavy sigh escaped Hart, the burdens he'd been carrying seemingly lightened, if only for a brief moment. Nestling his face deeper into the crook of Lupus's neck, he let out a whisper, "Thank you."

In the sincerity of their embrace, the fortress of ice around Hart's heart yielded, granting him a rare moment of peace in the steadiness of Lupus's arms around him.

An urgent knock on the door jolted Hart from his preparations. Taking his pocket watch out, he made his way to the front door. It was mere minutes before his planned departure to the council building.

Upon opening the door, Hart was met with an unexpected sight. "Lupus?" he called out, confusion lacing his voice.

Instead of a verbal response, Lupus barged in, his entrance so forceful it sent Hart stumbling back into the house. The door shut with a sharp snap behind him. Through a fleeting gap before the door closed, Hart caught a glimpse of a group of security officers assembled outside his residence. A frown etched itself into his brow as he faced Lupus, who looked uncharacteristically disheveled and slightly out of breath.

"What's going on?" Hart inquired, his voice filled with a mix of confusion and concern, as he sought answers in Lupus's eyes, which quivered with barely contained distress.

Taking a moment to compose himself, Lupus began, "The Hooves. They…" His voice faltered, the struggle evident as he grappled for the right words, his heavy breaths betraying his heightened emotions.

Hart's gaze then snapped to the crumpled piece of paper in Lupus's clenched fist. With a sense of foreboding tightening in his chest, he reached out and seized the paper—a motion so swift, it seemed to startle Lupus, who had perhaps forgotten it was even in his hand.

"Hart, that's–" Lupus started to protest, but his words were lost as Hart's attention became wholly consumed by the contents of the unfolded paper.

The poster's design was a clear echo of the ones used during Hart's senatorial campaign. At its heart, an illustration captured Hart's likeness with uncanny precision, down to the unique curvature of his antlers. It would have been a noble portrayal of a red stag terrian, much like Senator Redfern himself, had it not been marred by the disturbing black rectangle obscuring the eyes. Bold, accusatory lettering crowned the top as 'The Traitor

Stag,' while 'The Carnivore Pleaser' was emblazoned at the bottom in a script that seemed to condemn.

Hart's hands trembled, though he hadn't noticed until Lupus's steady hand came to rest on his shoulder, grounding him. The reality of the situation seeped in Lupus's voice broke through the shock, "They've spread lies overnight about the bison case, twisting the narrative to suggest you swayed the verdict in favor of a feral fox." He paused, the weight of his next words seeming to momentarily anchor him between the need to inform and the desire to spare Hart further distress. "These..." he continued, with a reluctant resolve, "were plastered across Downtown Wilfen by dawn."

As the weight of Lupus's words bore down on him, Hart's ears pressed flat against his head. His fingers curled around the poster with a desperate strength, only releasing their grip when Lupus carefully pried it away. Lupus turned the poster face down on a nearby table and guided Hart to the couch, softly insisting he sit. He then knelt, positioning one knee on the floor so he could meet Hart's gaze. "The head of the Wilfen Security Department has dispatched officers here and to the council building. They're seeking witnesses. The Bureau should've been notified by now."

Hart remained silent, a storm of emotions playing out on his face. Lupus's brow furrowed with concern, as he took Hart's cold, quivering hands in his own, trying to anchor the senator's gaze away from the abyss of his thoughts.

"Hart, look at me." Lupus urged, his voice a low rumble of determination. He tightened his hold on Hart's hand, tenderly cradling his cheek to steer his focus. When their eyes met, the wolf's predatory intensity seemed to cut through the fog, lending a semblance of clarity to Hart. The haze of panic in Hart's eyes began to recede, replaced by the sharp, resolute gaze Lupus knew well. "You have to stay strong. Don't let those cowards drag you down."

Hart didn't speak, but he nodded, his jaw clenching with newfound resolve, silently acknowledging Lupus's message.

A soft rustling from outside reached Lupus's keen ears, abruptly followed by a firm knock at the door. With a motion for Hart to stay put, Lupus cautiously opened the door a crack.

"Snowclaw,"he began, but his greeting was cut short as the director, visibly irate, pushed him into the house, followed by a couple of the Bureau agents. "Wilfen wasn't the only district plagued by the Hooves," she announced, her tail bristling with tension.

As she brushed past Lupus, he noticed she wasn't merely shoving him aside. He felt the deliberate press of a crumpled paper into his chest. Unfolding it, he was met with a chillingly familiar illustration. The leaflet, spreading lies about the case, now bore a stark, ominous message over Hart's image: 'Death to the Traitor.'

Luna shifted her focus to the stag. "Senator Redfern," she called out. Hart had risen from the couch, his posture exuding a calm authority that belied his recent distress.

"The Central Security Bureau will ensure your protection until we can disseminate corrections across all districts from the Capitol," Luna declared, with professional composure in her voice. "While the details of our investigation into the Hooves will remain confidential within the Bureau, only to be shared with the High Chancellor until the case's conclusion, we will keep you informed as necessary for your safety."

With his ears perked attentively towards the white wolf, Hart had shed his earlier panic. "Understood, Director Snowclaw," he nodded, his gaze briefly meeting that of Lupus, who stood silently behind her.

Noticing Hart's glance, Luna swiftly added, "Agent Lightfoot and Widetail will be your primary escorts." She gestured toward a coyote and badger terrian standing beside her. After Hart acknowledged them with a nod, the duo took their positions on either side of the senator.

"Mr. Greyfang would–" Hart started, but was abruptly interrupted.

"With all due respect, Senator, Sector Zero agents do not specialize in personal protection," Luna interjected firmly, her eyes locking with Lupus's. His green eyes, wide with dread, betrayed his awareness of her next words. "Agent Greyfang has been reassigned, effective immediately."

"Snowclaw!" The growl emanating from Lupus was low and threatening. He stepped forward, his entire demeanor, from his alert ears to his bristled tail, radiating fury.

Luna crossed her arm, her voice a venomous whisper. "You can thank me later. You weren't exactly happy with playing babysitter, as I recall," she snarled, her ears flicking with evident annoyance. "Agent Nutterson is expecting you at the Bureau. He'll fill you in."

"Snowclaw," Lupus growled, stepping closer to the other wolf, his fangs bared and fists quivering with tension. "You know that's not what I–"

"You were..."

Hart's incredulous whisper interrupted the angry gnarl from Lupus. Both wolves shifted their focus to Hart, whose face had paled considerably. The weight of the perceived betrayal heavy in his voice.

"You were an agent sent by the Bureau?" With each word, his voice wavered, teetering on the edge of breaking. His large brown eyes, now brimming with unshed tears, locked onto Lupus's, conveying a silent plea for an explanation. The pain in his eyes deepened as tears began to roll down his face.

"Is that why you became my guard? *To spy on me?*" The director's dismissive words echoed in Hart's mind, a painful reminder of how Lupus had been discontent with his assignment, relegated to what felt like *playing babysitter.*

The sharp pain of betrayal pierced his heart, tearing open the old scars of betrayal and abandonment he thought were beginning to heal with Lupus back in his life.

"I thought…" *you cared.* His voice broke, unable to complete the thought. The excruciating realization that the warmth in Lupus's green eyes was nothing but a facade was a dagger to his soul.

How naive, even pathetic, he must have looked in the wolf's eyes, opening up and showing his vulnerabilities when Lupus showed him a slight bit of pity with gentle smiles and friendly pats on the shoulder. It had always been clear that Lupus wanted nothing to do with Hart Redfern all these years. Yet, blinded by a desperate longing for approval and affection, Hart had fooled himself into believing otherwise.

He had clung to the hope that Lupus saw him as more than just a senator needing protection, that perhaps he was now deemed worthy of companionship. But it was all a cruel charade, a way for the wolf to stay close to

Hart. The 'pure luck' that had saved his life from the bear, the reason Lupus had become his guard, were nothing more than the Bureau's orders to keep an eye on Hart Redfern—*the first stag senator.*

Grief swiftly gave way to a tempest of anger and sorrow. Hart's fists clenched, his body trembling as tears clouded his vision. "Because I'm the stag senator, isn't it?" Hart stepped forward, his ears pinned back, brows furrowed in a tapestry of hurt and fury. "You thought I was with the Hooves," he spat, the accusation tearing through him as it left his lips.

"Hart, please," Lupus whimpered, his heart wrenching at the sight of the devastation in Hart's eyes. His own eyes glistened with the weight of the pain he had caused. He took a tentative step forward, his ears drooping, his voice heavy with remorse. "I can explain. I've never–"

"Senator Redfern." Luna's voice sliced through the tension with an authoritative tone. She positioned herself between them with a decisive stride, pushing Lupus back and locking eyes with the senator, her gaze carrying a trace of impatience. "The nature of this investigation is highly sensitive, as I've already mentioned. The Bureau is handling the inquiry, and once concluded, you'll be granted full access to our findings during an official hearing."

With a dismissive gesture towards Lupus, she turned on her heel toward the door. "We don't have all day,

Agent. Move out," the director commanded, her voice slicing through the air.

"Hart, believe me. This isn't what it looks like," Lupus pleaded, his voice laced with desperation. He stepped closer, reaching out in a futile attempt to steady Hart's trembling fist. But Hart recoiled, stepping back, his eyes brimming with more tears.

"I was a fool to believe you," The bitter edge to Hart's laugh barely masked the depth of his pain. His voice dropped to a pained whisper. "Please go. Don't make me more miserable than I already am."

Without another glance, he turned away from Lupus, his movement gentle yet dismissive as he nudged the badger agent aside and made his way deeper into the living room. His head bowed, cradled in one hand, as a deep, shaky sigh escaped him. The strong lines of his back, usually so steadfast and unyielding, now seemed to fold under the weight of his sorrow.

"Agent Greyfang," the director's voice growled from the doorway, laden with impatience.

Lupus gave Hart one lingering look, noting how diminished he seemed. Regret flooded his green eyes. "I'm so sorry, Hart," he murmured, his voice barely a whisper. He then followed the director, her ears twitching with every agitated step, out of the house.

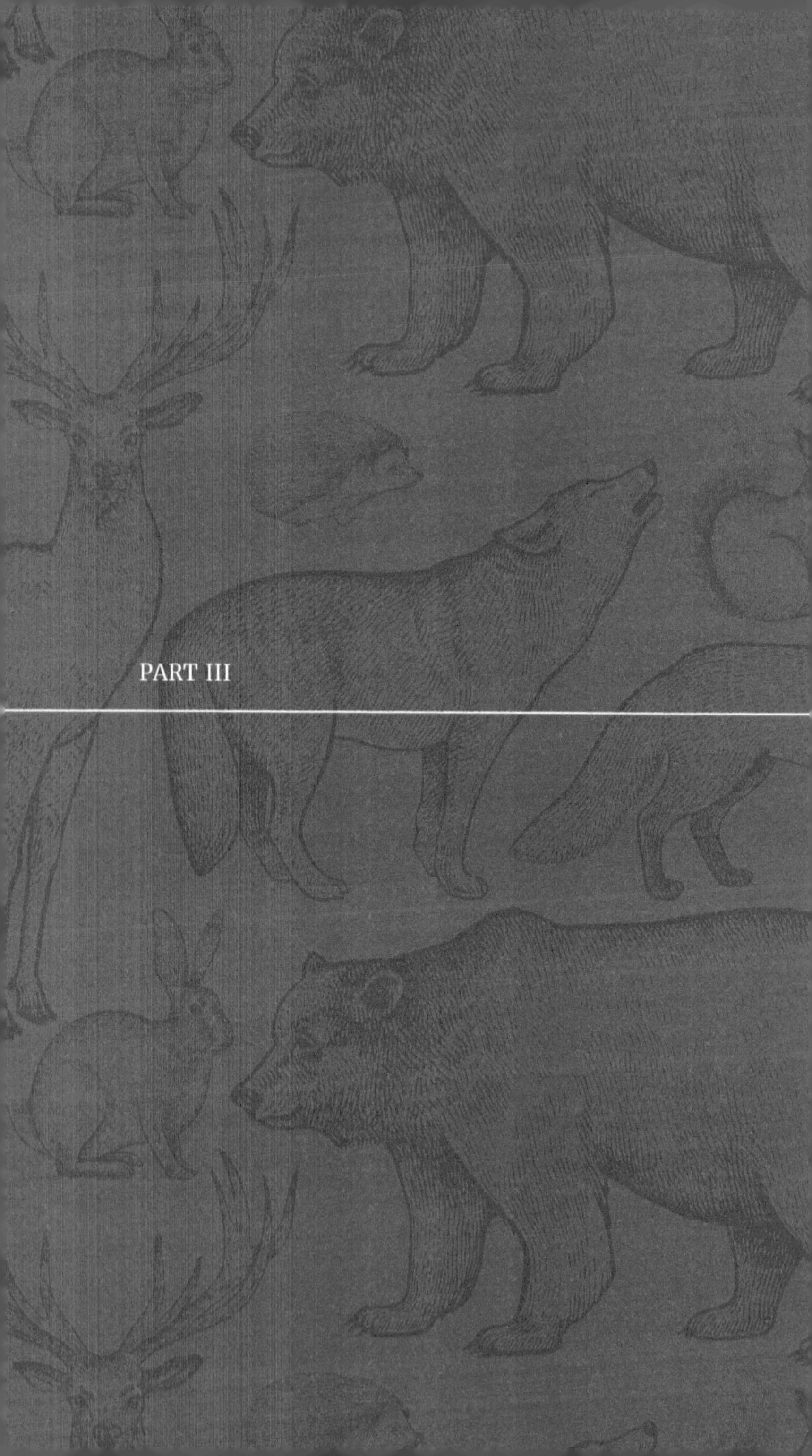

PART III

The Beasts
Among Us

The Abyss

The mournful resonance of a piano enveloped Rob as she was escorted into the Hart's residence by the Bureau agents. Her visit bore the official guise of conveying the Bureau's decision to temporarily relieve Hart of his duties for safety reasons, along with the necessary adjustments to his schedule. Unofficially, her concern for her friend weighed heavily on her, particularly after witnessing the incendiary propaganda posters smeared across Wilfen, all targeting Hart.

The Wilfen Council had issued an official statement, denouncing the baseless defamation against the senator and providing detailed clarification of the case. Yet, the general public seemed to adopt a stance of reticence, choosing silence over the risk of voicing concerns about the senator's troubling situation. Their silence was a tacit acknowledgement of a chilling realization the Hooves' relentless reach didn't stop at carnivores and would target anyone, even herbivores, who dared to deviate from their ideals.

Rob remembered Hart's meticulous piano recitals from their academy days. However, the sorrowful melodies now threading through the air carried a depth of emotion she had never before associated with her friend. It unsettled her.

Standing before Hart's door, Rob gave a gentle knock. The only reply was the uninterrupted, mournful cadence of the piano. There was no sign of Hart or Lupus; her presence went unacknowledged. A knot of anxiety tightened in her stomach. She knocked again, this time with more urgency, and called out, "Senator?"

"Just come in," came Hart's voice, tinged with melancholy, barely audible through the thick door. Rob cautiously entered the room, and the disarray inside immediately struck her. Unlike the immaculate spaces throughout the rest of the house, Hart's sanctuary was in chaos. Sheets of piano music lay scattered in disarray across the floor, and the heavy scent of alcohol hung in the air.

Seated at the piano, Hart had his face buried in his right hand, elbow resting on the keys, while his left hand listlessly coaxed mournful chords from the strings. A half-drained bottle of liquor stood atop the piano, beside a crystal glass holding its amber residue.

"You should be with your family," Hart mumbled, his gaze fixed elsewhere, not once shifting in Rob's direction. The uncharacteristic sluggishness and slowness of his voice made his level of intoxication evident, a fact all the more troubling given the early hour.

Rob's grip on her briefcase tightened, her concern deepening. "Hart, talk to me," she urged. "What's going on?" Despite the Hooves' slanderous campaign, she had never imagined it would impact him to this extent. It was more than just stripping away his senatorial composure; it was eroding his inherent self-assurance. Witnessing this unfamiliar side of him, marred by vulnerability, pained her.

With a weary sigh, Hart straightened up from the piano bench and poured another measure of liquor into his glass. Leaning against the piano, he turned to face Rob, his eyes a stormy blend of sorrow and the haze of alcohol. His curly hair was disheveled, and his tie loosened with the top buttons of his shirt undone, revealing a rawness Rob had never seen in him before. "You know what's going on," he replied, a bitter smirk accompanying his words as he raised the glass to his lips.

Rob took a deep, steadying breath, trying to carefully navigate the tumult of Hart's emotions. The faint tick of the floor clock, resonating through the house, caught her attention. She recalled the conversations between Hart and Lupus about this clock. Given how Hart's icy demeanor towards the wolf had been thawing, Lupus's conspicuous absence at this moment was disconcerting. Rob couldn't shake the feeling that it was entwined with the distress that clung to Hart like a shadow. "Where's Mr. Greyfang?" she asked, her voice tinged with worry.

Hart's eyes flickered, a storm of emotions passing through them. "He's…" He paused, the corners of his mouth turning downward in a fleeting grimace. "*Gone. The truth is, he was never really here. You should ask those Bureau agents, not me.*" A cynical smile flickered across his face, disappearing as quickly as it came, before he took another swig, seeking solace in the burn of the alcohol. Rob felt a chill run down her spine; Hart's demeanor was almost unsettling, beyond unfamiliar.

Closing the distance between them, Rob sought to pierce the veil of his anguish. "Hart, please, talk to me," she implored softly, her eyes earnestly searching his, which now seemed too void, too distant. "I can't understand the depth of your pain if you remain silent. You know you can trust me, not just as an aide, but as a friend."

"I appreciate your concern, Rob. Truly, I do," Hart murmured, his voice slow and thick with the influence of alcohol. His eyes, glossy with unshed tears, betrayed a profound sadness. "But I'm coping, in my own way." He paused, his gaze lingering on her. "For your own sake, perhaps you should consider aligning with a more promising politician. I'll write you any recommendation you need." With those melancholy words, he turned back to the bottle atop the piano, pouring another glass of the amber liquid.

Rob, jarred by the gravity of Hart's words, swiftly positioned herself beside the piano, ensuring she was squarely in his view. "You can't be serious, Redfern," she countered, her voice taut with a blend of worry and disbelief. The dramatic change in Hart's demeanor, coupled with his outlandish suggestions, had left her reeling. "You're not thinking clearly. Stop drinking, and get some rest." Her grip on her briefcase tightened, her heart pounding with a cocktail of rising frustration and concern.

"Tell me, Rob," Hart said, his eyes locking onto hers with unwavering intensity. "Do you honestly believe any of this would have happened if Councilor Nicholas Brew of *the Great Bears* had been in my place?" he sneered, bitterness evident in his tone. "None of this chaos would exist. Perhaps we might not even be dealing with the escalating Wild issues and the surge in criminal activities, just as the critics in The Wilfen Daily have been saying for months." His voice took on a self-mocking edge, but his eyes revealed the depth of his anguish and self-doubt.

Rob's voice softened, almost pleading, as she tried to reconnect with the stag she had admired and worked alongside for years. "Hart, you know those critics will say anything for attention. You can't blame yourself for everything happening in Wilfen."

For a fleeting moment, Rob's unwavering determination to reach Senator Redfern seemed to falter beneath his tormented gaze. In a whisper, barely audible against the backdrop of the room's thick tension, Hart murmured, "You should go." His voice, thick with emotion, hinted at a world of unresolved pain. "We can talk later, after the dust settles."

He took another prolonged sip from his glass, his other hand dancing over the piano keys, producing a haunting melody. With a shaky sigh, he closed his eyes, seeming to drift away, losing himself in the melancholic tune, each note resonating with his profound sorrow.

"I'll return later, alright?" Rob whispered, in one last attempt to reach him. Yet, her words seemed to dissolve into the poignant melody he played. She wished she could offer solace to his broken soul, lost somewhere deep in the seemingly bottomless pit of despair. With a heavy heart, she tightened her jaw and tenderly brushed Hart's shoulders, her touch lingering in a silent comfort before she turned to leave the room.

A light, rhythmic knock on the door woke Hart from a shallow slumber he hadn't realized he'd slipped into.

The blurred line between drunken stupor and fleeting consciousness had distorted his grasp on time. A brief glimpse at the window revealed the dark amber hues of late evening.

It had been a couple days since his official duties had been relieved, his current status teetering on the edge of house arrest, surrounded by the Bureau agents and security officers.

His solitude, however, wasn't peaceful. Spiraling thoughts and a cascade of self-doubt consumed him. Every time the alcohol's numbing grip started to weaken, the stabbing pain of the betrayal gnawed at him, carving fresh wounds into an already shredded heart.

Hart massaged his temples, grimacing as a piercing headache clamped down on him. He dragged a hand over his face, feeling the scratch of an unkempt beard against his fingertips. With a resigned sigh, he reached for the bottle on his bedside table, pouring another glass of the fiery liquid. He gulped it down, seeking a brief respite from his tumultuous emotions.

Yet the knocking persisted, only serving to fan the flames of his irritation. Hart assumed it was yet another guard with a trivial report. With a languid stride, he approached the door.

"Yes?" Hart's voice was gruff, an edge of annoyance unmistakable, as he flung the door open. To his surprise, he was met with the sight of a whitetail doe, simple yet elegantly dressed, her presence momentarily cutting through his haze.

"Senator Redfern," she greeted with genuine warmth, seemingly undeterred by her prolonged wait. Her smile was bright, bringing a gentle blush to her cheeks. "It's a privilege to meet you."

Pressing hard on his temples, Hart let out a deep sigh. He was painfully conscious of his disheveled state—the nightgown hanging off his frame, and the sharp scent of alcohol that clung to him. Striving to maintain a semblance of composure, he responded, voice slower and deeper than usual, "I must apologize, Miss. This isn't a… good time." As he spoke, a realization dawned on him. Her presence at his doorstep at such a late hour, without an appointment or prior notification from the Bureau agents, was highly unusual. She could have been anyone—a reporter, perhaps, eager to dismantle what was left of Senator Redfern's reputation. His grip on the doorknob tightened, suspicion casting a shadow over his features. "Please, schedule a visit during official hours with my aide. Have a good evening," he said, his tone edging toward dismissive.

Without affording the doe an opportunity to reply, Hart began to close the door. However, with swift grace, the doe wedged her fingers between the door and its frame, halting his action. "Senator," she urged, her voice laced with intensity, her furry ears pressed flat against her head. Her brows were slightly furrowed, her large eyes desperately searching Hart's, conveying an urgent plea. "My name is Rose. The Bureau sent me to see you." Noticing that the senator, though visibly taken aback by her boldness, hadn't outright rejected her, she gently pushed the door open further, her lips curving into a reassuring smile. "I'm here to offer comfort."

Hart's brow knitted together in confusion. "The Bureau?" The alcohol in his system muddled his thoughts, lowering his guard against the attractive stranger. He found himself tentatively accepting her claim, reasoning that with the heightened security, it was unlikely she could have entered without proper authorization. "What do you mean by 'comfort'?"

Before he could fully process her words, Rose was guiding him back into the room, her hand on his arm firm yet comforting. The door closed behind her with a soft, definitive click.

"I mean I'm here for you, for whatever you may need," Rose assured him, her voice taking on an allusive tone. The tension in the air, intertwined with Hart's intoxication, rendered the moment surreal. The small waltz of her rhythmic heels against the floor intertwined with his hesitant steps backward, setting his heart racing. When he felt the edge of the bed press against the backs of his knees, his breath hitched. In this moment of vulnerability, Rose's gentle nudge sent him toppling backward, his elbows catching his fall.

Taking a moment to collect his thoughts amidst the emotional maelstrom, Hart murmured, "Please, Ms. Rose, this isn't…" A flush crept up his cheeks, his expression a cocktail of bewilderment and surprise. Seeking to regain some semblance of control, he sat up, his movements gentle yet firm as he eased her hands away from his chest.

Her laughter, soft and enticing, filled the room. She guided his hand to rest upon her slender waist. "Don't be shy, Senator. Allow me to take care of you." With a graceful motion, Rose hitched up her dress just enough to slide her knee onto the bed, positioning herself atop his lap with deliberate ease.

A jolt of surprise shot through Hart, his ears and tail perking up. The rapid thud of his heartbeat seemed to amplify the effects of the alcohol, making the room tilt slightly.

"Your prime antlers are quite the sight. It must be hard shouldering such a weight," she mused, her voice laced with genuine admiration and empathy. Her fingers delicately wove through his hair, gently massaging the base of his antlers. Each touch heightened Hart's awareness, his ears twitching involuntarily as a sigh of pleasure and relief slipped from him. "Does that feel good?" she whispered, playful satisfaction in her smile. Her eyes, alight with amusement, locked onto his slightly dazed brown eyes, captivating him.

As Rose's touch traveled further down his neck, a pang of conscience tightened around Hart's chest. The gnawing unease of having someone in his bed by the order of the Bureau overwhelmed the fleeting pleasure her affectionate warmth provided.

Breaking their intense eye contact, he whispered, "Ms. Rose, please." His trembling hands encircled her wrists. With gentle firmness, he eased her hands away and subtly indicated for her to slide off him. "I appreciate your intentions, but I don't need your services," he assured her. Yet, his quivering voice betrayed the internal conflict he was fighting against. Deliberately, he continued to avert his eyes, avoiding her lingering, intense stare.

"You're only fooling yourself, Senator," she purred, her fingers deftly slipping from Hart's grasp. They tenderly traced his jawline, compelling him to meet her gaze. "Part of you may resist, you know you need someone to ease your burdens. I can feel it right here." Her soft touch contrasted with his ungroomed stubble as her hands glided down, parting the gown to reveal his broad chest. Despite his desperate attempts to resist, his body responded involuntarily, his heartbeat quickening and breath growing labored.

"No, I'm..." Hart's protest began, but his words faltered, dissolving into a guttural rumble as her fingertips traced teasing patterns across his bare chest. Their touch was soft, almost otherworldly, igniting a fire within his senses, further clouded by the haze of alcohol.

Rose leaned in, her lips brushing against his quivering furry ear. "There's nothing to prove by rejecting what you really need," she whispered, her voice a soft, seductive lure that grew more compelling with each word. Her fingers danced down his arms, guiding his hands back to the curve of her waist. The slightest brush of her fingertips sent a shiver down his spine, leaving goosebumps in their wake. "You've given so much, sacrificed even more. Why not allow yourself this moment of pleasure? An escape from the weight of the world, if only for a moment." The warmth of her breath and the subtle musk of her scent drew another deep groan from him, to which she responded with a light, teasing chuckle.

With practiced grace, she shifted, draping herself against his broad shoulders. Hart was acutely aware of her every movement, every curve pressing against him, every breath she took. The tension that had ensnared him began to melt under her touch, his breathing growing ragged with rising desire.

"I'm here for you, love." Her lips curved into a knowing smirk as she caught his gaze, now darkened with the raw, unbridled desire she had stirred to life. "You've earned this."

As her gaze dipped to his parted lips, Hart found himself surrendering to the tempest of passion she had kindled.

The fiery surge of pleasure erased everything: the burdens of his position, the ceaseless challenges to his integrity, the gnawing self-doubt, and above all, the raw pain of betrayal and the chilling realization of his absolute solitude.

Embraced deep in burning desire, the world was reduced to the soft warmth of the body pressed against him, each touch igniting waves of pleasure. He surrendered to his primal urges, unrestrained and unbridled. The allure was intoxicating, simple, and profoundly fulfilling. With increasing fervor, he chased the pinnacle of ecstasy time and again, craving the overpowering release of pleasure.

The intensity of the moment, however, was cruelly fleeting. It departed all too swiftly, leaving behind the scorching afterglow of pleasure and the dreamy haze of intoxication, only to be replaced by a chilling clarity about his own actions that loomed like an abyss.

The reflection staring back at him was one he scarcely recognized. It was primal, driven by raw instincts, a stark contrast to the principled, disciplined being he had always believed himself to be. He saw himself consumed by a potent, unchecked lust, stripped of emotional depth, love, or authentic connection—as if he was nothing more than a stag in a rut. How easily he had given in, allowing his animalistic desires to usurp control, rendering his lifelong struggle to rise above his inner animal seem trivial.

Perhaps he had been fighting against an inevitable truth—he was exactly what the world perceived him to be, and all his efforts to prove otherwise had been in vain. The weight of this realization was suffocating, rendering his struggles meaningless. What had he been trying to prove all these years? That he knew better than the rest of the world, that he is more than just a stag? Or was he just delaying the inevitable acceptance of a painful truth that had been apparent since the day Lupus left him?

Lost in the vast expanse of his own thoughts, Hart felt unmoored, as if he were adrift in an endless ocean, devoid of a guiding compass or a grounding anchor. Every endeavor, every sacrifice, every decision seemed trivial against the immutable backdrop of destiny. He grappled with the notion of whether his suffering had ever held any true significance.

Perched on the edge of the bed, emptying the last of the liquor bottle in his hand, his anguish poured out. His heavy head was buried in his palm, tears carving paths down his cheeks, pooling on the floor. Gentle hands snaked around him from behind, and the soft press of lips found the curve of his bare shoulder. Amidst the tempest of his emotions and doubts, her warmth was the one anchoring reality that he could grasp. Gratefully, he leaned into the comfort she provided, like a weary traveler seeking shelter from a storm.

As she gently coaxed him back into the bed, a cascade of apologies spilled from his lips. At first, it was a simple expression of regret for letting her witness such raw vulnerability. But as his words continued to flow, it became unclear what sins he sought absolution for. All the while, her hands, warm and reassuring, cradled him, drawing him closer.

"I'm sorry, love. This is nothing personal," she whispered, her apology lost in the whirlwind of his emotionally charged state. Before he could ponder its meaning, a sharp sensation pricked the back of his neck. There was a brief moment of stiffness, followed by a twinge of discomfort radiating across his shoulder.

"I see his ears moving," murmured a stranger in a hushed tone, "just about time."

It took Hart a few disorienting moments to realize that he was no longer in the familiar confines of his bed. It was as if entire chapters had been ripped from the book of his life. With a few blinks, he struggled to regain his senses, only to realize his eyes were blindfolded, his mouth gagged.

Confused, he tested his range of motion and found himself bound to a chair, his limbs weighed down as if filled with lead. His furry ears twitched and swiveled, and his breathing grew erratic with mounting anxiety. His fists clenched tight, straining for some vestige of control.

"I told you that was enough, considering how drunk he was when I got in," Rose's voice sliced through the fog, now chillingly devoid of the affection that had laced her words just moments before. Hart instinctively turned his head toward where her voice was coming from.

"Hey, love." she said, her voice softening, a trace of warmth seeping back in. She cradled his chin tenderly, her lips brushing a soft kiss on his forehead. "Good luck," she whispered, her words accompanied by a light, teasing chuckle. Her fingers danced across the back of his neck, soothing the spot where numbness still lingered.

"Let's move. They'll be here any minute," came another voice, distant and tinged with impatience.

"On my way," Rose replied, her touch lingering on Hart for a fleeting moment before the sound of her footsteps faded away.

Hart attempted to wriggle free, but his efforts proved futile. Hindered by his restricted mobility, he fought to calm his racing heart and take stock of his surroundings. Every detail—the unfamiliar scents, the ambient noises, the peculiar temperature, and the humidity—felt foreign to him.

Thoughts of Lupus crept into his mind, serving as a painful reminder of his solitude. He clenched his fists again, channeling his energy into grounding himself and plotting an escape. The soft patter of approaching footsteps caught his attention. A glimmer of hope ignited within him, fervently wishing for a miraculous rescue.

 # The Broken Crown 

Something was not right. Lupus felt his fur bristle, an uneasy, instinctive sensation gnawing at his stomach.

This was no mere flicker of paranoia; it was a primal alarm, blaring a warning of danger. The compulsion to check on Hart had become an overpowering force, an insistent drumbeat that silenced all other thoughts.

"Lupus," Nutterson called out, his voice laced with concern, cutting through Lupus's mounting dread. The slow sway of his bushy tail and the look in his eyes betrayed his own unease. "You need rest. You won't be of any help in this investigation if you're exhausted."

Nutterson's gaze followed the subtle shift in Lupus's posture, sensing a deepening anxiety in the wolf's green eyes.

Ever since the chilling threat from the Hooves against Senator Redfern, and Lupus's subsequent involvement in the joint investigation, his dedication had teetered on the brink of obsession. The wolf had become a fixture at the Bureau, and Nutterson struggled to remember when he last saw Lupus pause for food or sleep. The squirrel braced himself for the wolf's usual refusal, mentally lining up counter arguments for any protest Lupus might come up with.

To Nutterson's astonishment, however, Lupus responded with a terse nod. "You're right," he admitted, his voice quivering with barely contained anxiety. He pushed back from the table, which was buried under a mountain of newspapers, various ads, and notes on a growing list of terrians of interest. Rising, his hand shook visibly as he reached for his coat, betraying the turmoil within. "See you tomorrow, Nutterson. Thanks," he said, his voice barely above a whisper. A faint smile, a brief flash of gratitude, flickered across his otherwise stormy expression. With that, he turned and walked out, leaving behind the dim glow of oil lamps and the heavy silence that now enveloped the Bureau.

The rhythmic clatter of the late-night train wheels against the tracks was only a faint echo in Lupus's ears, drowned out by the tumult of his thoughts. He replayed the reassurances in his mind—Hart was in Wilfen, under the watchful eye of the Bureau's finest. Yet, the frantic pounding of his heart found no solace in that reasoning. With each passing tree and shadow that flickered past the train window, the knot of worry in his stomach tightened further.

Despite the memory of Hart's pained expression, which Lupus feared might now harbor anger or, worse, a haunting indifference, he yearned to see Hart again, safe and unharmed. He clung to the hope that his gut feeling was just a shadow of prolonged stress and not the harbinger of a looming threat. The train continued its journey through the night, carrying Lupus and his sea of worries towards an uncertain dawn.

"Senator Redfern has barely left his room," the badger agent remarked, a flicker of concern betraying itself as his tail twitched. He kept pace with Lupus's brisk strides. "He's requested a couple bottles of liquor the past couple of days, yet his meals remain largely untouched. Ms. Whites managed to coax him into having a bowl or two of soup, but that's about all he's had."

Before Lupus could probe deeper into the senator's worrisome behavior, Widetail continued, his hand pressing against the heavy oak of the front door, "He was...

resting, when we checked on him earlier this evening, to see if he would take his dinner." His voice trailed off, laden with the memory of the senator's pained expression in slumber, an errant tear still clinging to a long eyelash.

A heaviness settled in Widetail's chest, a reflection of the decline he had observed in Senator Redfern over the past days. The senator, once a figure of meticulousness and principle, with the proud bearing of a red stag, now bore a closer resemblance to a disheveled, drunken deer. His once broad shoulders sagged, seemingly crushed under the weight of his internal turmoil. The melancholic strains of piano that once sporadically filled the house had, over time, morphed into a series of eerie dissonances, echoing the senator's spiraling mental state.

Shivering his tail as he recalled the haunting piano notes from hours earlier, the badger added, "We left him undisturbed since then. No visitors either."

Crossing the threshold, Lupus was immediately struck by the change in the house's atmosphere. The cozy and inviting ambiance from just a few days earlier, once imbued with the senator's vibrant presence and the warmth of home, was now replaced by a pervasive sense of desolation. The only sound that dared break the oppressive silence was the rhythmic, somber ticking of the floor clock.

With each step he took up the stairs, Lupus felt a growing weight of dread pressing on his chest, constricting his breath. The gentle flicker of lamps along the staircase cast eerie, elongated shadows, as if reaching out to him with ghostly fingers. His heart raced, and his furry ears strained for any sign of Hart's presence, each creak of the old wooden stairs echoing in the stillness of the house.

The sight that greeted them at the top, however, was both unexpected and alarming. The coyote agent, tasked with guarding Hart's room, lay sprawled on the polished wood floor in the corner, an ominous indication of the chaos that had unfolded.

Lupus's instincts surged to the forefront. He spun, seizing the badger agent with one hand while his other hand shot to his combat knife with practiced ease. "Get reinforcements! Alert the Bureau—now!" he barked in a hushed yet sharp tone. With the badger hastening away, Lupus rushed to the coyote terrian on the floor. The agent was still breathing but lost in a deep, unsettling unconsciousness. A faint syringe mark on his neck was a clear sign: this was not an ordinary intrusion, but a well-planned and executed act.

His attention snapped to Hart's door, his hands quickly testing the handle. It was securely locked. Panic began to gnaw at his composure, leaving no room for the delicate work of lockpicking. Retreating a few paces, Lupus charged the door, his body driven by sheer desperation.

The sturdy door withstood his blows, each impact sending jolts of pain through Lupus's frame. Yet, he persisted, a frustrated snarl escaping through his grinding fangs. His ears were tuned to the subtle splintering of wood, each crack a beacon of hope amidst his growing despair. Finally, with a thundering crash, the lock gave way. The sound of fracturing wood echoed through the hall as the door flung open, revealing the disarray within.

A wave of chilling realization swept over him—*Hart had been taken*. Time seemed to dilate as Lupus's eyes scanned the room for clues of what had happened. The open window, with its curtains fluttering softly in the nocturnal breeze, drew his attention. An unsettling hush settled over the room, broken only by the occasional rustle of paper. The air was thick with the aroma of spilled liquors, yet Lupus's keen senses cut through it, identifying the distinct, heavy musk of Hart intertwined with that of another deer. The scent trail led him to the window and then upward, suggesting a route to the roof.

Lupus's hands, now shaking with a cocktail of dread and anxiety, clutched the windowsill. He turned around as his gaze lingered on the chaotic scene before him: bedsheets tangled and trailing on the floor, liquor bottles tossed carelessly about, and sheets of music scattered in disarray. This scene stood in stark contrast to the memories of the disciplined young stag he had watched grow under his guardianship, or the composed Senator Redfern he had guarded in recent months.

Every discordant detail in the room felt like a blade twisting in Lupus's heart. It served as a painful reminder of the isolation and despair that must have engulfed Hart. All the while, Lupus had been consumed by his investigation, haunted by the image of Hart's deep brown eyes filled with pain, since their last, strained confrontation.

He had been determined to clear Hart's name from any lingering association with the Hooves, to root out the Hooves who had audaciously smeared Hart's reputation with their vile propaganda, and to preempt their escalating threats. Once justice was served, he had envisioned a reunion with Hart, a time to lay bare the darkest corners of his past and to seek forgiveness, and perhaps, another chance to mend their fractured bond.

But as he stood there, amidst the tangible remnants of Hart's emotional turmoil, Lupus was forced to confront a devastating truth: He was already too late. His efforts to protect Hart had fallen short when it mattered most.

A crushing weight of guilt and fear plunged his heart into an abyss of despair, with the icy grip of dread seizing his frantic pulse, rendering his breaths shallow and ragged. Yet, the urgency of the moment snapped him back into focus. As security officers poured into the room, piecing together the scene, Lupus darted outside, trying to hold onto the faint trail of Hart's scent, praying fervently that he wasn't too late.

⚬⚬⚬

"I know it's been a taxing week," Moonlight whispered, his voice a blend of hushed excitement and soothing calm. He gently guided her into the building, his hands mindful not to let her stumble, and murmured, "I hope this gift will lift your spirits."

With his large hand easily covering both of her eyes, and the other steadying her by the waist, Stellar leaned back against his solid frame. Her own fingers curled around his arms for balance. A soft giggle, infused with the relief of this welcome diversion, escaped her lips.

The past week had been relentless. The unexpected district court ruling in favor of the feral fox had undeniably strengthened her position within the Hooves. She had seized the moment, swiftly quelling any dissent within the Hooves that previously questioned her leadership. With fiery resolve, she channeled her rage against the traitorous stag's assault on them. Under Stellar's command, the Hooves' determination had become unyielding, a solid front against their adversaries.

Yet, the burden of leadership weighed heavily on her shoulders. Moonlight's unexpected visit was a breath of fresh air, a steadfast support in these tumultuous times.

As they moved deeper into the building, Stellar was struck by the distinctive smell of ink. She instantly recognized it as one of their safehouses, the one housing their clandestine printing press. Once they were securely positioned, Moonlight leaned in gently, his lips almost grazing her furry ear. "Open your eyes now, S," he whispered softly, his hands moving away from her eyes to rest lightly on her shoulder.

Stellar's eyes slowly adjusted to the dim ambiance. With each blink, more details of the room emerged, until the centerpiece became unmistakably clear. In stark contrast to the littered propaganda images portraying a dignified Senator Redfern, there sat the stag himself, bound and vulnerable. A cloth masked his eyes and muffled any potential outcry.

Stellar's heart skipped a beat as she grasped the reality of the situation. She turned to lock eyes with Moonlight, her expression etched with a silent plea for an explanation.

His face, obscured in the shadow of his thick hood, was barely visible. Yet, the scant light was enough to reveal a mischievous smirk playing on his lips. "All yours," he whispered, his voice a soft echo in the stillness of the room. He extended his hand towards the captive senator, presenting him like a trophy with a gesture that was both grand and chilling.

As Stellar's initial shock subsided, her gaze returned to the stag. The scene before her painted a somber portrait of decline. Senator Redfern, once the embodiment of elegance and dignity, now appeared as a mere shadow of his former self. Clad in a simple nightgown, his ungroomed beard and tousled curly hair, coupled with the lingering scent of alcohol, told a story of a fall from grace.

Yet, beneath the disheveled exterior, the senator's inherent resilience flickered stubbornly. Bound and subdued, his composed breathing stood as the sole testament to an indomitable spirit that refused to be extinguished.

Moonlight, with a grim smile on his lips, let his hands drift down to settle on Stellar's waist. "Look at him," he remarked with a subtle gloat, his gaze fixed on the restrained senator. "It seems he thoroughly 'appreciated' your hard work, which seems to have shaken the very foundations of his mind." He relished the rapt attention in Stellar's eyes as he drew her closer, pressing his broad chest against her back. His fingers traced the contours of her waist, gently pressing against her pelvis. The warm breath against the soft fur of her ears stirred a complex dance of comfort and tension within her.

His amber eyes, darkened with malice, never left the restrained senator. The corners of his mouth twisted into a cruel smirk, betraying a sinister amusement. "We could make him pay for his treachery, show him that actions have consequences. And if his remorse remains absent..." Moonlight's voice, mingling with a low chuckle, sent a chilling promise. "We could toss him into an underground carnivore arena and watch how much he likes the predators when they dig their fangs into his flesh." The quiet sound of his swallow followed his words, sending a shiver down Stellar's spine. "A poetic end for a carnivore pleaser, wouldn't you agree?"

Pushing aside the ripples of anxiety that tugged at her gut, she focused on the traitorous stag before her—the one who had betrayed his own kind, who had threatened to drag her before the Bureau when she had sought his help to seek justice for her late brother. Memories of her brother's gentle smile, his warm embrace, and his untimely demise fueled a fire within her.

She leaned back into Moonlight's hold, her hands resting over his as they wrapped around her waist. Drawing from his warmth and strength, her voice emerged steady and full of conviction. "Absolutely."

"Perhaps we should begin by stripping him of those prime antlers, a symbol of status he hardly deserves," Moonlight suggested, his hushed voice now a deeper shade of menace as he produced a serrated saw from beneath his cloak.

Stellar's gaze lingered on the curvature of impressive antlers, almost ready for the blossom to shed their velvet. In a gesture both intimate and foreboding, Moonlight guided her fingers to the saw's handle, drawing her into the act, its sharp edges gleaming ominously in the dim light. As she accepted it, a tremor fluttered through her fingers, stilled only when Moonlight's hand enveloped hers, firm and reassuring. "Show him the strength of the Hooves, the true herbivores," he whispered, his gentle nudge against her back fueling her determination.

Haunted by memories of their previous encounter, Stellar advanced toward the senator. She could still feel the sting of humiliation and despair from when he had wielded his authority over her, crushing her spirit beneath his heel. *Such disgraceful terrian doesn't deserve the senator's title*, she thought, her jaw clenched in simmering rage. Grasping the saw with renewed purpose, her steps morphed from hesitant to resolute.

"Senator Redfern," she addressed him, her voice a low murmur to mask her identity. With feigned tenderness, she traced her fingers over his face, peeling away the cloth that muffled him. But even as words threatened to tumble from his lips, she seized an antler with sudden force, tilting his head back.

A raw cry of pain escaped from between Hart's gritted teeth, shattering the room's stifling stillness. Days of drowning his sorrows in alcohol had left Hart with a pounding headache as he was teetering on the precipice of sobriety. That agony was only amplified as the sensitive velvet of his antlers endured her brutal grip, a force that seemed almost intent on wrenching his skull from his neck.

Stellar, drunk on the potent cocktail of control and vengeance, leaned in until her lips barely brushed his ear. "Do you understand why you're here?" she whispered, her voice soft yet laced with menace.

"The Hooves," he growled defiantly, despite his compromised state. Even bound and constrained, the senator's indomitable spirit was undeniable. The muscles in his wrists bulged against the ropes as he demanded, "What do you want from me?"

His eyes might have been concealed, but an overpowering fervor radiated from him, filling the space between them. Stellar felt exposed, as if he could peer straight through her despite his blindfold, sending unsettling tremors down her spine.

Regaining her composure, she replied with a calculated coldness, "Our aim has always been justice. Unlike yours," she sneered, savoring the sight of the stag's face—etched with frustration and pain she had stirred. With a deliberate motion, she released his antler, pressing it downward with force, compelling him to bow. "Repent of your sins, Redfern. Perhaps then, you might leave this place intact."

Hart snapped his head up, his teeth gritted. "Justice? Is this your idea of justice?" he growled, seething with disdain. "You fuel prejudice and cast shadows upon the innocent based on nothing but lineage," he spat, each syllable a venomous dart aimed at her. "You spread fear, reducing society to primal instincts, manipulating them to serve your agenda. You aren't seeking justice, you insufferable zealot—you're a power-hungry fanatic."

Before she fully comprehended her own actions, the back of her hand struck his cheek with a sharp crack, sending his head snapping to the side. Stellar's eyes blazed with raw fury. "Shut your mouth, traitor," she hissed.

After a brief pause to regain her poise, she sneered, "In your world of privilege, you bask in adulation as the first herbivore senator. But I see through you. You are nothing but a mere pretender, yearning to join the ranks of the mighty Greats, obsessed only with their status," she reproached, her voice laced with scorn. "Theodore Brown and Freya Redtail—you helped these feral predators roam freely, abusing your authority. You're so desperate for their acceptance, aren't you?"

Her nostrils flared as she took a steadying breath, watching the stag carelessly spitting out blood pooled in his mouth. He turned his head back to her, his expression devoid of remorse or fear.

Moving to stand behind him, Stellar gripped his antler tightly, yanking it backward. She disregarded the pained grunt that escaped his clenched teeth, her grip on the antler tightening until her knuckles blanched, a surge of fury building within her that had been accumulating for months.

"You're nothing but a delusional deer. You'll never be one of them, no matter how pathetically you seek their approval," she whispered with a malevolent edge, positioning the jagged teeth of the saw beneath the brow tine. Despite the brave front the stag tried to maintain, she could see the rapid pulse throbbing at his throat. "Perhaps a small reminder of who you are is in order."

Despite being visibly shaken by the looming threat, Hart found a deeper well of courage within. His mind, which had once been consumed by an abyss of despair, now flared with defiance. "Do your worst, you coward," he growled, his teeth clenched and his body trembling in fearful anticipation. Yet, this raw, primal terror, in a paradoxical twist, only strengthened his resolve that had been teetering on the edge. "You may strip me of my antlers, but you'll never put a single dent on my belief in unity and true justice for every soul."

Stellar's fury surged, fueled by the audacity of the senator, now bound and defenseless before her. The sensation of power, having such a prominent figure at her mercy, was intoxicating. Her eyes flicked towards Moonlight, seeking his silent counsel. His smile and the subtle nod were all the confirmation she needed, a silent endorsement to continue.

"This will be a lesson you will never forget," she promised ominously. Tightening her grip on the antler and
the saw, she clenched her teeth. As the saw's serrated
edges began to cut into the soft velvet of the antler,
Hart's agonized scream tore through the room, his body
tensing against the chair's relentless hold, the scent of
fresh blood permeating the air.

The velvet-clad antler and its bone stood no chance
against the saw's sharp teeth. Each chilling cut ripped
through its soft velvet, bit by bit, on every relentless
slide, sending a fresh jolt of excruciating pain penetrating his core. The merciless vibration of bone scraping
against the saw's jagged teeth assaulted his eardrums
from within, smothering his own agonized cries spilled
past his gritted teeth along with the saliva saturating
his beard. His body convulsed, the intensity of his torment evident in the sweat and tears that soaked his
blindfold and gown.

Minutes stretched into what felt like a lifetime of torment, until the last slide of the saw cut through the
final strain of velvet, severing the antler from its place
of honor atop Senator Redfern's head.

Hart's breathing was ragged, each exhale a pained gasp.
He clenched his fists, struggling to keep his head upright, his body still trembling from the raw aftermath.
Each heartbeat sent waves of pain through his body,
pulsing blood out. Warm streaks of blood soaked his
hair and stained his features, the fabric over his eyes

becoming saturated. A primal dread gripped him at the loss of his antler, the unfamiliar imbalance on his head sending shivers down his spine. Yet, within this torment, a resilient spark ignited. Hart tightened his jaw and pressed his nails into the flesh of his palms, commanding himself to focus. *It's just an antler.* He forced his breaths to even out, seeking calm amid the chaos.

As her frantic breath settled, Stellar stared at her hand clutching Senator Redfern's prime antler, now smeared with blood. Momentarily overwhelmed by the gravity of her action, a tremor ran through her. Her quivering gaze glided down the bloodied saw, reflecting the dim light of the room. The entire act felt both surreal and disturbingly tangible, as if she was on a stage without an audience. She sensed a cracked line between her flesh and her soul, a divide that seemed to widen with each passing second.

Realizing the momentary silence from her, Hart spat a mouthful of blood, its metallic tang filling his senses. A shaky, unsettling laughter bubbled up from within him, capturing Stellar's drifting attention. "Look at you," he taunted, his voice raspy yet dripping with defiance, "nothing more than a pathetic criminal. Your actions don't intimidate me."

The sheer force behind his growled words, even in his vulnerable state, seemed to wrap around Stellar's throat, suffocating her. The resilience Senator Redfern displayed, even amidst excruciating pain, began to erode her resolve.

Struggling against the claws of doubt, Stellar forced herself to remember the vision of the Hooves, the trust placed in her leadership, and the promise of a land liberated from the terror and silent tyranny of carnivores over her kind. She clung to the justice she sought for her brother, vowing not to let his fate be repeated in this land.

Grasping the heavy antler with renewed determination, Stellar cast aside the bloodied saw, its blade clattering loudly against the cold floor. "Let's see if that defiant tongue of yours remains as sharp when you're at the mercy of feral carnivores," she hissed, her voice dripping with venom. With those chilling words, she started walking away from him.

"May All Father have mercy on your wretched soul," Hart growled after her retreating footstep, spitting out blood that had pooled in his mouth.

The full weight of her actions crashed over Stellar the moment she stepped outside. Her cruel mind replayed memories of her gently touching the soft, warm velvet of her brother's growing antlers, and his warm laughter when he saw the genuine awe in her eyes.

She flung the cold, blood-drenched antler aside, her stomach churning in revolt against the night's grim deeds. The cold night air stung her lungs, a sharp contrast to the turmoil burning within her. It was not the chill, however, but the action she had taken against one of her own kind that deeply unsettled her. The path she had once tread with unwavering certainty now lay before her, riddled with doubt and tinged with regret.

Moonlight approached, his footsteps soft against the gravel. "You were magnificent tonight, Stellar. You shone brighter than on any stage you've graced," he praised, his voice filled with genuine awe, as he gently wiped away the remnants of her distress from her face with a tender touch.

He pulled her close, offering solace in the form of a comforting embrace. His warm breath tickled her ear as he murmured, "Your strength, your determination... they've never been more evident," he whispered, planting a soothing kiss on her forehead. "Leave the rest to me."

He retrieved a steel flask from the depths of his inner coat, its surface chillingly shimmering in the dim streetlight. With the flask's contents, he dampened a handkerchief and tenderly wiped the blood from Stellar's hands, his movements deliberate and caring. The stinging scent of alcohol and the cold touch of the wet fabric sent shivers down her spine, making her teeth chatter.

Once her hands were clean, Moonlight offered the flask to her, noticing the internal turmoil she was enduring.

Stellar gratefully accepted it with quivering hands. Her shivering, wet brown eyes met Moonlight's intense gaze. Once warm and gentle, his amber eyes now held a fiery edge, threatening to engulf her soul and set her heart ablaze. Stellar clenched her eyes shut, the liquid inside providing fiery relief as it carved its way down her empty stomach, bolstered by Moonlight's supportive embrace.

When she lowered the empty flask, the world seemed to tilt, threatening to trip her if not for the strong arms around her waist. "Thank you," she whispered, her voice barely audible as she returned the flask. Her fingers trembled, but they found certainty in the solid presence of his arms, a solace that steadied her.

Moonlight's gaze softened, his eyes reflecting deep affection. "Anything for you," he whispered, his touch gentle as he caressed the back of her hand. He gently pressed his lips on her knuckles, guiding her toward the waiting carriage. "Rest now, my love. We'll speak soon."

She nodded, her fingers lingering on his, tracing the lines of strength even as she stepped into the carriage. Settling into the seat, she felt the comforting warmth of Moonlight's presence fade, leaving her in a solitary struggle with the fading echoes of her brother's laughter and the senator's defiant snarl still vying for dominance in her thoughts. Her eyes clung to the receding

silhouette of Moonlight, the last glimmer of his amber
eyes haunting her as the carriage pulled away.

The Blood Pack

"Sir, Mr. Greyfang, please," an elk officer implored, stepping hastily into Lupus's path. His voice carried a tremor of unease. The elk's large hands hovered in the air, hesitant between pushing Lupus back and gesturing a plea. "We've been ordered not to allow any visitors. Mr. Grounder is set for transfer to the Bureau tomorrow."

Lupus stood there, a figure of barely contained fury. His black tie was missing, lost somewhere in the last tumultuous hours. His shirt was quarter-way open, revealing a chest heaving with snarling breaths. His military tag and two metal rings hung around his neck, swaying slightly with each labored breath. The wolf, who had nearly destroyed the front door of the security office in his rage, glared with raw fury and determination. "Step aside, or I will make you," he growled, his voice a low rumble that seemed to make the walls themselves shudder.

Despite his towering stature, the elk officer felt a chill of primal fear snake down his spine. He had seen Senator Redfern's guard in calmer states during downtown visits, but this disheveled, furious wolf was a stranger. The air around them crackled with the menace radiating from the wolf with each snarling exhale. The elk swallowed hard, his voice faltering, "B-but the protocol-"

"That bison might have information on the senator's whereabouts. I don't have time for this shit!" Lupus's voice thundered through the corridor, his fists clenched so tightly his knuckles blanched, his tail bristled in aggression. His eyes, narrowed with frustration, flickered with an internal struggle to restrain the rage boiling within him, painfully aware that every second lost could be critical.

Then, a deep voice sliced through the tension like a knife. "Let Mr. Greyfang pass."

Both Lupus and the elk officer turned to see Chief Detective Bradford Brew of The Great Bears striding toward them, his presence commanding, flanked by a cadre of detectives and officers.

Bradford's gaze locked onto the elk officer. "I'll assume full responsibility. This is a matter of urgency."

Relief washed over the elk's features, his shoulders sagging slightly. He seemed all too ready to avoid the repercussions of barring an enraged wolf. "Yes, Chief," he acquiesced, his hands still trembling as he unlocked the door to the holding cells.

Lupus gave Bradford a curt nod, his expression softening marginally in gratitude. "Thank you, Chief Detective." The bear nodded back, a silent acknowledgment of the gravity of the situation, then turned to join his team in the adjacent briefing room.

Ground blinked groggily, the stillness of his cell shattered by the clunk of the heavy metal lock. The noise of his cell door being flung open barely registered before he was yanked from the corner where he'd been resting.

"What's... what's happening?" His words slurred, trailing off as he struggled to focus on his surroundings. But before he could find his bearings, he was shoved onto the cold, hard floor of the cell. A sharp pain shot through him as he winced, and when he raised his head, he was confronted by the piercing green eyes of a wolf—eyes that bore into him with menace.

"Safehouses. Capitol. *Now*," Lupus growled, his voice a low rumble, fury simmering just below the surface. His grip on Ground's collar tightened, pulling the bison close enough to feel the heat of Lupus's ragged breath.

The only objective in Lupus's mind was clear. The trail of Hart's scent led him to the Wilfen trainyard, but nowhere further. An operator had mentioned several freight trains departing in the past hours to various destinations; only one was rumored to be linked with the Hooves activity—the Capitol.

Confusion from sleep and panic from the abrupt awakening tangled in Grounder's mind. "I... I don't know what you're..." His feeble defense was cut short by a sharp slap across his face, so forceful it left him reeling, the taste of blood in his mouth from a bitten cheek.

Lupus leaned in close, his snarl barely above a whisper, "The Hooves' hideouts in the Capitol. You won't be asked nicely again." The dim light from the hallway's oil lamps cast a sinister glow on his sharp fangs, his dreadful shadow seeming to swallow the bison whole.

Ground's eyes clenched shut, avoiding the menacing glint in those dark green eyes. His massive frame quaked with fear. "You can't—this is illegal! I want my lawyer!" he cried out, his voice cracking with desperation. Tears threatened to spill as he cowered, overwhelmed by the raw, predatory intensity of the wolf looming over him. The sheer aggression clawed at his primary fear. His imposing bison stature, usually a source of strength, felt utterly irrelevant now. No Anthroterrian herbivore was meant to endure such terror. He felt powerless in the grip of a predator, his body shaking uncontrollably.

Lupus sneered down at him, his grin sending a chill through the air. "You want to play that game now, huh?" His voice dripped with mocking coldness, sending icy tendrils of dread down the bison's back.

Suddenly, Lupus released his hold, and for a fleeting moment, Grounder dared to hope for relief. But before he could even savor a breath, Lupus's hand shot out, snatching a fistful of his hair and wrenching a pained cry from his throat. With a brutal yank, Lupus dragged him across to the cell's desk, slamming Grounder's forehead against the hardwood.

"Fuck!" the bison gasped, struggling with renewed panic, the edges of his vision darkening as pain lanced through him.

"Last time, Grounder. Where are Hooves' safehouses in the Capitol?" Lupus's grip was unyielding, his other hand twisting the bison's wrist to the brink of fracture. The threat in Lupus's growl was unmistakable, "Speak now, or I'll snap it."

"AH! P-please, please, I, I..." Grounder's plea broke into a cry, his words tumbling out incoherently as a warm trickle of blood slid from his nostril, his entire being trembling with fear.

"GREYFANG!" A sharp shout cut through the air. Nutterson's voice was filled with desperate urgency as he charged forward, using the momentum to push the wolf off the bison.

Taken aback, Lupus staggered, his eyes aflame with a wild, untamed fury. Nutterson positioned himself as a shield between the incensed wolf and the quivering bison, gripping Lupus's shoulders, trying to pierce through the haze of rage clouding the wolf's judgment.

"Have you lost your goddamn mind?" Nutterson gasped, breathless yet resolute. "What are you doing, mauling him before we've even had a chance to interrogate him formally? You know the protocol, Greyfang. We need him intact!"

Lupus's reply was a guttural snarl, his menacing green eyes never leaving the trembling bison cowering behind Nutterson. "I don't give a fuck, Nutterson. Get out of my way." The wolf's nostrils flared, taking in the metallic smell of the bison's blood. Each ragged breath he took was laced with a low, threatening growl.

For a fleeting moment, Nutterson saw a feral creature in place of the wolf he knew—a being of instinct and violence, far removed from the composed and compassionate figure Greyfang had always been, even in the face of imminent danger. The once reassuring green eyes were now stormy, blinded with scorching rage.

"Greyfang, listen to me!" Nutterson's plea was tinged with desperation, an attempt to anchor Lupus back to reason. "Do you intend to cripple him just on a hunch?" The bison shuddered at the words, the weight of the accusation heavy in the air. "He's not even been confirmed as a Hooves affiliate."

"I've told you already." Lupus growled, his tone sharp and low, "I don't give a fuck."

Nutterson inhaled deeply, seeking composure, his mind racing for words that might penetrate the thick veil of Lupus's anger. "Are you going to put that dishonor under the senator's name?" The relentless fire in Lupus's gaze flickered at his words. The wolf's attention caught Nutterson's steady, probing eyes.

"Consider the fallout, Greyfang. Imagine the media frenzy if they learn a wolf has tortured an unconvicted herbivore on nothing but suspicion. The public's distrust of carnivores is already being stoked by the Hooves' propaganda. Do you wish to confirm their worst fears?" Nutterson's voice was a blend of desperation and persuasion, an urgent plea to the principles they both cherished. "You *know* what the senator stands for—what he's fought to uphold."

With a subtle gesture toward the frightened bison behind him, Nutterson continued, "This young terrian is one of his constituents, a resident of Wilfen. Would

Senator Redfern ever condone such brutality, especially under his name?"

The room was saturated with tension, the gravity of Nutterson's words lingering heavily. Gradually, the veil of fury that had obscured Lupus's judgment began to dissipate, tense aggression seeping out from his bristled furry ears and huffed up shoulders, revealing the vulnerable, weary wolf grappling with the raw anguish and concern. "Hart is in danger, Nutterson," Lupus finally whispered, his voice quivering with suppressed emotion as his trembling fingers anchored on the squirrel's arm. "We need to find him."

Nutterson stepped closer, placing a reassuring hand on Lupus's shoulder. "We will find him, Greyfang." he affirmed, locking eyes with Lupus, trying to convey a depth of certainty. He hesitated for a moment, choosing his words with care, "It's unlikely they would…" He trailed off, wary of igniting Lupus's already volatile emotions. "What I mean is, he's more valuable to them alive, especially if they intend to use him as leverage."

The weight of the unspoken implications settled heavily between them, but neither voiced the deeper fear that the Senator might still face harm.

"S-sir," the bison suddenly interjected, his voice quivering, his face a canvas of distress marked by a dried nosebleed and streaks of tears. "I… I've heard about a new, larger safehouse, somewhere near the east trainyard in the Capitol."

Nutterson and Lupus froze, processing the bison's unexpected yet potentially crucial intel. Lupus's eyes, trembling with a mix of hope and skepticism, searched the bison's face. "Are you…" he began, his voice barely above a whisper, as if afraid to shatter the fragile moment. "Are you telling us the truth?" The question hung in the air, a fragile whisper clinging to a thread of hope.

"I… I don't know any details beyond that," the bison murmured, his ears drooping, his throat tight with nervousness. "But I've heard that's where the printing press was."

"Why are you telling us this?" Nutterson asked gently, his tone more curious than accusatory, sensing the sincerity in the bison's demeanor. "You know we can't hold you to your words, invading your rights like this, if your intention is to distract us from you right now. But I don't think you are lying to us." His eyes softened, conveying a sense of understanding and empathy.

Grounder's gaze dropped as he fidgeted with the buttons on his shirt for a fleeting moment. "The senator, he… He wrote me a letter after the trial," the bison murmured, his thoughts racing back to Senator Redfern's letter and the days of contemplation that followed. "He knew… what I'd done that night. My actions and the intentions behind them, almost as if he had been in my head. Yet, despite everything, he didn't judge or scorn me—he showed me empathy." He paused, wiping away fresh tears of remorse. "He spoke of what unity truly means, for all of us, and for me personally. It felt… otherworldly. Every letter on the paper, every word, every sentence—it spoke to me, as if All Father himself was there, standing in front of me. Not to judge my sin, but to embrace my soul. It made me realize how immature and arrogant I have been, my mind clouded by lust and a false sense of superiority."

A shaky sigh escaped him, the weight of his reflections and guilt pressing heavily upon his heart. "I've always admired Senator Redfern. Now more than ever. I had no idea he was in danger…" He trailed off, the implication too heavy to voice. "I truly hope you can bring him to safety."

Nutterson glanced at his wristwatch, thoughts racing. "There's a freight train to the Capitol around midnight," he recalled, "Greyfang, we might be able to catch it when it slows near the main crossroad just outside downtown. You can search the trainyard while I get to the Bureau for backup." His words jolted Lupus from his reverie.

"That could work," Lupus replied, a flicker of hope sparking in his eyes. He clasped the bison's shoulder, gratitude evident in his gesture. "Thank you, Grounder." Without another word, he sprinted out of the holding cell, with Nutterson closely following behind.

Amidst a fierce thunderstorm that had begun to deluge the trainyard shortly before his arrival, Lupus clung tightly to the fading scent of Hart. The overwhelming odors of the trainyard—a concoction of dust, metal, and the nearby meat facility, all churned up by the torrential rain—threatened to drown out Hart's distinct musk.

Yet, as Lupus zeroed in on the scent's source, the chilling, metallic tang of blood began to dominate his senses. What had sparked as a hopeful lead upon first detecting Hart's scent now spiraled into visceral dread. Each crash of thunder echoed his escalating anxiety. Rain streamed from strands of his hair clinging to his forehead, mingling with the warm tears that blurred his vision. Desperately shaking off the mounting panic and pushing away the nightmarish images threatening to consume him, he narrowed his focus on pinpointing the scent's origin.

A faint splatter of blood in front of an old factory building, barely noticeable amidst the relentless downpour, caught his eye. As he swiftly approached, the overpowering scent of ink and blood eclipsed all else as he neared its entrance. His heart pounded as he pressed an ear against the small gap in the heavy metal door. Amidst the grumbling thunder and the continuous patter of rain on the metal roof, he sensed a fragile, erratic rhythm of breathing. With a hard swallow, Lupus cautiously nudged the metal door open; it creaked faintly, yielding to his touch without resistance.

In the dimly lit factory building, a shadowy figure was slumped at its heart. Yet, that was all Lupus needed to identify Hart, sitting on a chair with his head tilted to one side, his breathing shallow, *still alive.*

It took Lupus a fleeting moment, however, to fully comprehend the full extent of the horror before him as intermittent lightning strikes cast stark light on the grim scene. One of Hart's antlers, a noble emblem of Senator Redfern's authority and a proud testament to Hart's own growth, the graceful crowns that completed the majestic image of the red stag Lupus had so helplessly admired, was brutally cut off from its place. Blood, still oozing from the raw burr where the antler once stood, stained his blindfolded face and ungroomed beard. The crimson trail that had led Lupus to this place was Hart's own—a cruel betrayal of his fervent hopes.

A cold dread crept down Lupus's spine, making his heart falter and his limbs stiffen. Overwhelmed with horror, Lupus felt the world narrow, his ears pinned back, his breaths coming in frantic gasps. Time seemed to stand still, trapping him in his worst nightmare. For a moment that stretched into an eternity, he perceived nothing else, his entire existence fixated on the injured Hart before him.

It was then, Lupus was seized from behind. His wrists were cuffed behind his back before he could muster a defense, and he was roughly hauled in front of Hart. With unyielding force, his captors made him kneel, their hands clamping down like steel on his hair and shoulders.

"You're one hard wolf to corner, Konrad," a familiar voice sneered from behind him. The metallic clang of the door echoed through the room, followed swiftly by the heavy sound of a lock sliding into place. The measured footsteps of dress shoes clicked against the floor, approaching Lupus slowly. Soon, a statuesque black wolf, radiating malevolent confidence, stepped into view, a smirk playing on his lips. "Or do you go by *Lupus* now? Quite the mundane choice, don't you think?"

"Ulrich," Lupus growled, his voice thick with suppressed rage. The sporadic flashes of lightning briefly illuminated his snarling fangs. Despite his best efforts to break free, the combined strength of his captors held him firmly in place. His glare, fierce and unyielding, stayed fixed locked on Ulrich. "What have you done?"

"It's indeed a pleasure to see you again after all these years, *brother*." Ulrich gave a low chuckle, his amber gaze drilling into Lupus. He crouched to meet Lupus's fierce green eyes. "Hope you missed me as much as I did," Ulrich taunted, grasping his older brother's chin, scrutinizing the wounds and scars that marred his face. Lupus jerked his head away from Ulrich's leather-clad hand with a defiant snarl. The younger wolf simply scoffed as he rose to his full, imposing height.

With slow, predatory grace, Ulrich circled Hart, who was bound to a chair, a bloodstained blindfold obscuring his vision. "The Senator here seems a bit fatigued, not even welcoming his guest properly." Ulrich grasped Hart's remaining antler, yanking it violently. A pained cry escaped Hart, wrenching him from the depths of an unpeaceful rest, a mix of fatigue and pain.

"Let him go, Ulrich!" Lupus's voice thundered, every inch of him straining against his captors and the handcuffs.

"...Lupus?" The whisper was quiet and fragile, almost drowned out by the downpour's deafening echo within the building. Hart's breath trembled weakly, laden with confusion. Blinded and disoriented by lingering pain and the strength draining from his body with each drop of blood lost, he couldn't tell if the voice he heard was a cruel twist of reality or a figment of his tormented mind. The relentless drumming of rain on the metal roof only served to further muddle his senses. When he made a feeble attempt to shift, seeking clarity, a sharp and cruel tug on his antler served as a punishing reminder of his helplessness.

The pale, stricken look on Lupus's face, his green eyes wide with dread and fixed on the distressed stag, brought a smirk of satisfaction to Ulrich's lips. "This is the one, isn't it? The deer you'd *kill* to protect," he taunted, his words deliberately punctuated, making Lupus flinch. "Imagine my surprise upon realizing the infamous stag senator is *the very one* my misguided brother adores."

"Ulrich, please, let him go," Lupus pleaded, his whisper teetering on the edge of despair. "This is between you and me. He has no part in this."

The younger wolf clicked his tongue, a mocking sound that cut through the tense air. "Sorry to disappoint you, brother, but it was the Hooves who sealed his fate, not me. You've surely seen their posters around, haven't you?" Ulrich kicked one of the Hooves' posters featuring Senator Redfern with his dress shoe, sending it skidding to land near Lupus. "So this," he paused, his fingers playfully tapping the stag's swollen cheek, "isn't just between us. Not anymore." His voice was a blade of malice slicing through the air. "They stripped his antler. Now they want him thrown into the arena as bait, a lesson to humble the proud stag senator," the wolf smirked, shaking Hart's antler with a casual cruelty. Hart's head followed the motion involuntarily, a pained groan spilling from him. A flash of lightning briefly illuminated the sinister gleam in Ulrich's fangs. "It seems that's his fate, inescapable even after every-thing you've done."

His dark amber eyes locked onto Lupus's horrified expression as the older wolf's resistance seemed to vanish, stunned into silence by the gruesome reality of Ulrich's words.

"The so-called 'Greats' have pacified the masses to keep their reign, breeding a generation of entitled herbivores while systematically silencing and exploiting the powerless carnivores, guilting them into submission." Ulrich's voice descended into a menacing growl, his fury simmering just beneath the surface. "These herbivores, mere *prey*, now blinded by arrogance, prioritize their ideals over true justice." The wolf scoffed, his tone a dark blend of irritation and amusement. "The false promise of this nation that led you to betray your own country, your own blood," he snarled, his fingers tightening around the stag's neck, the surge of rage cutting off breath for a moment. "Look where it has landed the one deer you treasure most." The wolf pulled on the antler, drawing a pained groan. His fingers moved from the neck to the bloodied cheek, then to the severed end of the antler, deliberately staining his fingers with the stag's blood. "What a shame," Ulrich sneered, licking Hart's blood from his fingers, his menacing gaze lingering on his brother's ashen face, savoring every emotion etched upon it as the metallic tang of fresh deer blood danced on his tongue.

"Ulrich, brother," Lupus whispered, his voice quivering, the remnants of his defiance giving way to raw desperation. His green eyes, clouded with fear, shimmered with tears of helplessness. "Please. I beg you, let him go. I'll do anything you ask."

Ulrich's response was a dark, throaty laugh that reverberated ominously through the space. "I must admit, I do enjoy that look on your face, Konrad," he said, a cruel smirk twisting his lips, taking sadistic pleasure in the emotional chaos he had inflicted upon the older wolf. "Though I don't trust a word from a traitor."

The wolf tightened his grip on the antler and revealed a hand saw from beneath his coat. The blade caught the momentary flash of lightning, casting a sinister gleam. Ulrich dragged the saw's teeth over the brow tine slowly, almost playfully, eliciting a stifled cry from the stag, whose frame trembled with the effort to remain composed. "I think our Senator needs a matching set," Ulrich mused, his voice dripping with perverse anticipation. He positioned the saw near the burr, eyeing the perfect spot to mirror the already mutilated antler.

"ULRICH!" The sheer panic in Lupus's voice was raw, a desperate bark. His eyes, wide with terror, were fixated on the menacing saw. "Harm me instead, take my ear, do whatever you wish," he implored, his voice breaking with anguish, "but spare him, please."

The black wolf paused, his amber eyes alight with a dangerous gleam as he contemplated Lupus's offer. A sly smirk slowly curled his lips. "You'd trade your ear for his antler?" he mused, giving the antler a nonchalant shake. "You're aware these are... rather disposable, aren't you?"

"It's still in velvet. The pain would be unbearable," Lupus insisted, desperation evident in his voice. "You have me here, on my knees. Take my ear, Ulrich. Claim me as your trophy. Just... let him go unharmed."

"No, don't," Hart protested, his voice a rough whisper that sliced through the heavy air. "They can take my goddamn antler. It's–it's not that bad, Lupus," he stammered and let out a shaky chuckle, a feeble attempt to mask the terror of the excruciating pain he experienced not too long ago.

Despite the fog in his mind and the weakness in his limbs, Hart's thoughts were a tempest of emotion and reflection, stoked by the surrounding conversations and the raw emotions emanating from Lupus.

Even though Lupus was no longer his guard, he had found Hart faster than anyone else who might have been searching for the missing senator. Now, here he was, ready to sacrifice a part of himself to spare Hart from suffering. The sincerity in Lupus's concern pierced through the haze, bright and undeniable. It was a last strand of hope Hart had clung to in the deepest recesses of his mind, despite their tumultuous past. This revelation, this glimmer of genuine connection, cut through the darkness of what Hart had resigned himself to as a bleak existence, offering a beacon of hope to his weary soul.

"Hart," Lupus said, a hint of relief in his voice upon hearing Hart speak. But the deer's quivering furry ears, laid flat against his head, and trembling fists betrayed the depth of pain he'd endured with the loss of his antler. "Kid, it's okay. You'll be fine," Lupus gently assured, trying to soothe the distressed Hart.

"How touching, really," Ulrich sneered, his voice oozing sarcasm. "But your proposal, Konrad, is intriguing." He released Hart's antler and slowly strode over to Lupus, his eyes gleaming with malevolent delight. "You do know me very well, don't you?"

"No!" Hart's outcry was raw with desperation. He strained against the restraints binding him to the chair, mustering all his remaining strength. But the blood loss from his severed antler, coupled with the lingering pain, left him enfeebled. "Don't let him do this, Lupus! Please!" he pleaded, his voice breaking with sob erupted by helplessness.

With a flicker of irritation, Ulrich gestured subtly toward the stag. One of the captors restraining Lupus swiftly approached the stag. The lioness placed a cloth over his mouth, tying it firmly, effectively silencing Hart's protests.

"Thank you, Ulrich," Lupus whispered, his voice soft yet filled with a complex mix of gratitude and resignation. It cut through the sound of the relentless downpour against the metal ceiling, which seemed almost distant amidst the heavy tension of the moment. His eyes locked with the amber gaze of the imposing wolf, who towered over Lupus's submissive form.

In a gesture that sharply contrasted with his earlier malevolence, Ulrich reached out with unexpected gentleness to stroke the older wolf's lupin ear, prompting an involuntary flinch. "You are very welcome, brother." With swift precision, Ulrich pulled the ear taut and produced a pocket knife, snapping it open with a chilling snap.

Lupus braced himself, a suppressed groan escaping his lips. His teeth gritted, fists clenched behind his back, and eyes squeezed shut in anticipation of the inevitable.

Blindfolded, Hart was spared the sight but not the sound or the scent. The gut-wrenching sound of Lupus's suppressed groan, coupled with the metallic scent of fresh blood, paralyzed him with a terror that consumed his senses. The weight of Lupus's sacrifice bore down on him, a heavy burden that clenched his heart. A knot of despair and helplessness swelled in his throat, forcing him to choke back the sobs that threatened to spill over the fabric gagging his mouth. The cloth over his eyes grew damp with the tears he couldn't hold back.

"Beautiful," Ulrich murmured, a rich note of satisfaction in his voice. "Consider your debt of betrayal settled, Konrad," he added, the warmth in his tone belying the brutality of his actions. With meticulous care, Ulrich wrapped the severed ear in a handkerchief and placed it gently into his coat pocket.

"Th-thank you," Lupus managed to stammer, his voice quivering from the pulsating pain and the warm rivulets of blood that dripped, streaking across his face. His breaths came in ragged gasps, his body drenched in a cold sweat, fists clenched as he fought to anchor himself against the waves of agony. The loss of his lupine ear triggered an instinctive dread that shook his soul, sending shivers through his body. A high-pitched ringing assaulted his ears, disorienting him further.

Ulrich approached Hart with measured steps, casually wiping his knife on the fabric of Hart's gown draped over his shoulder. "You're free to go," he declared, his voice laced with malevolence, a smirk curling his lips. He signaled to the lionesses holding Lupus.

A fleeting sense of relief was quickly eclipsed by a surge of panic. "Wait!" he cried out, his voice raw as he was yanked to his feet and propelled toward the exit. "No, Ulrich, let him go!" Lupus demanded, struggling against the iron grip on his arm.

"Why should I?" Ulrich mused, caressing Hart's shoulders. This elicited a sharp wriggle and a growl from Hart, who was grappling with a whirlwind of emotions. "It would be a shame to squander such a prime gift, one that would certainly spice up the arena. Don't you agree?" he pondered aloud, his grip tightening on the stag's shoulder until he elicited a deep shiver of pain that Hart refused to vocalize.

"Ulrich, I beg you," Lupus's voice broke with desperation. He sank to his knees, fighting the hands that tried to pull him away. "I'll do whatever you ask, just name it. Please, let him go."

"Is that right?" Ulrich's lips curled into a sly smirk. With a subtle gesture, he signaled the lionesses to release Lupus, who collapsed onto the frigid floor. The younger wolf approached, his tail swaying with evident satisfaction. "There is something you can do for me."

"I'll do it, brother," Lupus vowed, pushing himself up to sit on his knees. He looked up at Ulrich, his eyes brimming with a mix of fear and hopeful desperation.

Ulrich lowered himself to one knee, bringing his fierce amber eyes level with Lupus's. "This country is on the brink of awakening," he began, his voice a soft yet commanding rumble. "I aim to lead a new world, one built on the rightful order of the universe—where we can embrace our true selves, where predators and prey reassume their natural roles, as dictated by mother nature."

He laid a firm hand on Lupus's shoulder. "I need you to forsake this country, the Bureau, and the Greats—those who have forsaken and betrayed our kind. Return to your blood pack, Konrad. Stand with me, and help me forge the nation our kind is owed, the *New Furrocia*," Ulrich solemnly intoned, his voice deepening to a growl.

His intense gaze never wavered from Lupus's face, now etched with the stark realization of Ulrich's intent. The gravity of Ulrich's proposition seemed all the more ominous, underscored by the backdrop of rolling thunder and relentless patter of rain.

"The revolution is on the horizon. You've felt its tremors, haven't you?" Ulrich's low voice wove a vivid tapestry in Lupus's mind, illustrating the growing unrest—from the marginalized carnivores to the Hooves' unjust assault on Senator Redfern, and the escalating distrust between species across the country.

"And when the storm hits, where will the stag senator stand? Will the Hooves spare one they've branded a 'traitor'? When our kind, suppressed for so long, finally rises, will they show mercy to a mere prey once seated at the high table, looking down upon them alongside the Greats? Would you put your faith in the Bureau and The Greats to even lift a finger to shield him when their dominion is threatened?"

Ulrich's fingers tightened on Lupus's shoulder, his gaze piercing. "I can offer sanctuary to your precious deer if you pledge your loyalty to me, to your pack. It *is* his only chance at safety when the storm shatters the very fabric of the society you know." With his ears perked and attentive, Ulrich subtly signaled, ordering to free Lupus from his restraints.

Lupus's thoughts swirled, consumed by Ulrich's words and the daunting challenge of ensuring Hart's safety. The Bureau's defenses had already faltered once, allowing the Hooves to abduct Hart. How could Lupus, on his own, hope to shield Hart from the multitude of threats that seemed to circle like vultures, each hinting at a grim fate for the stag senator?

What Ulrich offered, an organized protection, seemed the best option Lupus could afford, despite his visceral aversion to the idea of leaving Hart at Ulrich's mercy. The haunting memories and nightmares of Furrocia, that accursed land which had stripped him of all he held dear, stormed back, flooding his mind with haunting images.

"So, what will it be?" Ulrich began, shattering the tense silence, yanking Lupus from the depths of his inner turmoil. "Will you join me at the forefront of our revolution, the one our kind is so rightfully owed? Or will you stand by, powerless, as your cherished stag falls prey to the next opportunist seeking a sacrifice?" Ulrich removed his leather glove, extending his bare hand, a seemingly gentle smile playing on his lips, the glint of his fangs betraying the danger underneath.

Lupus hesitated, his gaze dropping to Ulrich's outstretched hand. A primal dread gnawed at him, a stark reminder that each choice laid before him bore the weight of irreversible consequences.

Hart, though bound and gagged, fought against his bonds with the last ounces of his strength left in his weakened frame. A lioness quickly stepped in, gripping both the chair and Hart's shoulder to stabilize him. Lupus's focus snapped to the lioness restraining Hart, visible just over Ulrich's shoulder.

Witnessing Lupus's evident struggle and indecision, Ulrich let out a snarl of dissatisfaction and rose abruptly, his demeanor turning chillingly cold. "How disappointing, Konrad," he said, his voice a sinister blend of calm and menace, snapping Lupus's attention back to him. "I forgave your betrayal, offered you a place in the pack, and this is how you repay my generosity? With this disrespectful hesitation?" His voice then descended into a menacing growl, his tail bristling with unmistakable rage. With a dismissive turn of his back to Lupus, he signaled for the older wolf to be taken away.

"No, Ulrich, wait! That's not–" Lupus's plea was cut with desperation, his words trailing off as he was dragged away from Hart. "I will join you, just—please, let me!"

"You were a traitor, after all. You spat on my unbound trust, trampled years of my work," Ulrich retorted, his voice seething with contempt. "You declared I was no brother of yours. A blood pack meant so little to you; why should I place my trust in you again?"

Now standing imperiously over Hart, Ulrich crossed his arms, his tail flicking with irritation. "Once you're back at your post, send my regards to the Greats and the Bureau," Ulrich sneered, his voice dripping with biting sarcasm. He cast a scornful glance over his shoulder, adding, "I imagine they'll be devastated to discover what's become of their precious stag senator."

In a surge of determination, Lupus broke free from the iron grip restraining him and lunged forward, nearly collapsing at the younger wolf's feet. "Ulrich, my brother," he gasped, his trembling hands clutching at Ulrich's polished shoes, even as the lionesses moved to seize him again. "I pledge my loyalty to you—on my life. Please, take me in," he implored, his voice wavering with the weight of his earnest plea.

Ulrich paused, taking a deliberate moment before turning slightly to look down at his older brother prostrate at his feet, meeting those trembling green eyes that swore a life's loyalty—a loyalty Ulrich had long desired. With a curt nod, he signaled his lionesses to stand down, releasing Lupus from their grasp.

"You're in luck, Konrad, that we have an honorable witness tonight," Ulrich said, stepping away from Lupus's desperate grasp. He positioned himself ominously behind the bound senator. With a swift, deliberate gesture, he removed the blindfold, exposing Hart's eyes to the dim light. "Perhaps you'd like to inform our esteemed guest from the Anthroterra Central Senate of your newfound loyalty?"

Blinking against the harsh, sporadic flashes of lightning that illuminated the factory's interior, Hart's weary eyes slowly adjusted. The sight that greeted him made his already erratic breathing hitch in dread: Lupus, his drenched and disheveled frame shivering, reduced to all fours, his expression contorted in anguish, and one of his lupine ears savagely halved, still oozing blood. The gravity of their situation pressed down on Hart, blurring his vision with tears. A muffled sob escaped him, his head shaking in a silent, desperate plea for Lupus to resist.

Lupus, now fully absorbing the sight of Hart, felt his heart clench with a storm of profound sorrow. Hart's pale and weary face, a canvas of exhaustion and blood loss, was smeared with blood, his once neatly groomed beard and mustache now matted and unkempt. Large brown eyes, brimming with tears, conveyed unspeakable pain, while quiet cries spilled from his gagged mouth.

His attention shifted to Ulrich looming behind the stag. The imposing wolf regarded him with a cold, amber stare, tinged with evident impatience, clearly waiting for Lupus to make his move. The silent ultimatum was clear to Lupus—this was the last chance Ulrich was offering.

With controlled breaths, Lupus steeled himself, recognizing this moment as potentially the last chance to alter the grim fate of Hart. It was no longer just about protecting Hart; it was about ensuring his safety against the impending storms. Lupus had been prepared to pay any price to keep Hart safe, ever since the moment he first met the brown eyes of the joyful young fawn all those years ago.

The older wolf moved his trembling limbs to kneel before Hart, cradling Hart's bound hands in his own. The contact of cold, quivering fingers felt like a piercing reminder of his failure to protect.

Hart clung to the offered warmth like a lifeline. For the first time in what felt like an eternity, he felt the raised scars and rough texture of Lupus's hands against the almost pristine skin of his own. Tears carved paths down Hart's cheeks as he shook his head vehemently, his eyes squeezed shut, his muffled cries growing more frantic.

"Senator Redfern," Lupus began, his voice quivering. A gentle squeeze on Hart's hands urged the stag to meet his gaze. In the green depths of Lupus's eyes, shimmering with unshed tears, Hart saw a depth of genuine concern that was boundless. "I've chosen to stand with my kind, with my blood pack. From this moment on, my allegiance to the United Districts of Anthroterra is severed." The declaration, heavy with pain, sent tears cascading down Lupus's cheeks. Hart responded with a muffled sob, his head shaking in denial.

"Focus, Senator," Ulrich whispered, his hand wrapping firmly around Hart's chin. His fingers clamped down, wrenching Hart's full attention back to Lupus, indifferent to the stag's labored breathing from the slight constriction of his windpipe. "Konrad, perhaps you'd enlighten our senator about where your loyalty lies?" Ulrich's low growl, rumbling like distant thunder, bore down on Lupus.

The grim reality of his choice, leaving Hart's life in Ulrich's hands, was now agonizingly clear. Lupus knew what needed to be done, to keep Hart safe.

"I pledge my unwavering loyalty to the pack, and to my brother, Ulrich Moonfur. I swear it on my life," Lupus avowed, his voice heavy with the gravity of his oath. He maintained eye contact with Hart, his gaze conveying a silent apology.

Hart blinked back a fresh wave of tears before closing his eyes, consumed by a tumult of helplessness and guilt.

"It's settled, then," Ulrich declared, a triumphant smirk playing on his lips as he released Hart's face and stepped closer to Lupus. "Welcome back to the pack, brother," he said, his grin broadening as he extended his hand in a gesture of reconciliation.

Lupus hesitated for a fleeting moment, his gaze still tethered to Hart, visibly torn. Then, with a resolve that fortified his soul, he met his brother's eyes and took his hand. The warmth of Ulrich's hand was a stark contrast to the coldness he felt from Hart. "Thank you, Ulrich," he murmured, his voice a mere whisper, yet resolute amidst the storm of his emotions.

As Ulrich helped Lupus to his feet, his other hand swiftly grabbed the military tag that quietly rattled against Lupus's chest. "You won't be needing your old owner's tag, will you?" Ulrich said with a smirk. Without waiting for a response, he yanked it free, the tag and metal rings clattering as he tossed them carelessly onto Hart's lap. Hart's gaze lowered to the metal tag, bearing the years of Lupus's life, reflecting the ominous lightning.

Ulrich placed a supportive hand on Lupus's shoulder, guiding him towards the exit. "The Bureau's agents and officers will likely arrive soon. Our esteemed senator will be in safe hands and back to full health after a good night's sleep," he intoned, nudging Lupus forward with a gentle press on the shoulder. "From now on, the Shadow Clan's finest will stay near him, ensuring his protection," he assured with a gentle smile. The gentleness and warmth in Ulrich's voice, reminiscent of the ones Lupus recalled from his distant memories, earned a nod of gratitude from Lupus.

A lioness promptly unlocked and swung open the imposing metal door, revealing the relentless downpour outside.

On the threshold, Lupus cast a final glance over his shoulder at Hart. Their gazes locked, and in Hart's eyes, Lupus saw not just despair but a flicker of determination.

With a heavy weight of his choice, Lupus stepped into the storm, clinging to the hope that he had made the right decision for Hart's safety amidst the looming turmoil, fervently wishing that the shadows of his past would never again darken Hart's path.

To my dear reader,

Hey there. This is Rat K.

Thank you, you beautiful soul, for dedicating your precious time to reading my book.

This journey began as a prolonged daydream about a world where the line between animals and humans blurs—a world where characters grapple with their identities, endure the pain of seeking life's meaning, and find solace in each other's company. This daydream lingered in my mind for so long that it eventually transformed into the story I was eager to share with you. Bringing the added element of animal traits of every terrian into the story was a joy, allowing me to explore how these traits might shape their thoughts, behaviors, and the unique challenges they encounter.

This book is the culmination of many early mornings and late nights throughout 2023, hours that filled me with the joys of storytelling, but also with the doubts of being a first-time author. Juggling a full-time position in tech and overcoming self-doubt, especially as someone who spent a lifetime reading mostly 'practical' books, there were countless moments when I questioned whether to continue writing. I often feared that I was wasting my life in something that might go unnoticed.

Yet, it was an inner drive that consistently brought me back to the storyboard, as if the characters themselves were eager to be discovered by you. And now, here I am, writing a thank you note to you. The rest of the series is in the works, with lots of edits and rewriting ahead. I hope you found the story of Hart, Lupus, and everyone around them interesting enough to keep you excited for the rest of the journey to come.

I sincerely hope you enjoyed reading this book as much as I enjoyed writing it. Thank you again. May All Father enlighten your way.

With love,